D0065996

By Bob Ottum

SEE THE KID RUN

THE TUESDAY BLADE

STAND ON IT

ALL RIGHT, EVERYBODY OFF THE PLANET

SEE THE KID RUN

A NOVEL BY
BOB OTTUM

SIMON AND SCHUSTER   NEW YORK

COPYRIGHT © 1978 BY BOB OTTUM
ALL RIGHTS RESERVED
INCLUDING THE RIGHT OF REPRODUCTION
IN WHOLE OR IN PART IN ANY FORM
PUBLISHED BY SIMON AND SCHUSTER
A DIVISION OF GULF & WESTERN CORPORATION
SIMON & SCHUSTER BUILDING
ROCKEFELLER CENTER
1230 AVENUE OF THE AMERICAS
NEW YORK, NEW YORK 10020

DESIGNED BY ELIZABETH WOLL
MANUFACTURED IN THE UNITED STATES OF AMERICA

1   2   3   4   5   6   7   8   9   10

LIBRARY OF CONGRESS CATALOGING IN PUBLICATION DATA

OTTUM, BOB.
    SEE THE KID RUN.

    I.   TITLE.
PZ4.O914se   [PS3565.T8]   813'.5'4   78–9174
ISBN 0–671–23095–6

ONE

1

THE KID

The Kid does tricks. He looks like he is walking, but he is really running. It takes a lot of practice.

That's just one of them. The Kid has got all of the good moves. So far, nobody knows how he does any of it, and he is not talking. It figures. If you do this thing right, then nobody sees you—and there's nobody to talk to. It's one of the ways it works.

Here is how The Kid does it:

He is easing through Rockefeller Center. He is pretending that there is a television camera truck rolling in the street alongside. The truck is tracking him; it keeps perfect pace. Now, then. From behind the TV camera up on the truck—looking through the viewfinder and following the scene—you can see that the camera picks up everybody on the sidewalk, The Kid included. Now you see him; now somebody steps between him and the camera, and then suddenly there he is again, a few feet away. That's it. The

Kid has learned that everybody flickers through life—in and out of sight.

Well. All right, so it's a little more sneaky than that, but the rest of it is all practice. The Kid also holds his face set just right. Zero emotion. Blank robot eyes. It is an abstract expression that you can use only in New York City. Try it in any small town in the country and they nail you. People in small towns always let their faces hang open. They do not have the same security problems that people have in New York City.

And that's it. The Kid is sliding on through. Just blink once—or glance the other way for a second—and you've lost him.

The Kid has had a good day.

In addition to being semi-invisible, The Kid steals money from office desks. Not from men. From women's purses: he now has three twenties, four fives and fifteen one-dollar bills in his right front pocket. Even now, while he is ghosting in and out of the crowd near Radio City Music Hall, secretaries in the Time-Life Building across the street are saying:

"No, really. Listen, I couldn't have been away from my desk any more than . . . listen, I swear. I just turned my *back* and all my money is gone, see? No, no. All the keys are still here. The apartment and all. And my credit cards. You know, look: the Bloomie's card, all of them. License, everything here. Just the money."

Exactly. Turn The Kid upside down and shake him and only paper money would fall out. Money is anonymous.

The Kid won't tell anybody about *that* trick, either.

He has this fantasy all worked out inside his head. Say that maybe the camera truck pulled to a sudden stop just in front of Sam Goody's record store on the corner of Sixth Avenue and Fifty-first, and the guys were to jump

8

off the truck with hand-held cameras and microphones. Say they were going to do a man-on-the-street thing. New Yorkers are very, very big on TV man-on-the-street segments. Point a microphone at anybody in Manhattan and he'll tell you everything.

The interview guy would be Walter Cronkite, maybe. No, not him. Nobody has ever seen him on his feet. Make it maybe Dan Rather holding the mike with the black sponge-rubber ball on the end of it. Dan Rather with the double-vented sportcoat.

The crew would get set up and The Kid would do his number: the flicker. He would slalom through the crowd in the background, head up, never once looking sideways at the camera. Now you see him, now you don't. Then he would turn around halfway down the block and do it all over again—just at the back of the crowd. It's important.

It's important because maybe just one time, somebody out there might be absently looking *into* the TV screen instead of at it. Just somebody, anybody. And he would turn to his wife and say:

"Uhh, I don't know if you saw it, Harriet—no, he's gone now—but there was a really nice-looking kid there in the crowd. He was . . . no, there he is again, see? No, you missed him. Anyway, it was a nice, normal-looking kid for once; jeez, the way they all look these days. It was, I don't know, something about him. You know, handsome and sort of, mmmm, sort of distant-looking, know what I mean?"

It would mean that The Kid had got it right.

End of fantasy.

He turns and walks toward Fifth, moving easy through the crowd. He doesn't look like he's got ninety-five dollars on him. But he also doesn't look stone-broke, either. It's part of the trick.

If there was only somebody to talk to; that is, if some-body could see him, The Kid would have a lot of things to say. Even about why he steals.

"Here's the way it works," The Kid would say. "I'm not doing this to get ahead. I'm doing it to catch *up*. I got off to a late start."

All right, then. It's about his distant look. Maybe it's hiding something. What does The Kid really feel on the inside?

He would tell the truth: "You tell me what I'm supposed to feel. Look: I can make up something nice for you; you know, I can make my eyes go all big. Or, if you want sad, I'll look sad. But the trouble is, I don't feel *any*thing. Nobody ever taught me that part, see? I mean, it doesn't just come with the *body*; it's not standard equipment. You got to learn all that when you're small—and when I was small, everybody was looking the other way."

The Kid stops and looks at the store window. He is not looking into it—at ladies' underwear—he is looking *off* the window at the reflections of the people walking past just behind him. A cop comes by and pauses. He looks in over The Kid's shoulder. The Kid doesn't flinch; he's too fast for that number. The cop moves on.

The Kid swings away from the window and looks both ways along the sidewalk.

Pick a grownup, any one of these big guys: The Kid would trade him lives straight across. It would solve the problem of getting off to a late start—and he wouldn't have to worry about being finished on time.

Like Dan Rather, especially. The Kid has spotted Dan Rather a couple of times coming out of his building on Sixth Avenue. He had followed him and had gotten it figured out: people all knew who Dan Rather was, but nobody came up and jumped on him. What it was, Dan Rather had his own space around him. He fit into the world.

10

Which is exactly what The Kid wants.

He starts walking again. The TV camera truck is wheeling alongside. The camera is rolling, videotaping The Kid's every move. It's a sort of protection: if you figure you're on camera all the time, you don't make any dumb mistakes and you stay safe.

And that's how The Kid does it.

He stops at the corner, waiting for the light. He is considering going down to Greenwich Village again. The only way to work all of this out is to get down to the Village. Even though terrible things are coming off down there.

The Kid is not into terrible stuff.

Well. Not yet, anyway.

It is 4 P.M.

2

MR. AND MRS. SOL HAVEN

4 P.M. in Greenwich Village:

Three more steps; hoo-boy, I'm telling you, three more steps to go. And two more and . . . one. She paused on the landing to catch her breath. She reached out with her right hand and patted the railing, then turned and squinted back down the stairs. It was hard to make him out; he looked all solid through the middle and all wavy around the edges.

"So come on, already, so shake a leg," she said. "I'll make us a cup of Brim. It'll give you strength."

He got fuzzier now. Closer. There was something in his step.

"Sol?" she said. "Sol?"

He looked heavier. It was these, hoo-boy, these eyeglasses. They were the cataract prescription glasses and the lenses were too thick. From the other side, for anybody looking at her, she knew that the thick glasses made her look like those old photographs of Harry Truman. She rubbed her hand on the railing again. The palm of her hand was suddenly cold.

He kept coming up, slow. It *was* his step that was different. That was it.

"Sol?" she said. "It's not you?" She took one step backward.

She could feel him now. It was like a heat coming. Something, something came out of the fuzziness. It was all wavy. It was coming toward her. A what? It was . . .

It was a hand. The index finger scratched down the center of her forehead, coming right down through the middle of her eyebrows, and it flicked. It flicked and her eyeglasses popped right off, the wire earpieces stinging the sides of her face. The glasses fell onto her chest, one soft bounce, and then they fell to the floor. Her pupils wouldn't dilate; they wouldn't contract, *any*thing, and the light turned all milky.

The hand came back. It was like a shadow now, a bird's wings flapping in the darkness, maybe. It landed on her neck and folded the wings around.

"Oh, Lord God," she said. "Oh, no."

The hand gave a push and she went backward, her skirt flying up, the back of her head hitting the plaster wall. She threw her arms out. The brown A&P grocery sack jumped away. Just jumped out of her hand in the milkish light. She could hear it hit the floor. The little jar of Brim could break; such a tiny little jar, too, and so expensive. Other, regular coffee, you could use the same grounds over and over again, but it got so it never tasted right. Once in a while, mmm, every other month, maybe, you could get some Brim. You know, some pennies off on the coupon when they put it in the paper. Well, you had it coming and . . .

No. Why was she thinking of this?

Her head. Her head hurt so. Where was . . . ?

She fell forward. All this was taking so *long*. What she

was doing was bouncing off the wall: *that* was it—and she still had all this time to *think*. She put her hands out. Stop the fall. She used to be, what? Acro*bat*ic, even, a young girl. So supple, everybody always said.

Sol could put his hands around her waist then and his thumbs would almost touch in the front. Right here. Sol could lift and hold her up over his head then, with never even so much as a tremble. "We could go into the circus," he would say then, walking around the bedroom and holding her up, her nightgown falling forward into his face.

Stop the fall. Oh, my *God*.

When she raised her head, she knew that her nose was bleeding. It bled so easily now. Sometimes she couldn't stop it, the bleeding—even pressing a cold, wet dishcloth at the back of her neck, like this, but still it bled and bled. And her teeth. She tightened her lips to get her upper plate back into position.

Sol could . . . no. She was too heavy now, too thick all through the waist. But it happens to you when you have so many kids.

Everything was so dim. This was more blood than usual; it wasn't just a bloody nose. It was a *hurt*, a broken something. The pain of it flared out into both cheekbones.

Her sides. A kicking at her sides. Sharp-toed shoes, too, and suddenly she couldn't breathe. She tried to squirm away on her stomach. The back of her skirt was up and there were holes in the backs of her stockings. Holes high up. Maybe he couldn't see the holes, this kicker. She should tell him that she really did have one good pair of stockings. But you don't wear your good stockings just to go out shopping. Just a little jar of Brim.

"Sol." She whispered it into the carpet.

The carpet was worn. None of the little fuzz-balls like it used to have when they first moved here. The carpet was burning her forehead.

14

The fluttering bird. No, no, it was a *hand*. Two hands now; two hands pulling at her arm where her purse was.

Seventeen dollars and forty-three cents. She knew.

Oh, God, no. Not the *money*, you grabbing hands. Not the money. Do you know what it's like living on this pension? Do you know, hands? Listen, you go down the stairs and get the check. A little lock on the mailbox down there. Not much of a lock; some lock. All right. Go to the bank and then to the store.

The young man at the bank. Nice young man, he could be Jewish: "How many times do I have to tell you, Missus Haven. You got to sign the check on the *back* here. Here where I always tell you, Missus Haven."

"So you know it's me already," she would say.

"You know. And I know. But the bank don't know."

She couldn't catch her breath now. All this blood from her nose. She couldn't see, even. Not even the light and the shadow.

The bank: of *course* she knew that she was supposed to sign the check; of course. It was just to make conversation. To have somebody to talk to. You talk to somebody, it means that you're a *person*. Otherwise, you tend to forget.

The bird doubled up its wings again and flew into the side of her face. Once, twice, clawing at her.

Her face was bouncing on the carpet and the skin was flaking off her cheekbone. It wouldn't have done that in the old days, but the carpet was so raggedy now, old and worn rough. So rough. If she could only breathe.

"Sol?" she said. "Sol?"

Maybe she wasn't really saying it; maybe she was thinking it. She wasn't sure now.

There was a flash. A light, bright and hot.

No. No light. It was the back of her head. Again: it was a crash. Like a cymbal, a beating against her head.

Goodness sakes: there was new blood now, and it was coming from the back of her head and running down *front*ward; frontward, curling around the tops of her ears and running down her cheeks.

The last crash against her head straightened her arms out. She didn't mean to straighten them out; didn't want to. They just went that way, and she could feel all of her fingers go straight. Her fingernails all hurt. Could that be possible? Yes: they all hurt. Feel that?

She listened. She could hear the blood swelling up and coming out of the back of her head now. Behind that, she could hear the footsteps going back down the stairs.

Down and down the stairs. With her purse.

Down to . . .

Sol had been so strong. Sol had smelled like Twenty Grand cigarettes. All his clothes. Sol had such a booming laugh; sometimes the neighbors would pound on the walls. Too loud a laugh.

He had gotten smaller as he had gotten older. More bent over, a little. But that was all right.

Listen to all that blood. Hear it? Such blood.

Her hearing was suddenly stronger now. She could still hear the going-away footsteps. Fainter. But there was something in them. Something different.

Goodness *sake*. Of course.

It was a *boy*. A young boy made that sound; it was the, you know, the young-boy way he put his feet down. She ought to know.

You bad boy. An old lady like me, too. How much was it? The purse, it was seventeen dollars and . . .

She couldn't remember now. It was hard to think with all the blood making that rushing noise. So bubbly, coming up and out the back of her head like that. A roaring, even.

She listened to it, face down, her arms outstretched.

It stopped roaring so much.

16

She listened carefully to her heart stop beating. It just plain stopped. Like that.

Sol? Is that you?

It was now 4:14 P.M. Not even dark out.

Sol was one landing down. Sol was also dead.

3

ICEPICK SALLY

It was now 4:30 P.M.

She said it out loud, so that the empty hallway could hear. It was a rite of exorcism to keep them all hidden away in the blackness. "I've got an icepick here," she said. "You come near me, I'll stick it right into your eyes. Icepick, and I know how to use it."

Her line of sight took in the stairway going down and, just opposite, the other stairs going up into the shadows. Nobody was coming up now, not even in stockinged feet —or barefoot, or anything. She knew, she could hear well. She had changed her route coming home. She had the treasures hidden in her red nylon knapsack. The knapsack was almost like new; it had just shown up one day in the garbage can out front. Too good to throw away like that. She had figured out how to work the shoulder straps and now she wore it all the time when she went out. Fine: it kept both hands free to fight.

Always keep both hands free. That part, and always changing the route back home. And the icepick.

She unlocked the lower lock on her door, listening to the dark.

She pulled the key out and shook the others around on the key ring, feeling for the one that fit the upper lock. She found it and half-turned and put it into the slot.

"An icepick," she yelled at the hallway. "And I've got both hands free, you hear?"

She turned the lock until she heard it click. Twenty-seven dollars it had cost to install that upper lock. Would the apartment pay? Course not. You got a lock on your door already, they had said. You got security. What do you think we got a buzzer downstairs for? She slid her hand down the door panel, feeling with the tips of her fingers now, and turned the knob. The door opened.

And he came out of the upper stairwell at the same time.

Oh, *no*. Not now.

He had been kneeling back there, there in the blackest part of the corner. Kneeling? Crouched? How could he move so fast?

No, you don't. Not to *me*.

There was a swish; she could sense it. A fast swoop of air, coming from top to bottom, just like *this*—and one of the straps on the knapsack gave away.

She still couldn't see him. Then a glimpse.

He was a boy. Just a boy.

She did a . . . what do you call them? She did a pirouette around the door and slammed it, pushing at both locks with the butts of both hands. Then she did the safety chain.

There was no icepick. There never had been an icepick.

She stepped back, one hand at her throat. She was gulping in air, moving her mouth open and closed in small kissing motions. She was watching the doorknob rattle. And then she could sense the soft force of the shoulder slamming against the other side of the door.

Watching it, she moved backward one step at a time, stooping and waving her left hand behind her back. She bumped into the end table. Without turning, she patted around the top of it until she found the Sony tape recorder. Still watching the door, she ran her fingertips over the top: one, two, the third key from the right. The volume was already set. She punched the key down. She waited.

And then the roar of the cassette-taped Doberman barks came out from behind her.

"And I've got a big dog in here, too," she yelled at the doorknob. "Big dog. A Doberman." She half turned and looked down at the tape recorder. "If he comes through that door, you kill him," she said. "Kill him, understand?"

She shook off her knapsack and let it fall to the floor.

"Kill, kill," she said.

The doorknob stopped rattling. There was a . . . oh, Lord, now what? A scratching of some kind on the other side of the door. Something scraping across the panel.

That was when she discovered why the shoulder strap had flicked away in the hall. The knapsack hadn't broken: it had been cut with one sweep. A big slice. And her Navy pea jacket. And sweater. Her dress. And the dress under that one. Right through the underwear. Right down through her shoulder.

She sank to her knees beside the knapsack and looked at the door, holding her shoulder with her right hand, cupping it to try and keep the blood in.

She fainted in that position, bending forward slowly, almost regally, until the top of her forehead rested on the linoleum. She went to sleep that way: a half-dazed sleep.

A knife cut this bad should be sewed up by a doctor. But . . .

But if you go out, if you dare to go out and get it sewed,

then they *really* cut you. Really. They know; maybe they know that you haven't got an icepick, those kids.

Icepick Sally, they yell, dancing all around you.

Icepick Sally eats out of garbage cans.

Which was true.

Icepick Sally eats dog food.

Which was also true. Well, once in a while, anyway. Once or twice last winter.

The kids would run up behind her and push her down; she had holes in her long underwear and skinned spots on both knees.

So, then. You can't just go outside and get the knife cut sewed up. Besides, it would cost too much, anyway.

And the doctor would no doubt grimace at the sight of her dirty brassiere straps.

So you fix the cut here.

You sprinkle something on it: flour, oatmeal, whatever you have in the cupboard. Dry oatmeal, then—and you tape it closed with the wide masking tape. Remember the tape that you found that day in the artist's garbage? He really turned out good garbage, vintage garbage. All right: the masking tape to seal the cut.

What do you suppose had been that scratching outside her door?

She would find out. But not now. Tomorrow, maybe. Right now, ummmm, where was she? She would get up and crawl over to the camelback couch and put the oatmeal on the cut and tape it shut. It would take time, because old blood coagulates so slowly.

She slept until the next night, holding her shoulder with her hand until they stuck together.

The message was waiting on the other side of the door when she finally opened it. It would be there for a long time. It had been scratched into the brown paint with the tip of a knife.

It said:
YOU NEXT.
And then it said:
YOU
      AIN'T
           GOT
                NO
                    DOG.

4

OFFICER KEITH LEE

Yessir, fine evening. Not too hot and better air today. It was now 6 P.M. on Tenth Street.

Mr. and Mrs. Sol Haven were extremely dead now, a whole lot deader than they had been when he had first found them—just about as dead as they would ever get. But they couldn't be moved off the stairway and boxed in everlasting peace until the Homicide guys got through. And the main Homicide guy was taking his time.

Not that Officer Keith Lee cared. He had done his part. He had gone back into the apartment and escorted them up the stairs, pausing at each body. First, Mr. Sol Haven, face up, with his legs gone all noodly, the slits from the stab wounds running at right angles to the stripes on his shirt. And then Mrs. Sol Haven, just outside their apartment on the top landing—lying face down with her arms spread out like she was hang-gliding. Her fingers were curled so strongly into the worn carpeting that she had cut scratches into the graying fibers. The blood on the back of her head had turned Dr Pepper-brown against the wispy white hair.

All right. Scratch two more senior citizens. Nice evening.

So he stood out in front of the apartment building now, looking both ways along the sidewalk, doing the Johnny Miller.

There was no way to miss it: Officer Keith Lee looked exactly like Johnny Miller, looked like him right through to the teeth—as if he had just this minute leaned his putter against a tree to go answer the phone and then stroll over here. Maybe nodding to his caddie: Don't let the tournament go on without me, Sambo, I'll be back in a minute. It's something about two old folks murdered on my beat, two hapless oldies, my boy. Just put a dime down on the green to mark where my ball was, all right?

Officer Keith Lee didn't play golf—*golf*, chrissakes? But he fostered the Johnny Miller by bleaching his hair in alternating strands every other week to get it into tawny layers. Like he had just played in the bright sun at Augusta and then in the misty rain the next week at Pebble. He also stretched out motionless and naked under a sunlamp for a half hour every night, Kennedy half-dollars over his eyes. He wore Sears Men's Store clothes, the Johnny Miller signature-model golf outfits. He had all twelve colors in the bell-sleeved sweaters and all the Johnny Miller slacks and knit shirts. Today he was wearing the red pants and tassel loafers and the Navy blue sweater over the white knit golf shirt.

He took good care of himself: he lifted weights every morning, and he took three kinds of vitamins. And he soaked both hands in salt water so that he wouldn't split his knuckles hitting kids in the head.

It's Johnny Miller standing there. Winning pro. Mormon

24

elder. All tanned and nice teeth. Such a sweet-looking man.

Except that Officer Keith Lee carried a Smith & Wesson .357 Combat Magnum tucked into his waistband, under the sweater and under the cotton golf shirt. It was nickel-plated, two-and-one-half-inch barrel, pearlescent grips—and it all slipped into the waistband holster with the soft chamois lining. You can do that in the Child Welfare Division when you are a youth-gang control officer.

The division was what a lot of people called an elite outfit, which didn't really mean much. It didn't mean any more money; it only meant that he hadn't worn his dress uniform since the last departmental funeral. That elite stuff had probably started with *The New York Times*.

"This is a small, disciplined outfit whose mission is to combat juvenile crime," the captain had said, quoting it from the newspaper. "That's us they're talking about. You know, plainclothes. Well, except for you, Lee. Will you for Christ's sake knock it off with the fag stuff, already? Anyway, okay. We got something like two hunnert sixty youth gangs. I don't mean here in the Sixth Precinct; in New *York*, I mean, and we got five intelligence officers and me. I spend, let's see, I spend half my time over at City trying to keep them from cutting my budget any more already. The other half of my time I spend giving interviews on television. Plus interviews to newspaper guys. Lissen: every reporter in this town is doing a series on kid crimes, and they're all quoting *me*. But, okay. Okay, the *other* half of my time I try to get some work out of you goddam clowns. Look at that arrest sheet there on the wall. No, don't look; just go out there and put some goddam numbers on it. Numbers, maybe I get more money. No numbers, you're all back in uniform somewheres."

Keith Lee looked at his watch again: 6:15 P.M.

So all right. He would, maybe tonight, he would nail

the one who had done this. The Homicide guys would do what they always do. They would take a lot of notes and then go away. And then it would be head-busting time around here.

He looked both ways along the sidewalk again and then back at his watch.

Bring in a kid killer, get a citation. They put it in your service record. Ace cop strikes again. Kid puts up a fight, they put your picture in the *Daily News* maybe. And he really photographed well. Last time, what? Two months ago now, women had seen his picture in the *News* and had been calling him at the station. Captain had hated it. Well, until he had spun off one of them on the captain.

What he really needed was a new kid. Strange one would be best; he had already locked up half this damn neighborhood. It would be even better if the kid was a mouth-breather who wouldn't know what had hit him. And not a chili-burner; he had too many of those on his record right now. Pretty soon the Puerto Rican Preservation Society would be on him again—whatever the name of that outfit was. But a kid; somebody.

One of the Homicide men came down. He stood on the sidewalk and began polishing his glasses, hah'hing on them and holding them up to the light. Then he put them on and jammed the handkerchief back into his pants pocket, looking sideways at Keith Lee.

"You know, you make this whole block look nice, just standing out here," he said.

"Ain't that the truth? Least I can do."

"Uhhh, lissen: where do you carry your handcuffs, you know, dressed like that?"

Keith Lee shrugged. "Back pocket here. No belt on these kind of pants."

The Homicide man nodded. "Nice. I suppose they're, you know, they're double-knit handcuffs, right? I mean, match the outfit and all."

"Your ass. Lissen: you guys catch the killer up there yet?"

"Who, me? You're the intelligence officer."

"So that don't mean I'm smart. Smart, I'd be in Homicide."

"Not dressed like that, you wouldn't. Lissen: like, I don't even dress like that, my day *off*."

"Okay, look," Keith Lee said. "Look: the perpetrator comes by here; you know, I mean right on this side of the *street* and all, okay. I'll catch him for you. No running though, you got it? Not in these loafers. And no chasing into the buildings."

The Homicide man half turned and looked back up the sandstone stairs. "I know. It was me, these apartments along here, you'd have to back me up with six guys carrying sawed-offs. Dark hallways." He looked around and lowered his voice. "And, you know, dark kids. Lissen: these old-timey buildings flat scare me to death."

"Scare me worse. It's why I'm standing out here."

"Yeah, well." The Homicide man stood staring into the street for a moment. "Anyway, so what else is new down here? You getting any strange stuff?"

"Me? Listen, old stuff, even. I gave it up for Lent. I'm damn near out of the habit now."

"Horseshit. You Youth guys. I know. Bring in all the boys and bang all the girls."

Keith Lee looked at his watch again. "Oh, kids. *Kids,* sure; hell, every day. All the time. I thought you meant, like, real ladies."

"Your ass, ladies. It's probably the faggy clothes. How come the sleeves are like that? I mean, see: all baggy around the wrist like that there and smaller up on top."

Keith Lee raised his left arm and looked at it. "It's *supposed* to be that way. Man, one thing: you got no class at all. This is a *golf* sweater. What the hell do you think it is, a walking-around-in sweater or something?"

"Fruity sleeves."

"Bet your ass they're fruity. I got guys spotted all over this neighborhood who want to get up inside these sleeves and take off all their clothes. I got a pink one of these sweaters at home, it drives them right out of their gourd. No class at all, Homicide."

"You carry a gun, Lee?"

Keith Lee nodded, patting his waist in front. "Chrome-dipped, I don't get my fingers dirty."

"I just wondered, for chrissakes. I thought maybe . . ."

They both heard the other Homicide man coming heavily down the stone stairs. The one in charge. They both straightened.

"Officer Lee." It was a statement, not a greeting.

"Sir."

"Well?"

"Sir?"

"Well, what can you tell us?"

"About . . . ?"

"Lee, I'm not talking about the weather. About those two senior citizens up there on the stairs. Both of them dead; perhaps you noticed. Damn, that place stinks up there. So?"

"Well, sir, I haven't really had time to . . ."

"Don't interrupt me. You know what's going to happen down here? You want to know? I'll tell you what's going to happen. You keep this up and we're not going to have any living person over sixty years *old* down here. Youth division. Intelligence officers. Good God. And another thing. Just what are you got up to be?"

"Sir?"

"You, I'm talking about. The clothes there. Is that a, is that a *neck*lace there?"

Keith Lee brought one hand to his throat. "Uhhh. No. Well, I mean it's, it's called pukka beads. It's like . . . well.

All the people down here in the Village, they . . . uhhh . . ."
He shrugged.

The bulky man continued to stare at him, his lips pulled in tightly. "The Youth division. My God. Well. You look like somebody, Lee. I can't quite . . . but somebody."

The other Homicide man coughed. "Johnny Miller," he said.

"Johnny . . . ?"

"It's a golfer."

"A golfer. Is that good or bad?"

"Well. I don't think it matters either way, sir," the man said.

The bulky one nodded. "Well, whatever. He certainly doesn't look like a policeman. I take it that's the idea around here. Now. Now, then. Your foolish costumes aside, Lee, what I want from you is . . ."

Wait. *Hold* it.

For Keith Lee, it was as if he was wearing antenna. There was something there. Something out of place.

He swung around, letting the Homicide man's voice roll along, half listening. He looked across the street and picked him out of the crowd instantly.

It was a new kid.

Walking along. Not too fast, not too slow. Blank face. Eyes looking nowhere; the kid didn't want to be noticed. Okay: jeans. Prefaded blue shirt, epaulets, button-down pockets. Puma running shoes, the two white stripes dipping down at mid-foot. Mussed-around hair and arched eyebrows. Say, mmmmm, say, thirteen or fourteen years, no more. He would go maybe hundred and twenty-eight, nine pounds.

Keith Lee tightened the muscles across his chest, watching.

". . . every apartment in this whole district if you have to," the Homicide man was saying. "And then report back to me when you . . ." He blinked. "Am I boring you, Officer Lee?"

Keith Lee swung his head back around. "Sir?"

"You seem suddenly distracted. I was saying . . ."

Something in the kid's bearing. It was an all-wound-up tight look. The kid paused at the corner, waiting for the light; looking noplace, focusing his eyes on some middle distance, letting the people swirl around him.

Keith Lee glanced at his watch again. And then back at the corner. The kid stepped off the curb and into the intersection. He was heading toward Sixth Avenue.

Okay, then. Just about right.

". . . speak up, Lee. What is it?"

Keith Lee took a half step, then turned back. "Excuse me," he said. "Excuse me, but it's someone I have to question. I just this minute saw him. It could . . . well. It might have some bearing on this case here. That boy over there, see? No, the one just crossing. I want to . . ."

"Well, that's more like it," the bulky one said. "Go on. Go on, get after him."

"Thank you, sir."

He sidestepped around behind a cab and headed for the other side of the street.

Behind him, he could hear the voice say, "Tell me again. Who the hell is Johnny whatever-his-name-is?"

And Officer Keith Lee fell in step. The kid's back was just up there ahead; in sight, out of sight. The kid was just easing through the crowd. Hard to keep him in sight.

Bugger. Little bugger had guilt stamped all over him. Catch up to this little bugger and run him into a hallway and he'd never know what hit him. Time he got through with him, the kid would confess to killing everybody in town. Fine.

But there had been something else. There had been something there the first time Keith Lee had looked across the street and spotted the kid. It was . . . well, he had a special police feel for these things; you develop it. You get so you can spot one of those types. They're sort of giving off waves of trouble. They're not ... what? Not malleable; they can't be bent and pounded into shape. There's trouble in the position of their damn heads in relation to their shoulders; trouble in the line of the way they *stand*, all sucked up inside. This new kid had it for fair, walking along there, trying not to show it. Touch him on the shoulder from behind and he would go up like a guided missile.

But, okay, so much for police science. You'd be all strung up tight like that, too, if you had just mugged and murdered two old people for a lousy few bucks.

The odds were very good—no, the odds were terrific—that this new kid hadn't done it. In fact, he looked all wrong for it. But the odds were even better that he was about to be *arrested* for it. And confess to it—if only to stop the pain of being hit repeatedly in the kidneys.

Up ahead, the slender shoulders suddenly squared. And stopped. The kid swung around, left to right, and looked back.

Keith Lee quickly looked down at the sidewalk. He gave it one beat, two beats. Then he looked up again.

Well, damn.

The kid had *made* him, just like that. All these people all milling around here and now the kid was looking at him. Directly. He had a sexy mouth, the kid. Brown eyes under the archy eyebrows.

But none of that startled-fawn routine. The kid was studying *him* now, taking all the measurements; weight, height, counting up the risks. Keeping some facts, throwing out others he wouldn't need. The kid wasn't blinking. Probably the little bugger wasn't even breathing.

Hell, of course. That was it. That was the air of whatever it was that he had spotted at first on the street back there. The kid knew exactly where everybody else was in relation to himself. He had them all made; everybody out there on the sidewalk with him.

And now the kid turned. He headed down Sixth toward the playground.

Okay. That did it. This would be the one. He had to go. It is very tough to be a smart-ass kid with your head all bent in.

Officer Keith Lee straightened his shoulders and moved ahead, the evening sunlight glinting off his golden hair.

But when he got to the corner, the kid was gone. Just like that.

5

MARION DOLAN

She made a distinct sound when she walked. It was because her thighs swelled up against the pressure of the
long-line girdle. The legs on the girdle came down to just
above her kneecaps. The raised elastic ribbing ran ver-
tically, and when Marion Dolan walked, her legs went
shhhhhppppp, shhhhhhpppp, shhhhhhpppp. She had
learned to adjust her thinking to the steady rasp of the
sound, and now it was natural, a musical pace.

She was thinking about the boy now, rhythmically, as
she walked toward the deli where they would meet. She
would buy two of the apple turnovers and carry them to
the round marble-topped table. One for him, one for her;
milk for him, coffee for her, and she would sit down and
wait. And he would come in, not seeming to look for her,
that lovely avalanche of hair spilling down over his forehead, his incredibly lovely mouth and all. And then he
would look directly at her from under the shadowy thick
eyelashes and his eyebrows would go up ever so slightly

in an arch. There was never a smile. He always wore a totally fathomless face. It was painfully delicate, the face of a young baby Doctor Faustus. And when he did smile, it was always bitterly—and his eyes would go half-closed. His eyeteeth were sharp, suitable for biting into souls.

In a way, shhhhppppp, shhhhhpppp, she loved him. No, no, not *physically*. Come on. Nothing that would fill the air with the musky, wet smells that she didn't care to smell. But, well. Love of a sort.

Marion Dolan often pictured herself sitting in a laboratory somewhere; somewhere *clinical*, in a swivel chair. White smock. And the boy would be sitting cross-legged on the floor, up close, with his back to her. That way she could open her legs and grip his shoulders with her mighty thighs. And then she would lean forward and lift open the top of his head, gently, and reach inside there and do wonderful things. She would lift out his lobes, perhaps, and hold them up to the overhead light and look through them at the facets all glittering—and then fix them with her psychic screwdriver: tiny, infinitely delicate adjustments that would . . . what? That would *tune* him back to the rest of the world. Then she would put everything back in place neatly and pat his hair back down. He would smile then, properly this time, with no bitterness, and thank her for it. And later, in years to come, she would be at her college and he would come to visit. She would have the memorial chair in psychology then, and tenure, and she would offer him around to her colleagues. Look what I wrought; see what I can do. Gaze upon the untroubled face of my boy.

She pushed open the door of the delicatessen and walked directly to the counter, looking for the turnovers among the pastries displayed under the glass-domed covers. The counterman had his back to her, but he turned when he heard the rustling of her legs. He knew what she was going to say, obviously. He knew by now, but he waited, looking pointedly at the outthrust of her stomach. It was his little game, that fiend.

"Two of the apple turnovers," Marion Dolan said. "One coffee, one milk. They're fresh?"

The counterman nodded. "Today, today. Always."

"Thank you."

"Sugar in the coffee?" He was playing the game again. She could kill him for this.

"No, thank you. I've got some substitute in my purse," she said.

"You're sure? That stuff makes it bitter, the coffee."

"No sugar, I said."

He shrugged. "S'your body. Fulla stuff, that junk. You know, what do you call it they put in there? *Additives.* A rat, you get cancer from it. But real sugar is . . ."

"Come *on,*" Marion Dolan said.

She put the two plates down on the table, and then the coffee mug and the glass of milk, arranging them so that she would be sitting side by side with her boy when he came in. She sat down heavily and glared across at the counterman. He grinned back at her, then puffed out his cheeks to make himself look fatter.

She could kill him. Stick a serving fork into his neck; something. The anger started welling up inside again, and suddenly the perspiration was thick under her arms— oozing right out through all the Ban Roll-On. She glanced down at her right wrist, there in the little inside hollow where they took your pulse, and she could see the vein starting to throb bigger and bigger. She took several deep breaths.

Easy now, easy. She picked up the thick white mug, holding it with both hands for steadiness, and took a sip of the coffee. Get it back under control. It's only a tendency toward tension. Nothing more; a lot of people can suffer from tension. It was nothing like the Director had written about her in her fitness report at the agency. Or had even said straight to her face one time.

"Miss Dolan," the Director had said, "you show remarkable signs of instability for a social worker. You must control these outbursts of temper; after all, you're dealing with children. There are times, I must say, when you seem positively homi*cid*al."

Well, no. She wasn't nearly that bad; not like he had said. Everybody had a touch of instability hidden away somewhere. And she could control hers. Absolutely. She took another sip of the coffee.

The sweat was turning cold now, curling in under her breasts.

Don't look at the counterman again; that's it. Look at the turnover.

Oh, God, the calories. Hundreds of them, just dancing around in there. She studied it, looking deeply into the thin layers of crust, and then at the trail of white frosting wiggling like a continuous Z across the top. And the apple filling; it always sat so perfectly on her tongue, sending out signals of creamy taste to both sides of her mouth. Anyway, besides, her boy loved them so. He would turn the plate around and around, studying the triangular shape and, finally, where there would be an outcropping from a bubble caused in the baking, he would eat that part first to bring the turnover back into balance.

She glanced over at the door.

No telling who he would be acting like today. Alistair Cooke. Or maybe Dan Rather. Either way, she knew that you were not supposed to notice; it was part of the routine.

The thing was, there was so much *to* the boy. He was made up of so many parts and sections. His personality was so chinked and splintered already that she never knew quite where to start on him.

36

Well, wait. That wasn't quite true.

She did know where to start, all right. Certainly. First, the article. Right. Start with the story.

She had taken the story outline to the offices of *New York* magazine yesterday. And the editor—well, at least the one they had let her see, the editor had said, No, there can't be a kid like the one you describe, Miss Dolan. Not a real person. Not fourteen years old. But, well, sure, the magazine was interested in such an article. Hell, yes, an idea like this could be dynamite for the magazine. If it worked—no promises now, but if it worked—he just might give her story lead play. Put it on the cover, even. Kids are big stuff now. Hell, Miss Dolan, they're running wild all over Manhattan. Mugging, killing. You'd think this place was Calcutta, you know what I mean?

Lovely, then. That would do it, the article.

Under the table now—to help herself think—she raised first her left leg, then her right, rubbing her thighs together, listening to the comforting shhhhhppppp, shhhhhppp, of the elastic ribbing.

Her proposed title had grabbed the editor right from the start, too: "Media Child in Manhattan." By Marion Dolan, social worker. No. By Dr. M. Dolan, B.A., M.A., soon-to-be Ph.D. It was her case and nobody else had it.

She squeezed her thighs together more tightly and rubbed them slowly, creating a longer, more drawn-out sound.

There would be the story in the magazine. Under the first column of type there would be the ruled line running across. And underneath the ruled line would be the explanation of who the writer was. They always did that, and in italics. They would know how to word it properly, of course. Something like: Marion Dolan is a psychologist and social worker. This is the true story of her most exceptional case. Most unusual case, maybe, or even fright-

37

ening; whatever. This case-story of Johnny D. (not his real name) will become part of Miss Dolan's doctoral dissertation in psychology.

Doctor Dolan.

And then. And *then* would come the college someplace —no more of this grubbing around as a social worker. A real college someplace in the East; counseling, whatever— no more filthy welfare kids whose smell clung to her clothes when she got home every night.

The thesis would do it. Plus the excerpt in *New York* magazine. Like, mmmmm, like Buckley had done with *Man and God at Yale*. Or was it God and Man? Well, who the hell cares? She would do better. She could be published in *Psychology Today*, maybe. My God, it could even be a television series. Or a movie: *Media Child*. Everything.

Shhhhhppppp!

"Like I said in my outline," she had told the editor, "this boy is perfect. It's because of his background—but it's also because of this day and age. My boy might be the nexus of an entire generation of children formed and shaped by the media. This one is best because he started out *hollow*; that is, he was born illegitimate and he was neglected, battered, all of that. It turned him *in*ward, do you follow me? And now, he's like an enormous sponge, a psychological sponge. He doesn't rely on people. He doesn't trust people. He relies on media. He pulls in impulses from the world around him. Television, mostly, but movies, too. And a few books; he doesn't read as well as he *watches*. He feeds on input. Some days he talks in TV dialogue. You understand this? No father figure, no family to influence his speech patterns or mannerisms. Some days he's tough; sometimes he's Henny Youngman, for heaven's sake. He tries certain lines of conversation on you just to watch your reaction. If you don't react the way he wants, he never does it again; it's out. When he's in direct contact with people, he soaks them up. You know: their gestures, the speech. It means that he's still assembling, putting together what he'll be when he grows up."

"Perfect," the editor had said. "We could do this shadowy painting for the cover, see? Multilayer the image; you know, however the artists do that sort of thing. And . . ."

"There's one more element," Marion Dolan had said, getting more excited about it. Her knees had been pumping up and down like alternating pistons underneath her skirt. "The boy manages to stand *outside* himself and look back in. It's as though he is watching his own life. Lately, he has taken to referring to himself in third person. Calls himself The Kid. 'The Kid is going,' he will say. Or something like that. He's living his life as if he was a character in it. And then comes the terrible part."

"There's a terrible part? Good."

"The terrible part," she had said, "is that he is watching himself disintegrate—and he's so fascinated by the drama in it that he can't stop watching. He wants to see how the life of The Kid turns out. He's into crime. Well. I mean, he steals things. You know. It could . . ."

The editor had nodded briskly at that. "Would you say, would you say, Miss Dolan, that it could deteriorate from there? From crime, say, to mugging. To dope? To, ummm, to rape? Murder?"

And she had nodded back. "It's possible, yes. I see what you're getting at. Yes, it's possible. And if there isn't a magazine story in that, I'll . . ."

"Got it, got it," the editor had said. "How soon can you let me see something?"

"Couple more interviews. We're into a very sensitive area right now," she had said. "And I've got to go carefully. The boy is not cooperating. And . . ."

"Tell me: is there any sex in it?"

She had blinked at him. "Any what?"

"Sex," the editor had said. "Surely, with all you've told me—you know, surely there's some sort of . . . well. What I mean is, you know, the kids today are all like, well, like dirty little animals, always doing it. And, ummmm. Well, frankly, it could use some sex. Now, I'm not trying to steer your article, Miss Dolan. Don't get me wrong. But it seems to me that if you're going to be a successful . . ."

That had done it. "I'll think of something," she had said. "But I'll have to be careful, as I just said. The boy is so volatile. And . . ."

"Unstable."

"Aren't we all," Marion Dolan had said.

Now she glanced down at her plate and suddenly realized that she had already eaten half of her apple turnover.

And when she looked up, guiltily, he was there.

He had come in quietly and now he stood looking down at her.

It was . . . what? It was the lighting. Good heavens, something, the reflections from the marble and chrome in here, but his eyelashes looked like *mink*. They were casting heavy shadows on his cheeks. His eyebrows went up slightly.

"Uhhhh, Press," she said. "*Press.*" She pulled back his chair, smiling up at him. "I was just this *minute* thinking about you. Sit down. Come on."

He sat. And he put both forearms on the tabletop and started turning the white plate around with his fingertips, studying the pastry from all sides, cocking his head slightly to look at it. The open collar of his shirt stood away from the back of his neck where the hair curled. She could see down inside. It was a new shirt, obviously: prefaded blue madras, with epaulets and button pockets. The label said . . . ummmmm, the label said Paul Stuart.

Paul *Stuart*, for heaven's sake?

"Nice shirt," she said. "That color is just right for you; you know, your olive skin and all."

He wouldn't look up at her.

"You . . . uhhhh. You bought . . . ?"

"Yes, ma'am. I bought the shirt," he said. He continued to turn the plate. "You can't steal shirts from Paul Stuart. They keep them in glass cases there."

She let out some of the breath that she had been holding. "Well. That's better. You know how I worry about how you . . . well. About how you . . ."

"Everybody worries about me," he said. The shadow of his eyelashes lay diagonally across his cheeks now. "It's the way it works. You; everybody. People stop me on the street and worry about me."

"Well," she said. "You know. I mean, I'm so glad that you actually bought the shirt. It's certainly a step in . . ."

Finally he looked up. The full, steady look: his eyes were the color of burnt umber straight through, with no definition of pupil or iris.

"Right, right," he said. "I bought the shirt." He put in the pause he always did when he wanted to get a sample reaction from her. "But first, I stole the money."

"Ohhhh, *Press*."

She could read tension in his face and the cords along his neck. He was giving off tension like it was a cologne.

She nodded. "Yes, well. We'll get back to that a little later," she said. "First, go ahead and eat your turnover. And the milk. Please, now."

"Thank you."

She wanted to reach over and put the palm of her left hand alongside his face and say: ease off. But she didn't.

Instead: "How have you been, Press?" she said.

He gave the slightest indication of a shrug. "Okay. Good, bad, same as always. Check one."

41

"Well, then. Ummmm, well. Press, listen: can we talk today? I mean, not like last week, all right? We've really got to talk. I've got a lot of material to cover. Really."

He glanced sideway at her and smiled.

She found herself staring at his eyeteeth. How could teeth be so white and perfect when he had never seen a dentist in his life? A dentist would cry, seeing those teeth.

He shook his head back and forth. "No," he said. He began chewing and there was a little fleck of the beige crust sticking to his lower lip. "You don't really want to talk. What you want to do is to ask me all those questions again. That's not talking to me."

"But, Press. See, I need to know . . ."

"No, you don't." He put down the fork and pushed the plate away, half the turnover still there. "No. You're supposed to be helping me; that's what you said. That was a long time ago, too. But . . . I don't know. Now, all you do is ask me stuff. Why do I talk this way or that way. What's going on inside my mind. Who am I pretending to be—junk like that. Well, that's not helping me." He shook his head again and the hair fell over his forehead.

Watching him, not taking her eyes from his, she reached over and patted around on the table until she felt his plate. She picked up the rest of his apple turnover with her fingertips. She swung her arm up and thrust all of the turnover into her mouth, tamping it in with her thumb, and began chewing. She started rubbing her thighs together.

He took a breath and went on: "You want to know too much. Stuff I don't even know what to tell you. What I *want* to tell you is that I hate the place where I'm staying now. Where you put me. It's bad. Like all the others, every foster place I've ever been. No. It's worse, even. But you won't talk to me about that. You want to know what I'm thinking about instead. That's dumb. What difference does it make? What I want to talk about is why don't you leave my head alone? Help me instead. And then . . . what are you doing? What's that?"

"What?" she said.

"Moving your legs like that. Making that sound."

She stopped her legs. "I'm thinking." She licked the frosting off the tip of each finger.

"Oh."

"You said you've been stealing again."

"I already told you that. Next, you're going to ask me why. 'Tell me, Press, who were you pretending to be when you stole the money to buy that shirt?' Right? Or, 'What was going through your mind then, Press?' "

"Well, I need to know."

"Wrong."

"You'll get caught. The police . . ."

"No way. I'm too fast to get caught. Put that down in your weekly report. What The Kid is thinking about when The Kid is out taking money is that he's too fast to get caught at it."

"All right: that report you mentioned. My report. Its purpose is to help you."

He shook his head no.

"It is, too, Press. Really."

"No, it's something else. You're up to something with the report; I can tell by the way the questions go. I don't know what it is you're doing. But something. Not to help me."

She could feel her blood starting to chase all around again. It was throbbing everywhere—her wrists, her temples. "Are you suggesting that I'm lying? Lying? Now, listen here, young man. Don't you even dare . . ."

He leaned forward. His eyes seemed to fill her entire field of vision. All that one color. What was it . . . the light from the windows, maybe? She could see her face reflected in his right eye—her face all roundish.

"What do you want from me?" he said.

"I'm gathering material to . . . well . . . to help you, Press. To, uhhh, to mend you."

"I'm not broken. It's something else."

She was starting to get short of breath now. The, mmmm, the instability factor again. Damn the Director for saying a thing like that. No, no, by God. She could control it; get her blood back under control. She put the tips of her fingers against her temples and pressed down hard.

"It's none of your business," she said. "When I want you to know something, I'll tell you. Understand? Now, then. Now we'll talk, like I said."

"Okay. Fine. You'll get me out of the place where I'm staying."

"We're *not* going to talk about that."

Shhhhhhhhppppppppppp. *Shhhhhhhppppppp.*

The man at the next table turned and looked at her.

"All right," Press said. "Then I guess we won't talk about anything."

"Oh, yes we will," she said. "There are things that I need to know."

"What's the matter?"

"What?"

He looked more closely at her. "Your face."

"Never *mind* my face. You hear me? Just for*get* my face. It's the blood. I just get . . . flushed. Just never mind, I said."

The man at the next table turned again. He was holding a toasted English muffin in one hand.

"Lady, *lady*," he said. "Will you stop, already? Will you stop it with that *sound*? You're some kind of a cricket or something? Knock it off with that rubbie-rubbie stuff; I'm going crazy already."

She blinked and stopped her thighs. "Sorry," she said. "I didn't realize that you could . . ."

44

"That *I* could? Lady, lissen: everybody in this whole *block* could."

"Sorry."

And when she turned back, the boy was gone.

Oh, no. Not now. Damn it all. The *thesis.* And the magazine article. Damn him.

Well, wait. Just calm down. Hold your legs still a minute and try to think. Well, maybe move them a little bit, softly.

Okay, then. She would start out all over again on him. She would open his head like peeling a banana until she could get inside there and get him figured out. She would tell the world about it, too. She would take his psyche and hammer it into shape. Or else.

But . . . well, damn him. Press Reynolds was all of it. He was her way out of here, for one thing. He was her media child; she had found him and nobody else. He was her doctorate.

He was, or else. Very idea. That little . . . little creature. We'll see.

Two things. One: Marion Dolan would *not* be crossed.

And would not be blocked. Never. And, Two: if she couldn't get him, nobody else would. Ever.

6

THE KID

Get just the right look on your face and people will never notice you. It's an expression that falls just between you-know-where-you-are and you-belong-there-anyway. People see that look and their mind runs a quick check on it and says: "Well, he's all right. I'm looking for somebody suspicious." The Kid was very good at it. He was the best.

He stood beside the gray metal desk. He was holding the Charles Delicatessen brown-paper bag in his left hand. The bag was sitting upright in his open palm. He breathed quietly, listening for office sounds. And then he bent slightly and gently rolled out the lower left-hand drawer on the desk, the file drawer.

Women always leave their purses in the lower left-hand drawer, the file drawer. Never another drawer; they always use that one. Count on it. They never take their wallets out of the purses and lock the wallets separately in the thin top-center drawer. Women never carry desk keys with them. They always have far too many keys on the ring anyway, and it's a bother. There are only four times a day when women take their purses with them into the ladies room: first when they get to work. Once just before they go to lunch. Once when they come back from lunch and the last time just before they go home. All women only pee four times a day. Bet on it. The rest of the time, when they leave the office, the purse is sitting just behind the files in that drawer.

Some women put a scarf over the purse to hide it. It doesn't matter.

The Kid glanced down to locate the clasp, then un-clicked the purse with his right hand. He reached inside quickly and came up with the folded-over wallet. He flicked open the snap with his thumbnail and then lifted out the bills with his thumb and index finger. He dropped the wallet back into the purse, snapped it closed, eased the drawer shut and stood erect. He put the folded-over money into his right jeans pocket without looking at it.

Things The Kid knew:

Never take checks.

Never take credit cards. No small change, ever.

Only take bills.

He stepped back out into the hall and turned right. He was holding the brown-paper bag like a serving tray, the label facing out. Always hold it that way—the bag is really the first thing they see. They will see you, but they won't really see you; you're only the delivery boy. He got to the end of the corridor and turned left.

He passed the floor-to-ceiling glass walls and a glass door that opened into a reception room. There was gold lettering on the door. Tan carpeting and two modern wooden desks. A shame, too: wooden desks always contained more money than the gray metal ones. He glanced at the desks and kept on walking.

No way. To go into an executive reception area would be dumb time on the Hudson.

He passed the elevator bank on his left and kept walking, glancing into the other offices. Holding the bag: label out.

"Young man."

Things The Kid knew:

When they say "Young man," you're home free. If they say "Hey" or "Hey, kid!" you're in some trouble, maybe a lot, maybe a little. If a man says, "Hold it right there," it's the end. But "Young man," never. Never.

He stopped and turned slowly, his eyebrows up.

"Ma'am?" he said.

It was a little lady, about his size. Gray hair knotted in back. Eyeglasses on silver chains, the glasses resting on her chest. Silky print dress, little pictures of owls. He glanced down: she was wearing low-heeled shoes with laces.

The shoes cinched it.

"May I ask exactly what you're doing here?" she said.

He smiled. The Kid nodded so that the toss of hair swirled down over his forehead. And he held out the bag a bit farther.

"Delivering," he said. "Charles Deli."

"Who is that for?"

He switched palms with the bag, keeping the label pointed toward the gray lady. He put his left hand into the jeans pocket and pulled up the order form. He unfolded it and looked at the name written on it, then looked up.

"Delaney," he said. "Nancy Delaney. Twenty fourteen. Two–oh–one–four."

And he handed the order to the little lady so that she could read it. She put on her glasses, the chains swinging down in half-circles in front of her ears. And she shook her head.

"Well, you're on the *wrong* floor," she said. "There's no

Nancy Delaney on this floor; there's no floor number written down here. What number did you say?"

"Twenty fourteen, ma'am."

"Well, this is twenty-*one*. You ought to know better than that, young man. I don't know about this. Perhaps I ought to call the . . ."

"Ma'am," The Kid said. "I wonder if you have a building directory here? Could we look at it for just a second?"

"Well. Mmmmm, here. Come here to my office."

Ta dah. He followed her to the office and stood beside the wooden desk. She leaned over and opened the left-hand drawer, the file drawer, to see if her purse was still there. It was under a silk scarf. She nodded and closed the drawer and then opened the thin center drawer and took out the directory.

"Delaney?"

He nodded, smiling. "D-E-L-A-N-E-Y. Delaney."

The little lady ran her index finger down the D's.

"You're right," she said. "Twenty fourteen. That's one floor down. It will be on the other side of the corridor, twenty fourteen."

"Thank you very much, ma'am."

She nodded and looked into The Kid's eyes for a long moment. Then she smiled back. "One floor down. Remember next time," she said. "Our security people could get upset."

"I will, ma'am."

She went to the door with him, holding his right elbow lightly with her fingertips. Their heads were at about the same level.

Other things The Kid knew:

The Litany:

"How old are you, young man?"

"Fourteen, ma'am."

"Why aren't you in school?"

"I am. It's vocational. We work some, go to school some."

"Do you like doing this?"

"Yes, ma'am. You get to meet a lot of interesting people."

"Well. You just keep at it. It's good to see ambition in young folks. We all have to start somewhere."

"Thank you. I'm trying."

"Do you have a card, young man? You know, a number; something? I might want a sandwich delivered some time."

"Can't afford cards," he said. "But just call the Charles Deli."

"Whom shall I ask for? That is, if I want you to deliver it personally?"

"Ask for The Kid."

"The . . . well. You have a real name, I suppose."

"Yes, ma'am. It's Reynolds. Press Reynolds. They just call me The Kid there."

"I can certainly see why. You're such a baby face. Such nice, warm eyes."

"Thank you."

"All right, then. One floor down. Remember, it will be in the other corridor."

"Yes, ma'am. And thanks for everything."

He let the elevator doors slide shut on his smile. He knew that, on the other side, the little gray lady would stand there for a few minutes, looking at where he had been.

He rode the car to the main floor, stepping to the back as it stopped at other floors to let people on. Then he walked through the lobby, out the swinging doors and onto the plaza. He found an open spot on the ledge around the fountain and sat down. He opened the bag and took out the sandwich and unwrapped it. He turned the hard roll around and around in his fingers until he found the uneven, unsymmetrical spot, and bit into it there. It was egg salad and bacon, the kind he always took on his building rounds. And he began to chew, watching the people passing by.

Hello, everybody. I can see you, but you can't see me.

What if one time he ran into the real Nancy Delaney back up there in the building somewhere? There really was one, a real Nancy Delaney, just like there was a real name in all the places he hit on Rockefeller Center. He was very careful to look them up and write the real names on the stolen deli order blanks. The names were always real; hell, so were the sandwiches that he bought with his own money—switching his business around from one deli to another, depending on what day they made their egg salad.

It was just that Nancy Delaney was his favorite. It was a name for a small girl. It was a kind of name you'd have if you were on television. But a variety show; you'd have to sing and dance with a name like that.

The real Nancy Delaney would turn out to be really dinky, probably. With blond curls all over her head. And little tiny boobs that you could see perfectly, dials and all.

"Yes, I'm Nancy Delaney," she would say.

There would be big security guys standing all around The Kid then, their heavy hands on The Kid's shoulders, the antennas of walkie-talkie radios sticking out of their back pockets.

"But, no," she would say, "I didn't order a sandwich."

The Kid would smile down at her and look exactly into her eyes. The Kid would be stone calm like Dan Rather.

"It's something of a gift, my dear," The Kid would say, all David Frost. Or, no. D'Art*agnan*, that's the way *he* would say it. You got to make your voice sound like you have a mustache. "We wanted you to try our new egg salad-and-bacon combination. No charge, of course."

"Oh," she would say. She would smile then and there would be dimples. Well, for sure, at least a dimple on one side. "Well, in that case . . ."

And Nancy Delaney would send the security guys away. They wouldn't like it, but they would go. The Kid would turn and watch them leave, a faint look of contempt forming on his . . . on his, ummm. On his aquiline lips. And then he would turn back to Nancy Delaney. And she would already have her blouse half unbuttoned, pulling it off her milk-white shoulders. No. Her alabaster shoulders.

She would say, so low that you really had to listen to catch it, "I want you to . . ."

Horseshit. He let the image dissolve; he didn't have time for any of that today.

Everything was going wrong again. Good God, your life was supposed to get better as you got older and could get your hands into it more. But, no.

How do you like your life so far, Kid?

Up yours. It started out lousy and it isn't getting any better. That's how The Kid likes it.

Hello, out there. Any one of you walking past the plaza. Talk to me, somebody.

It's me. See?

Okay, okay. Forget it. Nobody looks at anybody in this town. You could die. You could lie there; they would step over you. Maybe nodding to themselves, like New Yorkers do: Hmmm, there seem to be more bodies than usual today.

See what I mean, Dan Rather? Here I am, sitting right here on the edge of the fountain, eating this egg salad-and-bacon sandwich, and I'm invisible. It's what I was telling you about. Oh, sure, I guess I could jump up on this ledge here and drop my pants and flash a moon. But that's not it, see? What I want is to be like you—the guy with the microphone who interviews the guy who did the moon. That way you're somebody; he's not. You get to wink at the camera and give it a little shrug. You're sharing this gag with the audience, get it? And the viewers only remember you because you're the real person and he's not.

But, okay. Knock it off. Come on.

Time to move on.

In a minute here, he would go down to Paul Stuart's on Madison Avenue. The Kid would keep going into Paul Stuart's until he finally got it worked out.

Here's the thing: you make it in a store like that and you can make it anyplace. It's sort of like a school for The Kid. It's a rite of passage. There are a lot of big guys; a lot of grownups can't do it. They walk into the place and something inside them crumples and gives up.

Listen: Paul Stuart's stands for, uhh, how do you put it? Paul Stuart stands for something in life. You've got to dominate the store, kick it in the ass. When you leave the store, it should be belly-up.

See, the thing is that at Paul Stuart's they gently break your balls. The clerks do it all with just the slightest raise of an eyebrow. It's tricky stuff. They put just a little backspin on a sentence: they'll turn, just right, and lay the shirt on the counter and say, "Is *this* what you had in mind?"

And a little something dies in the customer. "Well, uhhh, yeah," he says. "More or less. You know."

And the clerk gives it the two-beat pause. "What do you plan to wear it with?" he asks.

But all right. He would hang in and he would get it figured out. One time; one day now and one of them would crack under The Kid's steady look. Their eyes would lock and hold, like this—and finally the clerk would cough and look away. And then The Kid could get on with the next step in his escape.

Later today he would go to the new neighborhood he had picked out. Down in the Village and you start at Eleventh Street and look around.

The Kid could melt right into the Village; he had been walking around his area for weeks now, looking. Picking out all the right spots. The Kid would never run again without knowing every back door in the place. Every runway between the buildings. Every rooftop.

Every time you ran away and the Welfare Department caught you and dumped you back, you learned a little something.

Right, Kid?

You got it, dummy.

It wouldn't be easy, running down there.

There was a cop down there trying not to look like a cop. That meant trouble. Big bastard with all streaky blond hair and fancy golf clothes and a lot of tan and big teeth.

The Kid had made the cop from a block away, easy.

And they had played a little catch-me-come-kiss-me, but The Kid had won. He had slipped between the buildings and had gone through the block. And then he had peeked around from half a block away, and watched the big cop looking around for him. The cop was working his hands open and closed nervously. That meant trouble, too. The cop was an ass-kicker, never mind the streaky fag hair and the tan.

You learn these things: fleecy sweaters don't make you soft.

But that would have to be the neighborhood, cop or not. For one thing, he couldn't take any more time. For another, nobody would ever make him down there; they were up to their armpits in kids down there now.

Another thing: Miss Dolan was about to fall out of her tree. You could sense it coming. There had been a time in the deli this morning when he thought she was going

54

to come over the table after him. Her face. It had gone all splotchy. She had been licking all her fingers and rubbing her legs together like she did—going rasp, rasp—and just sort of pulsating, all at the same time.

The Kid knew. You tick Miss Dolan in just the wrong way and she could make that cop look like goddam Rebecca of Sunnybrook Farm.

God knows what she was up to, Miss Dolan. Something. Asking, always asking. Trying to get inside his head where The Kid wouldn't let anybody go.

Okay, time to move. Give it maybe another week.

And The Kid would vanish forever.

He got up and stretched. He went over and put the crumpled paper bag into the wire garbage container. Littering was against the law and he liked to obey the law. And then he stepped out into the crowd, his face set just right.

Naturally, nobody noticed him.

7

OFFICER KEITH LEE

The truth was—no matter what he had told the guy from Homicide—the truth was that he really loved these dark hallways. The dark has a tactile luxury, like pure black cashmere. When it is just right it is rich and thick and it wraps all around protectively. It gets up your nose and into your ears; you can stand absolutely still and dissolve into the dark.

The thing people didn't understand about darkness, hallways and otherwise, was that it sheltered you just as it did *them:* anybody else waiting in the dark. It all depended on who got there first and whose eyes got adjusted and who stayed calm. He knew every upstairs hallway, every landing and every back stairwell in this block. He could move along his black paths on Neolite heels and composition soles without even swirling the air.

The only thing that ever marked the spot where Keith Lee had stood was the smell of his cologne. It was made by Dunhill and it smelled like a fresh, just unwrapped cigar. Nobody within miles of this block could afford it.

So now he waited, leaning comfortably in the corner in his dark green sweater, listening to the soft pad of footsteps coming up the stairs.

The padder was coming up carefully, putting full foot down to distribute the weight, keeping to the edge of the stairs where they didn't squeak. There was a pause at the landing, then a click.

That would be the switchblade knife snapping open.

The padding sound started up again, but now there was a slight hissing that went with it, coming toward him. It meant that the padder was sliding one shoulder along the wall.

Keith Lee eased his hands out of his pockets. He spread out all his fingers and flexed them. He smiled a small smile out at his unseeing audience in the dark.

The padder stopped. There was a sense of turning around; not quite a stirring of the heavy air. And the form, finally taking on blackish substance, backed into the corner. It backed directly into the waiting arms of Keith Lee.

He closed his grip quickly until he could hear cartilage popping, and he bent his head forward until he could feel and smell the back of the other head against his cheek. The hair was crispy. A little further forward and the edge of an ear touched his nose. Keith Lee could have, by just snapping, bitten off the ear. But he inclined his head more forward in a half nod and spoke. He kept his voice warmly intimate: "I knew you'd be back here, dummy," he said. "All I had to do was wait."

The struggle suddenly stopped inside the circle of his arms. The padder had not uttered a sound. Which was good; good for the padder. Keith Lee could feel the heart pulsing strongly against the butt of his right hand where it was now pressed against the upper ribs on the invisible chest. And now the head turned toward him, so that a smooth, unbearded cheek lay against the side of his nose.

"Man, you near scared me to . . . hey, *man*. Get off of me."

"You planning to cut me with that knife?" Keith Lee said.

"Hey! You hurtin' me." But the knife fell to the carpet. Keith Lee kicked it away into the dark.

"Lissen, man," the padder said. "I know what you doin' up here. But I . . . but you got the wrong dude. I didn't do no . . ."

"Somebody did it," Keith Lee said. "Might as well be you."

"Me, shee-it. You grabbin' me, you grabbin' trouble, man. You ain't gonna charge me with no . . ."

Keith Lee swung his left arm out, still encircling the chest with his right. He opened his hand, closing the fingers together like an ax blade.

"I do believe that you're talking back to me," he said.

He slashed the hand down diagonally. When he determined that he had the right spot, he swung it four more times. It created a muffled sound, like someone applauding wearing woolen mittens.

The body sagged inside his arm. He yanked it upright again. He kept his head bent forward and his tone quietly conversational:

"Know what that is?" he said. "That's the sound of a kidney imploding. Not *ex*ploding; there's a big difference. This one goes in. No marks on the outside. It's just that you're going to be pissing pure blood for a week."

The chest inside his arm filled with air.

"One more thing," Keith Lee said. "You yell—one goddam squeak out of you and I pinch you in half. And when I pinch, it'll be running down your leg. You got that part?"

The air went back out of the chest.

"Now. You ready for us to talk? Or do you want to talk back to me some more?"

The head nodded against his nose, its cheek sliding wetly up and down.

"At's better. Now tell me about killing the old folks."

"Wha' old folks?"

Keith Lee tightened down with his left arm and swung his right arm up in the dark and waved it around until it touched the top of the head next to his own. Then he dug his fingers into the thick hair and lifted up sharply. The padder came off his feet.

Putting his shoulder into it, Keith Lee swung the body around and slammed it into the wall. Then he eased it down until he could feel the toes touch the floor again. There was a sense of shuddering beneath his hand. A spray of something misted against his forearm.

"We seem to be having a little trouble communicating," he said. "But you just go right ahead; let me know when you're ready."

"Ohhhh, coño, man," the voice said. It had suddenly thickened, as if coming through fast-swelling lips. "My face, man. You done . . ."

Keith Lee pivoted on the balls of his feet and slammed the form into the wall again, harder.

"I got a lot of these," he said. "But you, you're running out of time."

"What, man. What?"

"Who killed the old couple? This time, you ask me what old couple and you get to fly down the stairs."

"No, man. Like, lissen to me: I didn't do it."

Keith Lee smiled into the dark. "I'm really sorry to hear you say that," he said. "You confess; you know, show some respect for the law, and maybe I can make it a little easier for you. You know how it is over there at Family Court. Tell them you're sorry about it and they let you go. You know how it goes at Family Court. You can say that the old couple attacked you. Right? Now, do I hear a confession? I'm listening real hard, now. You want to whisper it to me in the dark?"

The voice had grown thicker: "*Puñeta.* Didn't do it."

Keith Lee pivoted again, lifting sharply. He slammed the form into the wall and held it there, feet off the floor.

"Ooooooh, God," the voice said. "You breakin' my head."

"I know. Nice thing is, it stops hurting like this the minute you confess."

"Look, man. I was here, unnerstan' me? Like, I was *here* in the building when it happened, know what I mean? But I din't off no oldies. I was here, up here waiting for *her.* I mean, assin' me around like that."

"Assing you around, who?"

"*Don't,* man. You really hurtin' me."

"I said, who?"

"Old Icepick, tha's who."

Keith Lee blinked. "Ice . . . you mean Icepick *Sally* here? That's who?"

"Yeah. Tha's her door right over there. I wasn't upstairs wasting no oldies. I was right here waiting for *her*; you know, like right in this corner."

"What the hell are you talking about?"

"Awww, man. Like, she ain't got no dog. You dig it? And she ain't got no jive-ass icepick, man. Like, that barkin' behind the door and all. Nobody does me that way."

"Go on."

"Nobody. Like, I mean, she really got it comin', man. Old *coño.* She beat me to her door last time."

"Keep going."

"Man, leggo my head. Ain't no dog in there, like she says. And money all sewed to her underwear, they said."

"Who said?"

"I don't know. *Some*body said. You know."

"I know that. They've been saying that for years, and I don't see her driving a Caddie, you goddam dummy. But, okay. What about the old couple?"

"Not me, man. I was *here*, lookin' to get at the old icepick lady."

Keith Lee eased him down the wall, keeping the head in contact all the way.

"That's a real fine alibi," he said. "Too bad. You lose."

"Lose? Man, I tole you. It wasn't me. Man, like you don't *kill* old folks. Nobody do."

"Explain that to me."

"Aww, you know. They *old*. You unnerstan' what I'm saying to you? It ain't the same. They OLD. So you touch 'em up a little and maybe they just *die*. You don't kill 'em, like I said."

"They're not just as dead?"

"I ain't talkin' dead to you. I'm talkin' *dead*."

"So you didn't waste Mister or Missus Haven down there?"

"Uh uh. No way, man."

"You just touched them up a little, like you say, and *then* they died."

"No, man. I was right here. I tole you. Lissen: you just broke my teeth on that wall, man."

"I broke your teeth? *I* did? I think you've got it all wrong, my boy. What you mean to say is, you accidentally walked into the wall and broke your teeth. Isn't that what you mean?"

"I'm gonna tell. Man, I can't see you, but I know who you are. I know what you doin' over at the *play*ground and all."

Keith Lee leaned in closer and lowered his voice: "What am I doing at the playground?"

"I know."

"Come on. You can tell it to me. What?"

"Come *on*, man. Like, I see *them*—you know who I mean—and then I look around and I see *you*. You always there when they there."

"You understand, of course, that the playground is part of my area."

"Don't know nothin' about that."

"Well, if that's all you know," Keith Lee said, "then you don't know anything at all, right? But we're getting a little away from the subject at hand. It's about killing those old folks today. Poor things; they couldn't take a little touching up, as you put it."

"I didn't . . . it wasn't me. Like I said."

Keith Lee sighed. He raised his left arm and studied the luminous dial on his watch.

"Let me know when you're ready to confess," he said. "Go ahead and take your time; just let me know."

Then he reached out for the shadowy form.

When he checked the watch again to read the elapsed time, it had taken exactly four minutes and maybe thirteen seconds.

Not his all-time record for getting confessions. But not bad.

8

ICEPICK SALLY

Somebody has to do this. It is mean and disgusting work, especially in the heat. And dangerous. She said it out loud to confirm it, not shifting her head so that anyone would notice, but moving her eyes from side to side. "Dangerous," she said. "You all don't seem to understand the danger. But I do."

She was standing on the sidewalk in front of the stairs. She put her hands deep into the pockets of the Navy pea coat, sorting out the balled-up pieces of paper. She was wearing the red nylon knapsack. The strap that had been cut by the knife was fixed—she had overlapped the cut ends and had wound them tightly with six layers of wrapping cord. It made the knapsack hang crookedly, tilted up to the left.

The knife slash was still there just below the left shoulder on the pea coat. The cut was hanging open, almost perfectly matching the next cut on the gray wool sweater underneath. On both jacket and sweater, the fabric had turned black where the blood had dried. The edges were starting to curl.

The directions . . . let's see. The directions for today's route would be written on one of these slips of paper.

She wrote down the route every day before she left the apartment because otherwise by the time she got to the bottom of the stairs she might have forgotten again. That was because she had suffered a series of little strokes.

There was no medical confirmation of this.

But it had such a nice flair to it; such a nice cadence and ring. Like poetry, really: a series of little strokes. Ta da ta da ta dah.

Sometimes, when she felt more alert, she would explain her condition to people passing on the street: "If I seem disoriented," she would say, nodding and smiling to reassure them, "it is because I have suffered a series of little strokes."

They didn't believe it, any of them; the reflection of it came back from their faces.

She knew that big strokes are disabling, sometimes totally. Big strokes often leave you paralyzed. And then you can smile with only half a mouth, a terrible thing to see, while uncontrolled waters seep out the other side. You can wiggle only the fingers on one hand while the opposite hand lies there, fingers curled permanently into talons.

But not the small, piercing flashes. *Transient ischemic attacks,* the TIA's. Brief bursts to the head, sometimes by day, most often by night, could be survived. It is a matter of strength and of rallying the other forces of the body. The remaining active sections of your brain simply take over more duties. Those areas burned by a series of small strokes are gone forever. Blackened tendrils sticking up inside your brain like sections of burned-out underbrush.

But the work is still there; the work doesn't go away.

And somebody had to do it. No matter how dangerous. She . . .

Ahhh. Here we are.

She unfolded the paper torn from the yellow-lined note pad and read what she had written upstairs: Go right along Tenth to Sixth Avenue and down to Third Street. Be home before dark.

She turned right and started to walk, matching the imbalance of the knapsack by raising her right shoulder slightly. She put the little piece of paper back into the right-side jacket pocket. That would be in case she forgot again.

It's all in the timing. The route is keyed to garbage-collection days. If you work the route properly, you get there before the sanitation men do, so that you can study the contents of the galvanized-steel garbage cans. And the dark green Hefty trash bags, too.

She stopped now and moved up close against the building, just before the sidewalk turned around the corner. She waited, sniffing the air. And then, a small step at a time, she edged forward and peered around the corner.

The garbage cans were there, the four big ones that were supposed to be there, their lids held on by the wrap-around coiled springs. There also were three of the green plastic bags today. A good day for research.

But dangerous: she crossed the sidewalk obliquely, conscious of the people making faces and sidestepping on both sides to get away from her. She stepped up to the cans. She bent quickly at the first one, right hand grasping the side handle, left hand on the lid. Then she lifted up sharply and snapped the lid free, letting the force of the spring carry the lid around to the side. A gray haze of gnats came rising up with the sweetish smell, and she blinked to keep them out of her eyes.

There was a lot of bread today. A lot of crusts, which

were really the best part. By studying the crusts, you could tell where the diners had torn out the doughy part and eaten it, pushing the crusts away and piling them at the sides of their plate while they tore open more bread. She sorted them out with the tips of her fingers, pushing aside the ones on which red wine had been spilled. It wasn't the taste exactly, it was the color. Red wine always dried on bread like blood. Still bent over, she lifted her arm out of the can. She reached up to her shoulder and dropped two of the big crusts into the knapsack.

Last night's special had been *Osso Buco*. They did it good here. And the big, knucklelike bones made such good soup. She sorted through them and picked two, the ones with the most white gristle left. One must not be greedy. She dropped them into the knapsack and then straightened. She eased the lid back up on top of the garbage can, holding it carefully so that the spring wouldn't snap too hard. Sometimes it stung her fingers when it did that.

But no papers. Nothing for the research, the history. No columns of figures or names jotted down on the paper cocktail napkins. No matchbook covers with telephone numbers written on the inside. Or the matchbooks with the good advertisements that were historically important: *Special Bicentennial Doll Offer From Reddi Wip*. Sometimes there were wadded-up *Playbills* where people had doodled or perhaps written comments on the play, and then had taken the *Playbills* to dinner. And then they had—of course, who wouldn't?—then they had left them on the table with their empty plates.

Hmmm. That's odd. All restaurants; well, Italian restaurants especially, but all restaurants contribute to history in the contents of the garbage they leave out front. Well, maybe one of the plastic bags.

She lifted up the nearest one, resting it back down gently on her toes, and started to work on the twist fastener. It was tricky, unwinding the little paper-covered wire where someone else had wound it up so carefully, trying to get the two ends to come out evenly. But then she paused, bent over. She stopped the unwinding and held perfectly still. She could sense him coming out the door across the sidewalk behind her. The enemy.

The tiny muscles at the backs of her knees began to tremble.

"Icepick!" he said.

She half turned and looked at him.

He looked particularly mean today: his eyebrows seemed to form one thick black line across the top of his face. He always looked meanest the day after they had had *Osso Buco*. And now he took two more steps into the middle of the sidewalk and stopped. He held out both hands, the palms up.

"Get away from the garbage," he said. "Come on. I told you; I *told* you. The hell's a matter with you? Go wan, now. Jesus."

She nodded at him.

"I'll just do this clasp back on here," she said.

"No clasp, no clasp. Just forget about . . . look: screw the goddam clasp, whatever. Just *go*, will ya? Jesus, Icepick, come *on*. I told you already. I got people—I got people coming in and out of here. Look: this is *lunch* now. I mean, what am I? I'm running a business here and I got this? People eat here. And so I got an old lady standing out in front going through my *gar*bage. Christ's sake, Sally. I told you all the time. You want food? Fine: food I'll give. Come around in back, I'll give you food. But, look: not the goddam garbage, all right?"

"It's more than just the garbage," she said.

"It's *gar*bage, is what it is. That's all. Excuse me, folks. No, just move along. I can handle this. Come on, Sally. Jeez, you're drawing a crowd already."

She straightened, nodding at him. Then the backs of her

thighs knotted and she half stooped again, rubbing them.

"I'll go," she said. "Just one minute."

He started to turn and then did a half swing back toward her. "So what happened to your coat?"

She blinked. "Coat?"

"Coat, *coat*. What the hell coat am I talking about? Everybody else here in shirt-sleeves and you in a heavy winter coat. *Your* coat there. The sleeve."

"It was cut," she said. "With a knife."

"You bled on it," he said. "It went deep?"

"Pretty deep, yes."

"A mugger?"

"Yes. Just a boy."

He shrugged. "They're all over here, these kids. Lissen: me, I got to hire a guy. Did you call the cops?"

"Would they come?"

He put both hands into his pockets. Then he lifted out his right hand and glanced down at it. He folded the bill over and took two steps back across the sidewalk, holding the hand out. "Here. I'm sorry about the cut. Here. No, come on. Look: just take it, the money, and go. And . . . lissen to me, and be careful, all right? I shouldn't have to keep telling you. You live down here."

She straightened as much as she could. She put both hands at the small of her back and pressed down where her kidneys hurt. Her kidneys shouldn't hurt like this.

"No," she said. "No, thank you. I happen not to need money, thank you. I am a woman of . . . of *parts*. You needn't feel that you have to offer me money. The mere fact that I sometimes seem disoriented is that I have . . . well, I have suffered a series of little strokes."

He nodded. "I know, I know. Strokes. You told me before."

"Well?"

"Well, so take the money already," he said.

68

"Thank you, sir. I will send someone around to pay you back, of course."

"Of course. Look, Sally: would you just go now?"

She nodded, shifting the money from her left hand to her right and slipping the hand inside where the pea jacket doubled over. She worked the hand in underneath the gray wool sweater, which buttoned the other way, and then in underneath the jersey dress. And then under and into the inside of the long underwear, where the little homemade pocket was. She had sewn it in there herself with a hand stitch, overlapping, like buttonholing. The pocket would never work loose. It was full of money. All bills.

"Thank you," she said.

Behind her, she could hear him turn and click back into his door. He wore taps on his heels. Italian gentlemen did that a lot in Greenwich Village.

She walked down Sixth Avenue to Third Street, adjusting her shoulders to allow for the tilt of the knapsack. There was room for a lot more in there before she finished the route. But she was behind schedule now. What was it again? Something she was trying to remember. Something that . . .

She pulled the ball of yellow-lined paper out of her right pocket and unwadded it again. Then she turned so that the light was better over her shoulder, and she held both arms out all the way so that she could focus on it. Something she was trying to remember. Ahhhhh.

Be home before dark.

She turned again, folding the paper and putting it back into the right-side pocket.

She walked on. Twenty paces from the corner, where the little kids always clustered on the brownstone stoop, she began to angle out toward the curbing.

These were not quite the deadly ones; they were still

too small. They were beginning killers, still in training. Still in the grade school of crime. They studied religiously on purse-snatching and tormenting, gathering speed and courage while their bodies grew stronger on the food-stamp diet. A year at the most; next summer they would be bigger, their little palms grown to fit the knives. Nobody had yet seemed to discover that a fortune could be made in New York providing switchblades scaled for the tiny hands of children.

There were seven in this pack. They fell silent, watching her as she passed.

"Stay right where you are," she said. "I've got an ice-pick here and I've got both hands free."

The one who looked most like the Botticelli angel grabbed the front of his short pants at the crotch and said, "Eat it, Sally."

She kept walking past, turning her head to watch them.

Next stop: the garbage cans were drawn into a half circle like a fortress on the sidewalk in front of the Chinese restaurant and in front of O'Halloran's Bar next door. She sidestepped into them carefully, sorting them out by smell. Ahh, there: third from the end. She stooped over it and reached inside.

The thing is: you have to be selective at a stop like this one; it is an art form. Chinese restaurants have absolutely *nothing* to offer in the way of a social picture of America at ease. The leavings from a Chinese restaurant are runny beyond belief—uniformly brown and wet. Any papers in there are soaked. Sprouted things seem to shoot and grow, slimy tentacles reaching back to seize your fingers.

Ahhh. But O'Halloran's Bar. And Grill, of course—though she felt that perhaps the food was not up to much. But the bar threw out treasure.

Let the world take note: broken glass of all bright

colors and a wealth of whiskey labels. Always a bloodied handkerchief, sometimes more after a big night. Coins rolled around in the snuff, and once the rhinestone-studded heel of a woman's pump. Cigar butts still showing the force of broad, blunt teeth. Cigarettes so savagely stamped out that they seemed to open at the tips and bloom like flowers. Torn-up tickets from the OTB parlor—such nice printing. And once—she had the exact day marked down somewhere back in the apartment—once she had found the tip of a human ear. Just the lobe, really, bitten off and possibly spat into the sawdust. It was still pink, too, though bloodless—as though the color went straight through. For several days after that she had stood outside the bar, looking intently at the customers for that one unsymmetrical head—but they had finally chased her away.

She brought her hand up from the can and looked at the longer-than-usual cigar. The band was still intact: Rigoletto, a brand much preferred in the afternoon by men of Italian ancestry. The end of the cigar was still smoothly round and undented by teeth marks. There was no darker circle of a saliva stain, as though whoever had lit the cigar had suffered from a dry mouth. Possibly the cigar had been rested on the edge of the ashtray and allowed to go out—as if the owner had been distracted. Perhaps the smoker of the cigar had been sitting on a stool by the window, staring out at the playground across the street.

But an unchewed, seventy-five-cent cigar from *this* bar? No. No, that wouldn't do at all.

Nobody knew as much about this neighborhood as Icepick Sally. Nobody.

She reached to her shoulder and dropped the cigar into the knapsack. And then she leaned the heels of both hands on the rim of the can and looked across the street, re-creating the line of sight from O'Halloran's window behind her. What could the smoker have been looking at so bemusedly that he had let his cigar grow cold?

Let's see, here:

There were four park benches. The slats on one of them had been broken so that just the concrete supports remained. And beyond the benches the basketball game was going on.

The players were running fluidly, the ball moving through them as if it had a life of its own. The action seemed to flow liquidly from one basket to the other; it was almost as if forces at each end were tipping the blacktop court back and forth between them.

But, no. It wasn't the game that the watcher would be watching. She brought her focus in closer to the benches again.

Of course. That was it: the exchange was taking place. She should have thought of that.

The two men were sitting side by side, second bench from the left. She could see the backs of their heads. They were watching the basketball game.

Well, not really. They had come into the square from opposite sides, the way they always did. That one, the small fattish one, from MacDougal Street. The other one, leaner and younger, from Sixth Avenue here. Each man carried his shopping bag. Both bags were from D'Agostino's.

She had seen it all many times:

They would shake hands when they met. The younger one always feinted a little, like a boxer, bobbing his head and shoulders. He would fake a punch at the older one, who would draw back, laughing. But she could tell by the tense way the older man held his head that he secretly didn't think that it was all that funny. They would sit down on the bench, putting the shopping bags between them. Upright and side by side, the four little cord handles arched neatly in a row.

It was very carefully done and you had to watch. No one else did. Certainly not the basketball players. Not the people walking through the park on the curving sidewalk.

The younger man would look into the bag, then reach in and take out two cans of beer. He would hold one between his knees temporarily while he popped the top on the first one, throwing the pull tab over his shoulder. He would hand the beer to the older man, then take the other one and open it and drink deeply.

Now the older man would look into his bag and then reach in and lift out the two sandwiches: wax-paper-wrapped from the shop over on MacDougal. He would hand one over before peeling back the paper on his own sandwich for the first bite. And then he would shrug, chewing, as if apologizing for the quality of the meatballs. Then, mouth still full, he would sip more delicately at his can of beer. They would watch the game, their heads moving back and forth in unison, their jaws chewing. Some days the younger man would slump down more and stretch out his arms along the back of the bench, beer in one hand, sandwich in the other.

Ten, possibly twelve minutes. And then, sandwiches finished, the wax paper balled up and dropped on the sidewalk; beer cans tossed over toward the wire trash basket, they would get up and leave. Shaking hands first. Sometimes the younger one would cuff the fattish one on the arm. The older man smiled, of course, but he didn't think that was very funny, either. Then they would walk away, each back in the same direction from which he had appeared. Each one carrying his shopping bag. A lot of people in the Village carried shopping bags.

But one thing: neither man was carrying the same bag that he had brought with him to the playground.

And that would be what the man had been watching from the bar window, his cigar going out.

She watched the men leave. And then she sidestepped over to the next garbage can and bent over it. Enough of this idling the time away. There was important work to be done and she had to be back in the apartment before dark.

The traffic rolled on just on the other side of her little fortress of cans. Occasionally a driver, having stopped to wait for the light, would glance over at her and watch her pick out items, inspect them and drop them into the knapsack.

Across the street the basketball game went on in the slanting afternoon light.

Above and behind her, where she couldn't see, the man stood looking down. He was in the second story above O'Halloran's Bar, standing at the windows in the empty rooms that had been a massage parlor the week before. He was deeply tanned and blue-eyed, with tawny, streaky hair. His face was pleasantly relaxed in a celebrity posture.

He was not looking down at Icepick Sally. The man was watching the two men leave with their shopping bags. He had his hands thrust into the pockets of his Johnny Miller slacks, jingling his coins.

From that position at the window, the man couldn't see directly below—either the bar or the Chinese restaurant.

And behind the windows of the Chinese restaurant, the young boy watched, swirl of hair down across his forehead.

The Kid wasn't watching the basketball game. Or the bag men. The Kid was watching Icepick Sally.

9

OFFICER KEITH LEE

Ahh, yes. There you are, my little flower of the Village. Been looking all over for you. You with the tilted-up, almond-shaped eyes and the absolutely, ab-so-*lute*-ly, totally perfect, flawless skin. The only way to get a skin shade like yours is to mix it in an electric blender, adding spoons of malted milk—and then spray it on. You are some kind of girl. Your black hair seems to soak up the sun. There is no reflecting shine; stand off to one side and there is only a sort of halo. Your walk is an easy glide, no hip movement. And your footfall leaves no sound.

And you've got a gun tucked right inside the waistband of your cutoff jeans, down inside the elastic top of your bubble-gum-colored panties. Up tight against your caramel belly.

Keith Lee fell in step behind her, half a block back. Parade time.

This is called keeping your area under control. He smiled at the back of her head.

Funny. She usually carried a snap knife. She was very damned good with her knife, but he had heard about the stolen gun this noon. It was a .22-caliber target pistol, which works wonders up close. And if there ever was anybody guaranteed to get right up close—maybe with the end of the barrel inside your right nostril—she was the one.

It figured that she would probably be good with the gun, too.

The girl stopped outside the Stride Rite shoe store and looked in the window.

Keith Lee stopped and leaned against the building. She would turn and look around in a minute, but she wouldn't see him through all the pedestrians.

He sniffed the air, watching her.

People wonder what this smell is. Graduate engineers and pollution experts will tell you that it's carbo, which is too easy—and which is also wrong. It isn't carbo. It's the smell of violence and fear, and on a hot day in Greenwich Village it will make the hair stand up along the backs of your hands.

Give her a little more time. She was still trying to make up her mind. It wouldn't really matter in the end.

When you're a Youth cop, you learn these things. What she would do was go in and try on shoes. It could take a little while, depending on how many people were in the store. The clerk would be sitting there on his little Naugahyde-topped stool, looking down and pinching with his fingers along the sides of her foot to check the fit. And when he looked up, there would be this gun barrel just across from his right eye.

The girl glanced over her shoulder, then squared back her shoulders and went into the store.

Keith Lee came away from the wall. He moved loosely. Plenty of time.

Let's see. Jewel Rodriguez. She had had twenty-two

arrests starting when she was nine years old and she was now eleven. Almost eleven. Assault was her specialty; she was a cutter. You'd never know it. Everybody loved her in Kiddie Court. She knew her Miranda by heart. If an officer stumbled over it while reading from the notebook, she could correct him. And she also knew the ruling that had come *after* the Miranda: a youth's confession is invalid unless it is made in the presence of a parent or other friendly adult.

He unbuttoned the yellow golf sweater and let it swing open.

Presence of a parent, all right. Jewel's mother was selling the Family Ass uptown, and her father . . . ho, ho.

The last time Keith Lee had brought her in, the court officer had patted her on the head and said, "Who is your father, child?"

"Well, now," Jewel had said. "Say that you're playin' with a buzz saw, man, and you get nicked. Now how are you gonna know what tooth it was that cut you?"

She had been ACD'd from Family Court again last week: Adjourned in Contemplation of Dismissal. She had come dancing back to the block, flashing him the finger and saying, "Got me another A. C. *Dee*, big pig-man."

Keith Lee had also smiled and patted her on the head that day. The pat on the head had sent her down the last flight of stairs at the building where she lived. She had lain at the bottom for a few moments, sneezing blood. He had walked down leisurely until he had stood over her. He had nudged her a bit with the toe of one golf shoe, watching her wince away.

"What was that name, again?" he had said.

"Pig," she said. "Jive-ass pig-man."

He had nudged a bit harder. "Let me know when you're ready."

She had doubled into a smaller ball. Finally: "Officer Lee," she had said.

"You won't forget it again?"

"You're . . . God, you're breakin' my back," she had said.

"I asked you a question, is all."

"Okay. Won't forget."

"Forget what?"

"Wait! Man, don't do it no more. I won't forget, I said. It's Officer *Lee*, man. God, man, *stop* it."

Keith Lee had stopped. Well. One more nudge to seal the memory into her perfect, absolutely perfect little caramel-colored ass.

And now two women came out of the shoe store. They turned toward him and, when they came alongside, he gave them the smile. It stopped them, as always.

"Excuse me, ladies," he said. "Is it very crowded in there?"

"In where?"

"The store. In there, in the shoe store."

They both thought about it, blinking.

"No, no, I think we were the only ones in there," the left woman said.

"No," said the right one. "Little girl came in."

He smiled again. "Thanks so much."

They sighed like a matched set.

"Don't mention it," said Left.

"Pleasure, I'm sure," said Right.

He let their steps fall away behind him and then he took the last four steps fast. He pushed the door open with the flat of his left hand. His right hand pulled the Magnum out of his waistband. It came up in a sweep of chrome.

"Freeze," he said.

Jewel Rodriguez and the clerk were facing: she had one foot up on the slanted board in front of the stool. The clerk was holding a shoe in each hand, his arms down limply. The toes of the shoes were touching the floor.

He didn't turn his head.

That was because Jewel had the target pistol up under the clerk's chin. The end of the barrel was pushing a dented hollow into his throat.

She turned her head now, but she didn't blink. Her skin was perfectly cream-beige in the fluorescent display lights.

Keith Lee looked into the almond eyes.

"Don't do what you're thinking," he said. "In fact, don't even think about it. You even twitch—you take a breath—and I blow your head off."

Then he waited. The two of them could have been cast in iron. Seated figures, facing.

Finally, slowly, she brought the pistol down. The dented-in spot stayed on the clerk's throat. It was white with a round red hole embossed in the middle of it.

Keith Lee stepped over and put the barrel of the Magnum precisely at the bridge of her nose, between her eyes. He squeezed in slightly with his index finger.

"Now, then," he said. "Just open your little hand and let the gun drop to the floor. You don't have to hand it up to me. Just let it fall. That's a girl, just like that. Now. Stand up nice and slow. You got it, kid. Up we go. You know, going all cross-eyed like that sure spoils your looks."

"Eat it, pig," she said.

"Now, now. Mustn't talk dirty in front of the store man here."

He reached over slowly with his left hand, the fingers all spread open. He brought it down slowly on top of her blue-black hair. He curled in all the fingers and then swung her up off her feet.

He eased the Magnum back into his waistband. He held her out at arm's length so that her kicks couldn't reach his crotch. When she wouldn't stop kicking, he shook her. The bones in her neck cracked.

"Okay," he said to the clerk. "Okay, already. You can

breathe. Come *on*, man: breathe. It's all over now. Your face is turning all cordovan. Little shoe-store joke there. You know—cordovan."

The man nodded, swallowing.

Keith Lee turned back at the door, swinging the girl around.

"Be back in a few minutes to get a report," he said. "Just leave the pistol there. Go ahead, sell shoes; whatever you want, I don't care. Just hang in. I'll be back."

Outside, he lowered her just enough so that she could lope along on her tiptoes. He glanced down at her.

"Okay," he said. "One more time. You have the right to remain . . ."

"You got it wrong," she said. "You got to say that other part first."

"Do tell."

They waited for the light at the corner. He ignored the stares.

"Hurtin' me," she said.

"I know."

"Man, come *on*. My neck, you *puñeta*. You *maricón*."

"You've forgotten my name again."

"Officer Lee. *Sir*. Please. You're really hurtin' on me."

"That's better," he said. He lowered her until she could walk.

Next corner: "Listen," she said.

And halfway down Eleventh: "Well, what I meant was," she said, "like, you're always lookin' at me. You know. I mean: I walk away, I can feel you lookin' at me."

He slowed the pace. "So?"

"So, you know, man. How'd you like to see all of it? Like, tiny brown *buns*, man. Each one jus' fit into the palm of your *hand*, know what I mean? *Mira*, we could work something out. You know, all of it. I didn't shoot nobody. I didn't get no *money* from that store man."

He glanced sideways.

Creamy malted milk. He could smell her perspiration now. Her hair was thick under his hand.

"Make you so happy, man," she said.

He took a deep breath. "Not me, you won't. Keep walking."

"Know a spot," she said. "I go there. Just up the block here. Upstairs. Up on top. They got a skylight there. The light comes down like this. I mean: man, the light comes down in, like, big kind of dusty *beams*, man. You unnerstan' what I'm saying? The glass in that ol' skylight gone all yellowish now."

He blinked several times. "Knock it off. Just walk."

The top of her head was giving off heat. The palm of his hand was getting slippery.

She turned at the stairs where she had been pointing.

"Dusty old beams of light," she said. "Just coming down from that old skylight. Afternoon sun."

She raised her tee shirt and rubbed her tummy.

He glanced down at the hand moving circularly.

"And I go up there," she said. "Up there, all by myself sometimes. And I stand under that skylight. And I take off all my clothes, man. All my clothes, everything. And I stand there, just right, man. And you know what?"

He narrowed his eyes. "What?"

"I turn pure gold in that light. Man, pure gold all over."

He let go of her hair. He took her by the hand.

And together they walked up the stairs and into the building.

10

THE CAT MAN

It was 9 p.m. and shadowy. It would be officially dark in maybe twenty minutes.

They stood at the top of the stairs facing the street, leaning their backs against the outer door to hold it slightly open behind them. They both checked the sidewalk and the cars on the street, this way, that way.

Directly across the street from them the old lady was weaving slowly up her stairs. She was bent forward and tilted to her left, picking up the front of her long skirt with one hand so that she could step up, holding the other arm out for balance. The red nylon knapsack was full. She paused at the top of her stoop and looked over her shoulder before she reached into the pea-coat pocket for her keys.

They waited, watching her, until she moved into her foyer and closed the door behind her.

And then they swung around into the hallway, the shorter one first, the taller one easing the door shut behind. They paused at the bottom of the stairs for a moment, looking up into the darkness. Then they started up, walking side by side. The tall one was carrying a clear plastic bag in his right hand. The bag was gathered tightly at the top. It swung gently as he went up the stairs. It had a cat in it.

At the first landing, the smaller one pointed, then stepped ahead, leading the way. He stopped at Apartment 102 and half turned, looking at the boy with the bag.

"*Qué pasa, está allí?*" he said

The tall one nodded. "He's there, all right."

The little one reached up and pushed the buzzer. They waited.

"You sure he's home?" the small one said.

"*Cállate*. He home, all right. Where he gonna go, his leg all twisted up like that? No, he home. That *viejo* just sittin' over there by the window and looking down at the street. All day like that, jus' looking. *Aguanta*. He got to get his old ass up and pick up that ol' cane and come slidin' over to the door."

They heard the thumping of the cane. The voice was muffled from the other side of the door: "Who's there?"

The taller one leaned in closely, his lips near the door frame. He held the plastic bag down beside his leg. The bag jumped as the cat struggled.

"Old man," he said. "I got your cat here."

"My . . . ?"

"Cat. Your old cat. Open up."

They both stepped back, watching the doorknob, listening to the upper and lower locks clicking. Then the door eased open to the length of the brass chain. A vertical, four-inch slice of the old man's face showed through. One eyeglass was visible. The eye was blinking.

"How nice of you," he said. "That old cat hasn't been up to anything bad, has he? Old Lawrence, he . . ."

"No, man. No, he's fine. Open up, I'm gonna give him on over to you."

The head shook back and forth, first one spectacled eye and then the other showing up and vanishing in the narrow space. "No, no, afraid I can't do that. I'm just an old man alone here; just me and old Lawrence left. Lawrence is part Siamese. Some folks say they're mean, Siamese. But not him. I suppose that's because he's mostly just cat, Lawrence. But I call him Lawrence of Siam; it's for him I do it. Where is he?"

"I got him right here. Doan worry. Just open . . ."

"Well, you're a good boy, but I can't open the door. Here, now. Look: if you'll just let him slip right through this space here, why he'll be just . . . he's done it before, Lawrence. Yessir. He knows I'm all by my . . . he knows, that old rascal. You know how old Lawrence is? Fourteen years next week. Fourteen *years*. You know how many years that figures out in human life? They say the ratio is seven cat years to one people year. It adds up to . . . well, that makes him out to be ninety-eight years old. And . . ."

"Come *on*," the tall one said.

". . . and he's still full of vinegar. He goes out the window there beside my chair. Over there, where I sit. And he walks along the ledge there, Lawrence. Heh. One full story above the ground and it doesn't faze him one bit. Heh. Walks that ledge over to the Hedlick's balcony there; you know, next door there. And I strongly suspect that he shits in her begonias, heh. Well, then he goes on around to the other side and he jumps back in through that high window down there at the end of this hallway. Down there by the janitor's closet. And he comes right up to this door . . . he knows just exactly which door it is that's his door. And he scratches once or twice and then he waits. Good cat for an old man to have. I can't walk him any more, this bad leg of mine. Can I, old Lawrence? Where are you, buddy-cat? Now, if you'll just let him slip right through the open . . ."

"You gonna open this jive-ass door, old man? You keep this up—this *talkin'*, man, you makin' my head hurt."

"... I, well. *Wait* a minute. Is everything all right? Where is he? Lawrence. Lawrence? Are you ... ?"

The tall one took one step back and brought up his right arm. He slowly swung the plastic bag over to where it could be seen through the four-inch slot.

The cat was on its back inside the bag. He was tightly doubled up, hind feet pressed against his white chest. He was making slow swimming motions with his front paws. His eyes were round with fear and his mouth kept opening and closing. His whiskers on both sides were bent where the bag narrowed. But there was no sound; just the faintest rustle of plastic as the bag swung back and forth below the hand.

The one spectacled eye pressed into the space at the door. Below it, there was a corner of white mustache.

"My God! Lawrence," the old man said. "He ..."

The tall boy shrugged. "Shut up, man. Cut it off," he said. "Now, lissen. You see this here old cat? Well, man, I'm gonna tell you what. This here old cat is for *sale*. How much money you got in there?"

The cat's tail was up under its right front leg. Beads of moisture were beginning to form on the inside of the plastic. The wedge of light coming through the slitted door fell diagonally across the bag. It made the cat's eyes distort, first round, then slitted, as the bag twisted slowly. The cat's mouth continued to open and close without sound.

The old man pulled his head back a bit. The sharp edge of the door had embossed a vertical line up the side of his forehead. Then he pressed close to the opening again.

"Let him *go*, boy. He can't, he can't *breathe* in there. Lawrence, can you hear me? Law—"

"Look: you wanna buy a old cat or not? Your time is runnin' out, old cripple."

"Let him go! The police. I'll call the . . . no, wait. I can't get back to my tele . . ."

"How much money you got?"

"But I haven't . . ."

The tall boy shrugged. He dipped his left hand into his pants pocket. He eased it back out and held it down beside his thigh, then made the click. The blade of the knife snapped out and around.

"Okay. Time's up," he said.

He swung the knife up, holding it dagger-style now, and let the shaft of light play on the chromed blade. And then he swung his arm down, lazily, and plunged the blade into the plastic bag.

The blade went into the plastic bag without a sound, directly into the cat's abdomen between the curled-up back paws. The cat tried to straighten, sawing at the air with its front feet. It closed both eyes for a moment, then opened them again. A drop of clear fluid appeared at each nostril.

The boy brought the arm up again. The knife blade was rusty-red almost up to the handle. He glanced over at the spectacled eye peering through the slit.

"Price goin' up on this here cat," he said. "You better hurry."

And then he swung again, harder this time, and drove the knife blade into the bag again.

It went into the cat's white chest. The force of the new thrust pumped up a spray of blood from the first cut. The blood splashed against the inside of the plastic and clung to the surface, shining like droplets of reddish oil.

The boy pulled the blade out and raised his arm again.

The door slammed, echoing like a shot in the dark hallway, and they could hear the old man clawing frantically at the brass chain. Finally it swung free, rattling in an arc, and he yanked the door open.

"Lawrence! Lawrence, I . . ."

That's when the little one stepped around from beside the door and pushed, both hands out flat.

The door swung all the way open and the old man fell backward, skidding deep into the room on his shoulders. His cane flew away, clattering against the chair pulled up beside the window.

The little one ran in after him and began kicking. He kicked methodically, taking careful aim with each foot, shifting his weight from side to side to keep his balance.

The tall one walked in slowly. He turned and closed the door behind him. Then he swung the bloody bag lazily and let it go. It made a curving arc and hit the wall before falling to the floor. The cat lay twitching inside, its fur quickly matting.

The smaller boy continued kicking. He was scowling, concentrating.

The tall one walked over to the window, reached up and pulled down the green canvas shade. He stooped and wiped the knife blade clean on the arm of the overstuffed chair, knocking the lace doily to the floor. He closed the knife and put it back into his pocket, turning to look around the room.

He ignored the little one and the muffled sounds coming from the floor.

"Got to be some money in here somewheres," he said. "Got to be something; pay me for goin' to all this trouble."

11

OFFICER KEITH LEE

"I know," Keith Lee said. "You told me before."

The captain continued to pace, kicking up puffs of feathers from the ripped-open pillows. "I don't care. I'll tell you again. *Animals* is what we're dealing with down here, these goddam kids. We can't, they're wild animals and they run in packs. We can't stamp them out, you got that part? Cops? Jesus, I could run in an army down here, I wouldn't bet on them winning against these animal kids. You got it? They'd *lose*, the army."

"Maybe guys in tanks. You know, those things where they spray fire up and down the street."

"Tanks? Your ass, tanks. Listen—you come around the *corner* down there on Tenth Street and these goddam kids would steal the iron treads right off your tank. Whatever those things are called; you know, where it goes around like a belt. I don't know. Hell, *look* at this place. You ever see anything like this place?"

"I see it a lot," Keith Lee said. "I see this kind of stuff all the time, remember? You don't always come around."

They stood in the middle of the small room, shoulders touching, and looked around.

He had, indeed, seen a lot of it. And this place was just about average, the way the Cat Man and Feets had left it the night before.

The chair was upside down beside the open window, dissected, the padding pulled out. The mattress on the twin bed had been laid open with one continuous diagonal slash and then emptied. Chunks of gray foam fanned out in a half-circle. The two pillows had been sliced open and shaken out on the floor. The four drawers had been pulled out of the dresser and spilled.

The old man had not had much in the way of possessions.

Most of the framed old-time vaudeville photographs were still on the walls, but each one had been stabbed through the middle, the force exploding the glass outward in fine spiderwebbing.

The cat had almost made it over to where the old man had been lying before it had died. The cat was rigored solid now, lying on its right side. The claws were all unsheathed, the last, reflexive grab at life that cats make. The smear of blood ran from the mouth of the plastic bag directly up to the cat. It went under and out of sight at the cat's stomach.

About average. No more, no less. Sometimes when he got there, the cats didn't have heads.

"I don't know," the captain said. "What do you suppose they got out of all of this?"

Keith Lee shrugged. "Couldn't have been much. It never is. The old man had, what? Extra pair of pants, one shirt. Half a bottle of Tokay in the fridge there. Probably what they got is pretty much what you see here."

"And the cat there. They killed the guy's *cat*, for Christ's sake. Listen: does someone come—who comes and takes away cats like that?"

"I don't."

"Who would *do* a thing like this? You can't, what you can't figure is the mentality here. What we're dealing with."

"Animals."

"I *said* that already. So what did you hear on the old man? Whoever?"

Keith Lee pulled the notebook out of his back pocket and flipped it open. "Name's Severson. He's eighty, maybe; nothing around here to check it out. He had a bad leg going in. So he's got two bad legs now because they broke his pelvis. Plus, you know, he's all covered over with abrasions and contusions, all that kicking and stomping. Whoever did it was probably wearing Cuban fence-climbers."

"Cuban . . . ?"

"Boots. Pointy toes. High heels; they zip up the inside here. They're very big around this part of town. Hell, I don't think anybody down here wears loafers except maybe me."

"I know, I know. And you got like fifteen pairs. But that was it: they stomped him. Boots. Jesus. What else did the doctors say?"

"They don't know. The old guy may live, maybe not. The doc said his lungs keep filling with stuff, fluids. They'll run a hose in there and drain him and then see what happens. He's listed critical. And that's about it."

The captain walked over to the window and looked out, his hands in his pockets. "Animals, these kids." He turned and looked back. "Listen: how do you stand it? What I mean is, you *live* down here. What? Maybe a block away. How the hell can you *stand* it? Kids, you know, kid gangs all over the place. Stamp 'em out here and they pop up over there. I mean, they got *names* on them, identify them-

90

selves as gangs. Right on their jackets. What? Diablos, and like that. We can't, there's no controlling this situation any more. Me, I can get away at night. Subway across the river. Hell, I'm not so sure I'm safe over on that side. But you. Savages running wild all around here, you got to go and *live* down here. Not bad enough, you got to go and dress like some Los Angeles fairy, for Christ's sake. All that, Lee, you got some kind of guts."

"Guts?" Keith Lee shifted his weight to his right leg, then lifted his left foot and picked the feathers out of the tassels on the shoe. "Hell, no. It's stubbornness. Meanness, maybe. Look, captain: I got here first. This is mine. I was born right here in the Village. Always lived here. It's *my* turf, not theirs. Used to be all nice here, all white. And now goddam spades, chili-burners overrunning the place now. If anybody goes, *they* go. Diablos my ass. And the clothes, my clothes. You don't see anybody snicker, right?"

The captain nodded. "Right. I got to admit you got 'em scared. You kick a lot of ass around here. What I mean is, you're one of the best, maybe the best cop I got down here and you got a good record and all. Citations. It's just that I worry."

"Hell, so do I."

"So all right. Let's get the hell out of here. Somebody, you're sure somebody does something about dead cats. Comes, hauls them away, whatever?"

"Sure, somebody. I'll call."

He took one last look at the room before closing the door and adjusting the POLICE INVESTIGATION sign. They went down the stairs together.

The captain stood out in front looking across the street. He spoke without turning his head: "Who's that one again?"

"Who?"

"Over there. That old broad across the street there with the surplus sailor coat on. Going through the garbage."

"Oh, her. It's Sally something or other. No last name, far as I know. She lives over there. Icepick Sally. She's heading off on her rounds. Eats garbage."

"Yeah, I remember. Think maybe she saw something? You know, I mean about the old man back upstairs?"

Keith Lee shrugged. "You could walk over and ask her. She smells so bad, I can't get close enough to her to talk."

"Well. If you're not gonna, I'm sure as hell not gonna. Listen—you want a beer?"

"You're buying?"

The captain looked at him, eyebrows up. "You mean you pay for drinks here? What kind of cop are you?"

"I pay. Well. I keep a, you know, a tab. Come on. I got a place around the corner here."

The captain fell in step. He looked up at the brownstones on both sides, checking the windows. Then he looked back over his shoulder at the street.

"You know what I miss?" he said.

"Mmmmmm?"

"What I miss is a good old-fashioned burglary. It's funny, right? I mean: what I miss is, you know, plain burglary the way they used to do it in the old days. Burglar waits until the guy is gone from the apartment; he takes a tool and he breaks in. Steals whatever it is, and goes. No kid gangs, for Christ's sake. No kicking the shit out of helpless old people. Goddam animal, nickel-and-dime assault and robbery. A good burglary, you should have seen my arrest sheet when I was back doing burglars. I could catch, I knew where to go to collar them. Now, I don't know, now it's all changed. *Kids.* It's all different now. You know what I am? Scared is what I am. Like I said, I don't know how you stand it."

Keith Lee nodded back at the captain, smiling and letting the sun glint off his teeth.

Oh, he could stand it, all right. He could stand it because sooner or later he was going to break every goddam chili-burning head in this block. It is very hard to prey on old folks when you got a spongy liver; it takes a lot of the snap out of a kid.

Animals, all right.

But, fine. He would break up the Diablos. Get another citation; they would put it in his record. Keep moving, maybe one day take over the division. It was important. Staying in the Village was important. The pay was too good to get transferred out of the Village. Not the police pay; you kidding me with the police pay? The extra pay. It adds up.

And as soon as it added up high enough, he would turn the whole damn place over to the animals.

12

MARION DOLAN

"Dirty kid," she said. "Nobody thwarts me. No way. You smart-ass. Stand in *my* way."

She let the refrigerator door swing shut and walked back to the counter and slammed down the Pyrex dish. "Dirty kid. Try and dog me around. Hold *me* back. We'll see."

Marion Dolan was naked. Her legs and torso were heavily welted and imprinted from the foundation garment. The pattern looked like it had been tattooed in with mauve ink. Her breasts rested on her stomach, with the aureoles and nipples looking down.

"Stupid kid, anyway. Damn him."

She peeled back the Saran wrap from the Pyrex dish. She put a slice of white bread on the counter beside it and began heaping the leftover mashed potatoes onto the bread with a spoon. She patted it firmly all around, shaping the potatoes into a hill that peaked in the middle. She dipped the spoon into the mayonnaise jar and spread that on top of the potatoes. She licked the spoon clean. Then she dipped it into the sugar bowl and, tapping it with her forefinger, sprinkled sugar evenly over the mayonnaise. She licked the spoon again, tossed it into the sink and then picked up the bread and bit into it.

This is the way to get even: Eat.

She leaned into the counter, chewing and staring out the window above the sink.

Damn you, Press Reynolds. Today had just about done it. She may have gone too far with the boy—well, certainly by the prescribed agency standards she had gone too far—but she by-God had his full attention now. Little bugger. After today there would be no more messing around over what she wanted and what she didn't want. Fink kid. At least that part was over and done with. A person can stand just so much and that's it.

She pushed the last of the bread into her mouth and then sucked the mayonnaise off her fingertips, one by one.

Too much bread is bad for you. Except for a piece or two in the morning, one slice a day has all the nutrition a girl needs.

She pulled the bowl of mashed potatoes closer. She got a clean spoon out of the drawer and plopped more mayonnaise into the bowl. She added three spoons of sugar and started stirring, holding the spoon upright like a dagger. Then, when she got it to the right creaminess, she changed her grip and began to eat.

She would make fettuccine for dinner. That would show them.

She bent forward and put both forearms on the countertop, rising for a moment to swing her breasts up so that they rested on the cool formica, then settling down again. She pulled the *New York* magazine over closer and began turning the pages.

The article on Press would be a little easier to do now. Well, now, after what had happened today. The tricky part would be to settle on just the right tone in which to tell it.

It shouldn't sound too professorish. No, too professional. But it shouldn't sound too really cute either, like maybe Gael Greene interviewing a meatloaf.

"Just tell the story in your own words," the editor had told her. "We'll go over it and put it into shape; we have people who do that. And then we'll both go over the changes together."

Well, all right. She should march right into the story. Get the reader's attention right away. Lord knows, once they read about her boy, they would sit right up.

And maybe a stuffed, breaded pork chop. No, two. There were two left in the freezer part.

She stood up and put the spoon and empty bowl into the sink and ran it full of water. Then, rubbing her fingertips across her buttocks, she walked into the other room.

The things were set up and waiting on the coffee table where she had arranged them when she had come in:

The tape recorder, full spool.

The microphone on its black plastic stand, its cord plugged into the proper spot on the side of the recorder.

The gray case-file folder.

The Johnson's baby powder.

She sat down facing the microphone, her knees lightly touching the coffee table.

Trial run. Who? You know, Phyllis George does this all the time.

"All right," she said. " 'Media Child in Manhattan.' Ummm. Mmmmm, 'Media Child *Stalks* Manhattan.' No. The, uhhh, 'The First of the Media Children,' a new generation of formless children who . . . no. A new generation of *empty* children. Empty kids who feed on your input, gorging themselves on the misguided violence of your television and your movies and . . . uhhhhhh. You have created a monster here with no feelings, only *reactions*. He may never learn to feel anything the way you and I do. Monster. Hmmmm: 'How to Make a Monster Child.' 'The Making of a . . .' no. Nuts. I don't know; maybe you don't do the title first."

She leaned forward and, with her thumb and index finger, pushed down the switches to start recording. Then she tapped the silvery end of the microphone with her fingernail, looking to see if the audio needle bounced properly. She sat back again and cleared her throat.

"This is Marion Dolan," she said. "No. This is *Doctor* Marion Dolan and this is my story:

"The first time I saw Press Reynolds was eleven years ago, long before I was assigned to his case. He was three and one-half years old then. He was sitting on the bench, the long bench outside our offices when I came in that morning. He had the biggest, brownest eyes I think I have ever seen in my life, all fringed with thick, thick lashes. And he was so thin, so tiny through the shoulders. He was wearing a dirty little undershirt, all big and sloppy-fitting around the neck so that you could see the sharp ridges of his collarbones. And jockey-style underwear, so dirty you couldn't believe it. I mean, gray. And he . . . well. First, I should tell you the reason that he was dressed like that was because that was all he *had*. That was it; it was what he had been wearing when the Morals Squad had gone over and arrested his mother. When they raided the place where she was work . . . no. Where she was entertaining a *client*.

"Now, I have seen a lot of children sitting on that bench in my time as a social worker. Our section chief calls it the Boulevard of Broken Dreams; that's from an old song. But, you know, I really have seen a lot of them and most of the time they are raising absolute hell out there: shouting and screaming, and there's an awful lot of crying goes on at that bench. But Press was sitting there, perfectly composed, looking around with those . . . I should tell you now that Press doesn't blink much. Or doesn't seem to. But he was looking all around with those big, luminous eyes and he swung his head around and looked right at me and he . . ."

She leaned forward and looked at the tape counter, then sat back again.

"Before I forget, I'd better make it clear that Press was not perfectly composed. He only *looks* perfectly composed all the time. Even now. It's a thing he does—one of the things he knows he can do. He does it to put you off, to rattle you. He's like a little *vam*pire that way. But, anyway . . ."

No, no, no. By the time they got all this set into type and put into the magazine, the reader would probably be turning the pages looking for the movie reviews or something. No, what you have to do is go for the throat right off, just jump right out of the page after them. How do these people do it?

She reached over and flipped open the file folder. She reread what she had written in the office after seeing him. She hadn't written down *all* that had happened, but all right. That part was between her and Press. Now, then. You tell the story fast, like a journalist would, and the reader sort of sits back and says, uhhhh, Good Lord, to himself and then you've got him. She licked her lips and looked at the microphone again.

New start:

"There really is no Press Reynolds," she said. "There is only this fourteen-and-a half-year-old boy who is loose upon us, who even now is a walking bomb. One day, one time, you could look up and Press Reynolds would *be* there—and God knows what he might do to you. And that's your fault; all our faults, really, because nobody got to him in time. Whatever he is today, he made up by himself. He *stole* it, a piece at a time. A bit here and a bit there—and he made it into a personality. All of which would be fine. Ordinarily, that is. But what you *don't* know—and what Press Reynolds doesn't understand—is that he is furious about it. He is angry, totally outraged, at a world that would make him do this, a world that would force a child to go out and make himself into a *person.* Without any help from anybody. There was no guidance, you see? Nobody cared. When he needed to know how to react; how to *feel,* there was nobody to teach him. Tenderness isn't in*her*ited, it's taught. Same for any character trait, you see? Now, *listen* to me, God damn it: *a person can't do this by himself.* Just can't. Press Reynolds taught himself how to react—but not to feel. Boy, oh, boy, can he ever react. But it's all imitations, imitations of what he has seen. What? Father Knows Best. The Brady Bunch. Waltons, whatever. You name it, he's seen it on television.

"He's perfect at it. Happy: Press will look happy on cue if he figures the situation calls for it. Sad? Remorse? He'll break your heart. Interest? Listen to me: he'll give you his *undivided* attention and there are times when you've got to him at last—you feel. But what he's doing is playing it out for you. He's reacting, but he doesn't feel a thing. He . . ."

She pressed her legs together. Now we're cooking.

". . . he can't get it right. Maybe he never will. Maybe it's too late. I hope not. What remains inside him is this steady anger at the world.

"One day Press Reynolds will kill somebody. Or . . ."

She squeezed her legs harder. She put the palms of her hands on the outside of her thighs and pressed inward.

". . . or something bad. And you won't have to wonder what made him do it. What you'll wonder is: How does he feel about it? What did he feel when he pulled the trigger? When he thrust home the, uhhh, the dagger?

"Are you sorry now, Press? Press, it's me. Doctor Dolan.

What do you feel now? Something honest? A social pain? Press, listen to me: I *love* you. I've always loved you, but you've got to talk to me. Tell me what you feel.

"And you know what? I'll tell you what: he'll look at me with that serene face, that wonderful, hurtingly handsome face, and he'll say, 'Well, just tell me how I should feel, Miss Dolan, and I'll do a few frames of it for you.' Oh, God."

No, no, no.

She bent forward and turned off the recorder.

She was sweating heavily now, through the deodorant coated under her arms, all along her upper lip. Her kneecaps were shiny with it.

Oreos. The super new ones with the double layer of the frosting. She would eat some Oreos. But this first.

She bent forward and picked up the can of baby powder. She twisted the top to line up the holes.

The heat rash was getting worse on the inside of her thighs. It always did at this time of year. She slid her wet buttocks forward on the couch and spread her legs apart. The ridged welts from the girdle were still bright.

The insides of her thighs were all pinkish and the rash moved down and around out of sight. Prickly heat: an efflorescence on the skin. All those hundreds of tiny red dots, each one distinct, the size of a pinprick.

She shook the can of powder into her lap with her left hand and began to rub with her right hand: small clockwise circles. The smell of it came up, an imprinted scent from years ago. Mother used to do that. Mother had patted her with the baby powder after every bath, even when she had grown up. Later, she had even taken large cans of her own baby powder along when she went to college. She had sprinkled it on and rubbed it in every night before bed. Her last roomie, what was her name? Meredith. Meredith had complained about it. "Christ, Dolan, no wonder you never get any men," she had said.

"You go around all the time smelling like the goddam Gerber baby." Now she shook on more powder and rubbed harder, widening the circles.

The outside edge and the knuckles of her right hand still hurt where she had hit him.

They had been sitting in her car outside the house in Bayside, Queens.

Marion Dolan wouldn't go inside any more. She hated the house—it was wettish dark in there and it always smelled like cold knockwurst—and she hated the Becks. She was half convinced that they shouldn't be allowed in the foster-home plan. So she always called ahead to say that she was coming and for Mrs. Beck to have Press come outside to the car to talk to her.

It was such a depressing neighborhood: all those thin, dark houses sitting side by side on the narrow lots. They were all two-story houses, all with the fake red-brick siding that was really tar paper, now turning grayish-black. There was a white plastic flamingo in every other yard and the yellowing lawns were spotted with dog crap.

Press had been outside waiting for her when she had pulled up in the Pinto. She had looked at him sort of obliquely from behind her dark glasses while going through the routine, first seesawing the car up to the curbing, then putting the gearshift lever into *park* and turning off the key. There was the familiar, sudden thrust to her stomach when she saw his hair and the line of his neck.

She had smiled at him and shrugged.

He had walked around to the side, gotten in and sat there, looking at her full on and waiting for his cue.

So she had smiled at him again and shrugged more elaborately; it was an apologetic shrug. He smiled back. He was waiting for her opening line. Get it right and it would determine how the session would go.

And now, playing it all back through her mind, she could remember all the dialogue, everything that had happened:

"Look," she said. "I'm really sorry about last week. You know. What happened at the deli, I mean."

"Me, too," he said.

Fine. So far, so good. "So tell me why you ran away like that?" She forced herself to smile again, holding her eyebrows as far up as she could get them.

"You were getting all red in the face. And that guy at the next table was yelling and all. All that stuff just gets to me." He smiled again. "You know."

"Okay. I know. Uhhh, look: we're friends again, right?"

"If you say."

"Good, good. You know, I went by the school this morning. I hadn't planned on coming all the way out here. But you weren't there. Naturally."

He looked away. "I had to work. I was in town."

"In the city? In Manhattan?"

"Uh huh. I said."

"Doing what?"

"Delivering things. Sandwiches. You know: coffee and sandwiches and things."

"Are you saving the money you earn?"

He swung his head back and grinned at her. "Some. I get more money some days than I do other days. Depends on the building."

"But mostly you spend it all. Right?"

He nodded. "Mostly."

"You go down to Paul Stuart and buy shirts." She reached across the space between them and rested her fingertips lightly on the epaulet on his left shoulder. The shirt was an imported Indian madras in yellow. "They're terribly expensive, Paul Stuart."

He just nodded back at her, smiling.

102

"Look," she said. "Why don't you just go over to, I don't know, go to a J. C. Penney or some place like that, and buy all the shirts you want, and still have some money left over to save? It makes sense, right?"

"Wrong."

"You're too good to wear Penney's or whatever? Is that it?"

He shook his head, thinking about it. "No, no. This is *important*, that's all. I just want to be somebody who can buy his shirts at Paul Stuart." He shrugged again, looking directly into her eyes to see if she understood him. "That's all."

"I don't understand you," she said.

He looked away again.

"And another thing. Stealing. You're not stealing things like you said, are you?"

"Things? Well . . . no. I'm not stealing things."

"Well, you *said* . . ."

"I was just talking when I said it. You never pay much attention any more."

"I'm sorry, Press." She wanted to reach out at him. Maybe with both hands, but that would spook him. Perhaps just to lay the palm of one hand on the top of his head. In this light, his hair looked like layers of puffy, polished satin. "I'm here to help."

"Sure."

"No, really. At the school today, the principal said you are really very, very smart. If only you'd bear down, he told me, the principal. Bear down and you could do it all. And . . ."

He swung his head back around, the satiny hair swirling down. Then he took a deep breath, blinking at her and started, picking up speed as he went:

" 'The principal said. He said.' Look: it isn't the school. The school isn't anything. What is it that I'm supposed to bear down *on*? John Greenleaf *Whittier*? The last class I was in—it was, oh, I don't know, I was supposed to be memorizing 'Snowbound.' Listen: that's *it*. And all the kids there have got plenty of *time* to do that kind of stuff. They can go home and recite it to Grandma: 'Shut in from all the world with*out*, we sat the clean-winged *hearth* about,' and she'll probably give them a damn Mallomar. Because they're families, see? But me. What I've got is this—this *house* here where you put me. I told you about it, but you won't listen any more. They're chipping away at me in there. You know why? Because they don't take me as a real people, they see me as a thing. A thing that is to be controlled. Keep them out of sight and keep them shut up, that's the number. All foster kids are idiots, otherwise they wouldn't be foster kids, right? All welfare kids wet the bed. So they've got a rubber sheet on my bed up there and Missus Beck checks it every morning. You ever sleep on a rubber sheet? Try it; it makes you less of a people and more of a . . . whatever."

"Press," she said. "Press, *listen*. Stop talking so fast. Listen: these take-in-kid homes are hard to *find*. And with your record of running away . . . well. Now, I know you don't like the Becks. And maybe they're not the best, as you say. But surely you can take . . ."

He nodded again, narrowing his eyes. "Right. Absolutely. I can *take* it. That's not the point. I can take all of this stuff. The Kid will be all right. The Kid can take all of this except the, uhhh . . . you know. The . . ."

"Injustice?"

"No."

"Ill treatment?"

"No, no. What they're doing. They look right through me. Nobody has ever taken the time to find out if there's anybody *in* here."

"The dehumanizing."

He squinted, then nodded. "Again?"

"Dehumanizing."

"That's it. Listen: there are three of us in that one little room. You already know that part, I think. But there are three of us and one of them, Freddy, one of them is retarded. He's . . . well. He really needs the rubber sheet. So is the other one; maybe not quite as bad. But he's got this bone disease. The whole front of his leg is open here—all along the shinbone. They have to leave it that way so it can *drain;* I don't know. But it smells. How do you like it so far?"

"You're exaggerating again. You make it sound like something out of Dickens."

"Dickens sucks."

"Watch it, watch it. Well, now. It all sounds dreadful, I agree. But what would you have me do about it?"

He shrugged. "Get me out."

"There'll only be another place. Maybe better, maybe even worse. Or an institution."

"Look, Miss Dolan, look: you don't really dig any of this, do you? I don't *care* if it's worse. The Kid will get by all right. All I want is to . . . look. All I want is to become a people."

"A person. And you are."

"Not in there. They're dehumanizing me."

"Oh, Lord. That's all I need: to add another word to your vocabulary. And, as it happens, by the way, Dickens definitely does *not* suck. To use your crudity. Charles Dickens just happens to be the greatest . . ."

"Well, if he isn't any better than John Greenleaf, uhh, you know, puke on him."

"Ohhh, *Press.* Come off it. Where do you learn this sort of thing? But, all right, all right. I'll tell you what I'll do. I'm going to explain something to you, something I haven't told you. And then, and then if you agree to help me, I'll try to help you. Fair exchange, right? All right? Well?"

He nodded.

"All right, then. First of all, I think you're unique. I

thought so when I first saw you. You don't even remember that."

"I remember everything."

"All right. And I thought so even more when you were assigned to me. And then I really thought so after I read all your charts. You are a unique child trapped in a certain situation."

"But human."

"Well, uhh, yes. Human. Now, then. I'm doing a paper on you. And if all goes well, it will . . ."

"What's a *paper*?"

". . . if all goes well, uhhh. It's a special report on one subject. A thesis. A dissertation. If I do it well and it's accepted, I'll get another degree. I'll become *Doctor* Dolan. That's important. Are you with me? Now, then. The paper is in*tense*ly psychological. I propose to lay bare . . . no. Let me rephrase that. I propose to set forth all of the innermost thoughts and reactions and reasonings of my subject. To get inside his mind, if you will. To search out motivations and the very thoughts that accompany that motivation. In orderly progression: motivation to thought to *deed*. It will be a scientifically *beautiful* paper. There's also a chance that it would be published in a magazine; a very good chance. It's even possible, if that's the case, that there would be a little money in it for you. Not much, maybe, but a little money. All right?"

"I don't want money," he said. "I want out."

"But you'll cooperate fully?"

He sighed. "So far, I don't even know what you're talking about."

"Yes you do. I can tell by the look in your eyes. But, all right. I'll give you a little example . . ."

She began rubbing her thighs together.

". . . all right? Now. We've been together long enough now. You can talk to me; I'm your *counselor*. You can tell me *every*thing. Everything that goes on in your mind. It will be easy if you try. Just relax and tell me everything."

She leaned slightly to her right, looking at him, and lowered her voice. She continued to rub her thighs, listening to the shhhhhpppppp, shhhhhpppppp. When she started to talk again, it was in an almost-whisper, and he bent his head forward, close to hers. She could smell him now, the scent rising up from the open collar of his shirt. He smelled salty and faintly wet. His, oh, God, his ribs would be shiny with it. Her mouth was too dry. She ran her tongue around her lips. For some strange reason she was starting to get light-headed.

"All right, here we go," she said. "I'm going to ask you something very *in*timate because that's the point I've reached in the report so far. I've stated the facts; now I take the reader on the first full step into your mind, see? The reason we start with an *in*-timate observation like this is because it's strictly *Freudian* and—well, you couldn't be expected to know about it—but everything starts with this. It is basic to human nature and it will tell us a lot."

He was sitting very still now. She was staring into the front of the crisp madras shirt and she could see his chest rise and fall rhythmically. Without consciously thinking about it, she adjusted the rubbing of her thighs to keep pace with his breathing.

"What I want you to tell me now," she said, "is what you fantasize about when you . . . uhhh, when you play . . . when you fondle yourself. That is, what thoughts run through your mind; what images play inside there while you're doing it. You must know, of course, that everybody does this. Well, all young *men*, I mean. Girls don't. So there's no need to feel embarrassed. And scientists have long regarded masturbatory fantasy as important to the psyche. I want you to tell me in your own words. I understand, of course, that you must dream about something while you're . . . uhhhh, *doing* it. It is a girl that you know, perhaps? Maybe a girl from your class at school?"

She licked her lips again.

"Or is it a cheerleader? Cheerleaders are very, very good, I'm told. With their supple little bodies and, and the swirly little skirts. Accordion pleats; those brief flashes of underpants. Pom-poms on the tops of their saddle shoes. Or is it—can you hear me all right?—is it an *older* woman? Possibly one of your teachers? Studies have shown that teachers rank second in this category. And *counselors*. You know: an older woman of, well, of *soft* authority. Maybe it's the way she stands at the blackboard. Or the, uhh, the gentle sway of her hips when she crosses the room. Or bending over your desk. Possibly you can look into the front of her blouse and see her ... and see her."

She was suddenly aware of the pulse at her throat now; it felt like a swollen cord running down into her collarbone. She had to listen hard for the shhhhhppppp, shhhhhpppp of her legs.

"Just tell me in your own words," she said.

In the silence that followed, she could sense the roaring of the thickening cord in the throat. She wondered if he could hear it. Finally she looked up.

His face was perfectly impassive. Composed—the look that he could don as easily as pulling on a rubber mask. His eyes were half-closed and the shadow of his eyelashes lay diagonally across his cheeks. He was not blinking.

"Well?" she whispered. "Tell me."

"I'll tell you," he said. "You're ..."

Shhhhhpppppp. "I want to hear it."

"You're crazy," he said. "God *damn*. I thought you were going to help me. But no. You're one of *them*."

And suddenly she was upright in the car seat, swinging hard and chopping blindly at him with the outer edge of her right hand. She could feel the sting of it radiating up into her bicep. She chopped harder, letting her arm swing out to full length inside the car, her fingertips brushing against the windshield as she brought her arm around.

A burst of blood came from his nose, forced out in a fountain. He pulled his head back sharply, opening his mouth, and all of his upper teeth were stained pink, each tooth outlined with a darker red line.

"Not crazy! I'm not *either* crazy!" she said. "It's—for—the—thesis. It's for me!"

But then he was gone, leaving the car door swinging open.

The tan imitation-leather seat was flecked with blood where he had been sitting.

And now, leaning back farther, feeling the clipped-velvet of the couch across the backs of her shoulders, she held the can of baby powder higher over her lap, shaking it hard, squinting into the falling haze of white powder. She rubbed harder with her right hand, a larger circle that went up across her abdomen and down between her thighs into the heat rash.

Lazy, sweet-swelling circles.

She would make fettuccine for dinner, too.

She rubbed faster, squinting.

"Oh, Press," she said. "Presssss. I didn't mean to hurt you. That wasn't it at all. It was just the article. And I wanted . . . no, they wanted. You see? My *baby*. Baby. Oh. Your eyes; the *lashes*. That look on your face: I hope this doesn't trigger something, some explosion inside you. Because I really love you. I do. Oh. Ohhhh, my baby-Press. My baby-love-boy-baby-Press-child. My boy. My, oh . . . my *boy*."

It was 9 P.M.

13

THE KID

The blood was dripping down on Mrs. Beck's tomato plants, spotting the dark green leaves. Way to go, Kid. When Mrs. Beck came out to see them it would be daylight; she checked the tomato plants first thing every morning, kneeling down beside them and cooing to them. And when she saw all the blood on the leaves, she would sit back on her heels and look up at the sky, wondering where it had come from. Had there been a blood-rain last night?

The Kid's nose was broken, straight through the main bone.

He leaned against the garage, bending forward to let the blood drip down. He was breathing through his mouth and watching the house.

His left eye was swollen almost shut now and getting worse. The puffy part was moving down his cheek toward his mouth. It felt like something was pulling his head to one side.

The dining-room lights were on. Shadows were flickering against the drawn shades, someone walking around the table in there. The upstairs windows were dark.

His lower lip was split, the cut running horizontally, the long way, almost to the corner of his mouth. There was a matching rip on the inside, caused by his teeth. The lip was puffed out so far that blood and spit kept pooling on the inside. He bent his head forward further and ladled it out with his tongue.

Everything hurt now, even his shoulders where he had tried to twist away from her. It had hurt worse when she had been hitting him with the edge of her hand. The bone in his nose had gone off with a crack you could hear—but she had kept on swinging. But maybe what was worse had been the look on her face: she had gone all crazy, blackish all around both eyes. She would have kept it up until he was dead. No, longer than that. Until after he was dead.

So long, everybody.

The Hunchback of Notre Dame had looked like this in the movie. But he had looked like this going *in*. For starters. What was his . . . ? Mmmm, Anthony Quinn.

Okay. He pushed away from the garage and moved toward the house. He stepped carefully in the tall grass, still bent forward, staying close to the dark line of fence. He stopped and took off his shoes, not stooping any further, putting the toe of one against the heel of the other and lifting out his foot. There were holes in the toes of both sweatsocks. He swung his head around to check the alley one more time, then turned. He climbed up to the porch railing, stood up on it quickly and grabbed the overhead rain gutter and then pulled himself up, swinging one leg. Then he lay on his stomach on the porch roof, licking the blood out of his lower lip and looking back down over the edge.

This thing would go a whole lot faster if the blood would only dry up. He spit a long, pinkish string of it down and watched it splatter on the porch railing.

The new shirt was all shot, too, the stains going all across the front and halfway under each arm. The good imported madras, too, damn it. Whatever madras was. But the good stuff.

Come *on.* He got to his feet and went across the roof to the bathroom window. He eased it up slowly, then bent inside. Shampoo bottles, hair-spray bottles, creme-rinse conditioner. Vaseline lotion and a blue Air-Wick thing. He cleared off the windowsill by taking them one at a time and throwing them over his shoulder into the grass below. Then he stepped inside the bathroom, right leg first. He stood for a moment in the Lysol smell, blinking it away, then opened the door and padded down the hall. He stepped around the grating of the hot-air register in the floor. The light from the dining room below came up in small squares through the copper grating.

There was a new smell now, like warm vinegar. It meant that Freddy had done it behind their door again. He pushed the door open, inching it to just the part where it always squeaked, then led with his left shoulder and slipped in sideways.

"Easy, *easy,*" Bill said. "Where you been, anyway? You, uhhhh . . . Jeez. What happened? Somebody beat . . ."

"Forget it. I haven't got any time. So what's with Freddy?"

Bill was sitting on the edge of Freddy's cot and Freddy was face down, crying again, hiding his head under the pillow.

"He's okay. Lissen: sometimes you're gonna get caught, out alla time like this. Get us all in a mess again," Bill said. "I told you already."

The Kid took a breath, looking around the room. He unbuttoned the shirt and pulled it up out of his pants, then wadded it up and wiped the blood off his face with it. "Never mind. Doesn't matter any more. It's all over now." He threw the shirt down.

"You going?"

"I'm gone. Listen, I said: What's with Freddy?"

"He wants you, is all," Bill said. "He thinks that every time you don't come right home at night like this, that you won't ever come back. You know. Jeez, your *face*. It's all rooned. You should see it."

"It feels like it." He bent forward and lifted the edge of the pillow, squinting into the darkness under it. "It's okay, Freddy," he said. "I'm here now. The Kid is back. So you can stop crying."

Freddy twisted around and leaned out and hugged him around the knees with both arms. He began rubbing his face back and forth, leaving a smear of spit. "Kid lef' me all alone and Kid din' ever come back."

"No, I didn't leave you. I was just out late and now I'm back." He stooped and pulled Freddy's arms away. He looked back at Bill. "Why'd you let him go and pee behind the door again?"

"Look, I can't stop him," Bill said. "I can't be on him all the damn time." He put the palms of his hands on the cot and pushed himself up, then hopped back to his own cot, his leg bent. He picked up his crutches and got them braced under his arms, leaning heavily. "I can't stop him from doing it. You know. Like, he's afraid of the bathroom when it's all dark in there at night and he can't find where the string is to turn on the light. You know. He keeps swinging his hand in the dark like you told him, but he forgets where you're supposed to swing your hand to hit the string. Then he gets all scared booger-man's going to get him and he runs back in here. He thinks that if you piss behind the door that nobody will ever find it."

"Well, clean it the hell up. Come on. I can't leave you clowns alone around here. Old lady Beck finds it and you guys will be up all night with the Lysol again. Go on, get on it. I'm in a hurry."

There were three drawers in the unfinished pine chest:

Freddy, Bill and The Kid. He pulled out the bottom one, lifted up a fresh shirt and shook it out. He wiped across his nose with the back of his hand, looked at it for fresh blood, then put the shirt on.

"Kid goin' again. Gonna leave me." Freddy was peeking out from under the pillow.

"No, no. Go on back to sleep." He zipped up the jeans and fastened his belt, looking back down into the open drawer.

There were two new shirts in there, still all pinned up, the collars just right. Two separate practice trips to Paul Stuart: twenty-two bucks, twenty-eight bucks. But, okay. The hell with it; it was too late now.

His nose was starting to really throb now, pumping the pain in waves into his check. But at least the blood had stopped.

"Kid?"

He didn't turn around. "Hmmmm?"

"Who hit you? Hit Kid?"

"Doesn't matter."

"Fat lady," Freddy said. "Fat lady in the Pinto."

He licked at the outside of his lower lip. It was starting to crust up into a hard ridge now. "Yeah," he said. "Fat lady. Now, go back to sleep."

He stooped again and reached in under the underwear and socks.

No. Goddammit, no. He swung around and looked at Bill. "Who's been in here? In my drawer?"

"Miz' Beck was," Bill said. He shifted his position on the crutches and shrugged. "You know, like earlier. She was, she went all through everything."

"Did you see her take . . . aww, Christ. Did she say anything about money?"

Bill nodded. "Something. Uh huh."

"What? Come on, dummy."

He wrinkled his forehead. "She said, uhh, like it was

wrong for you, you know, for a welfare kid to have money when people were out of work all over. Like that, she said. I think that was what she said. Welfare kids shouldn't have any money, she said. She told me not to tell."

The cut inside his lip started to bleed again. He had bitten it open.

Forty-two dollars. A twenty, two tens and two ones. He swallowed some of the blood.

"Where are they now?"

"Who?"

"The *Becks*. The goddam Becks, dummy."

Bill shrugged again. "They're down there in the dining room. They just sent out for Chinese food again. It was just before you got back here. I heard the guy at the door. And, you know. They're down there. . . ."

"They what?"

"Chinese food. Sent out for it. Like, you know the whole number by now. I mean: I fixed up your cot like always. And old lady Beck came up here and stood outside the door there for, you know, for a long time. And then she stuck her head in here to make sure we were all asleep."

"Didn't turn on the light?"

"No."

"And Freddy?"

"Well, he *was* asleep then. But then he woke up asking for you and you was gone. You remember that."

The Kid put the back of his right hand gently against the lip, then pulled it away and looked at it. "I can't . . . I can't b*elieve* any of this stuff. Dickens? Holy Christ. Okay, okay. So what did you do?"

Bill blinked at him. "Who? Do what?"

"*You*, meathead. What did you do? I suppose that you got right up off that cot and went right downstairs. And you stood there with that bullshit iron brace on your leg and, what? And I suppose you said, 'Oh, boy, Chinese *food*. If there's anything that foster kids love, it's that good old, mothering Chinese food. I think I'll just gimp right over to the table and join you.' Right? Your ass you did. And then. And then, I suppose you said, 'Wait, hold everything a minute and I'll just call Freddy downstairs. Lord, if there's *any*thing that old Freddy loves, it's ...' "

"Come on, Kid. Off my ass."

Freddy looked up, swinging his shaggy head to look at both of them. His nose was still running and he stuck out his tongue and licked at his upper lip, guiding the fluids back into his mouth. He was blinking. "Food? Chin*ee* food?"

"Oh, God," Bill said.

Oh, God, right. He kneeled down beside the cot and took Freddy by the shoulders. He squeezed in hard with his fingers. "Food? You bet your simple ass, Chin*ee* food. Listen, Freddy: *spare*ribs. You like that? And fried *rice*. All those little things mixed in it. Does Freddy ever love fried rice?"

"Yesssss. Freddy loves ..."

"Fine. But you can't have any."

Freddy started to cry again. "Come on. Want some, want some fried *rice*, Kid. Come on."

"No, Freddy. Forget it. And I'll tell you ... you want to know why? The Kid will tell you: because you're in a goddam foster home. Because nobody else'll have you. You're dehumanized. You like that word? De-*human*ized. You're a ward of the *state;* it's how they dehumanize you. And *they* eat Chinese food down there about once a week —after you've gone to sleep. But they don't want you down there."

"Want some, Kid."

"No, Freddy. Too bad. But ... but I'll tell you what I'll do. The Kid will do this for you. You want to *see* it?"

"Hey," Bill said. "Hey, no, Kid. Come on."

Freddy nodded, licking all around his mouth now. "Freddy want to see it. Eat it."

"Don't do it," Bill said.

"Screw off. This is the end of it all." He turned back to Freddy. "Okay, then, come on. Come on, get up. You know the hot-air register? Sure you do. You know: right out in the hall there, remember? Right where you stand in the winter to put your clothes on; where the heat comes up through the floor. Sure, you remember. Okay, look: the register is right over the dining-room table. You remember *that*. Well, then. All you got to do is to go out in the hall there and . . ."

"Awwww, *no*," Bill said. "Lissen, Kid, you'll get us all in . . ."

"Stuff it, I said. Now, listen to me, Freddy. Do what The Kid tells you. Go on out in the hall and look down through the hot-air register and you can see it. See all the pretty food. Go on, now."

Freddy got off the cot and sluffed out into the hall. His boxer shorts swung loosely in the back, all stained brown.

He got down on his knees heavily, sniffing and wagging his head back and forth, putting one hand on each side of the brass latticework of the register. Then he flopped down on his stomach and pressed his face tightly against the grid, looking down into the dining room. And then he shuddered, pulling all his fingers up into fists. He began to cry again.

The tears and spit started to drip down into the room below.

"Awww, Christ," Bill said. "Now you gone and got us . . ."

The Kid's left eye was totally closed now. Even by raising his eyebrow he couldn't get it back open. He could feel, what was it? He could feel water oozing out of it, and even that felt scratchy rolling slowly down the puffed cheek.

He ran out into the hall and stood over Freddy, one leg on each side of his waist.

"Way to go," he said. "Way to *go*, Freddy. Go on and cry. Cry into their goddam food, Freddy-boy. Drool. Go ahead. Barf on 'em, Freddy."

Then he wheeled and ran down the stairs.

They were seated at the dining-room table. They were both frozen into position, white plastic forks in their hands. They were both looking up at the long, stringing drips coming down from the ceiling. Some of it was plopping steadily into the white cardboard container of chop suey. The container was open, its little brass-wire handle swung down out of the way and the fold-over flaps open like wings.

He pulled to a stop and looked at them.

The old man finally closed his mouth. Then he slowly put down his fork. He looked down at the containers of food, blinking, and then looked up at the register again. And then he slapped both hands hard on the table, making all the white containers jump.

"I'll be a dirty name," he said. "I'll be a son of a bitch. That little, that little cretin up there is drooling into the *food*. I mean, you see that? What the hell."

It was hard to make them out with one eye. Their faces kept advancing and retreating, throbbing fuzzily with his heartbeats.

"He's *cry*ing, too," The Kid said. "Not just drool, no. Freddy's crying into the food and he's drooling and all of it. Because you know why? Because you fat-asses won't give him any. You goddam *night* eaters. Won't the foster home money buy enough for everybody? Listen: it's my food you're eating. No, wait. No, it's Freddy's food, really, because Freddy's only been here forever."

The old man started to push his chair back. "You again," he said. "Mister Smart Alex. So what happened to you? You run over by a beer truck or something?"

"Somebody pound the smarty-pants out of him," Mrs.

118

Beck said. She was still chewing, watching him. "He finally got what he deserves."

They were getting more blurred. His eye was running full tears now, stinging. He took four steps toward the dining-room table, holding both arms out parallel to his shoulders.

"Watch this one, Freddy," he said. "You want to see all the pretty food? Well, watch."

And he took one more step, point-after-touchdown, swung his right leg up and kicked the table over on its side. The shock stung up to his kneecap. Never kick a table over in your stocking feet.

Mr. Beck tried to get up on one knee, slipping in the chow mein. There were grains of rice and bits of browned pork sticking to his head. The bits of pork looked like freckles against the shining white skin.

"You dirty . . ." he said.

"Right. Right, you got it: bastard. It's why I'm here in this place."

"I told Miss Dolan about you," Mrs. Beck said. "Mister Big Shot bad boy. Mister know it already."

"Did you tell Miss Dolan that you stole my money, too?"

She shrugged. "I suppose you're supposed to have money? I was holding it for you."

"Sure you were."

She shrugged again.

He waved for them to stay put. Then he tilted his head back and looked up at the register in the ceiling. "You hear me up there, Freddy? This is it; I gotta go now. You be a good boy and don't forget The Kid, Freddy."

He sidestepped around toward the kitchen. At the door he paused again.

"Do one last thing for The Kid, Freddy," he said.

He squinted at Mrs. Beck.

"The Kid is gone," he said. "Nobody here ever sees The Kid again. That ought to make you happy."

He looked up at the register again.

"Okay, Freddy," he said. "Listen to me now. Get up on your knees now, Freddy. You got that? Hurry up, do what The Kid tells you. Okay, Freddy, whip it out. Now, pee on them, Freddy. Right on through the register. Go ahead and whiz on them and their goddam night food."

They were all looking up at the register now. They were blinking at what they saw.

"Way to go, Freddy," he said. "I knew you could do it."

And he wheeled fast and ran out the door.

It was 11:55 P.M.

14

MARION DOLAN

She rolled over on her back, blinking up into the dark and wondering what it was that had awakened her. She turned her head, making all the paper night curlers rustle, and squinted at the clock radio.

It was 1:35 A.M.

There it was again. A something there.

Then the hand came down hard across her mouth. The fingers pinched in on one side and the thumb on the other side, just up under her cheekbones—and the palm of the hand pushed down heavily.

She squeezed her eyes shut, then opened them to try to get him into some kind of focus. But without her contact lenses in, his face seemed rippled and wide, like looking at it through shallow water. He was standing beside her at the edge of the bed, bent forward with all of his weight pressing down. There was something shiny in his other hand.

She pushed back with her shoulders against the bed

and arched her back, trying to breathe. The web of his hand was twisting her nose. She couldn't get her mouth open to bite at it.

Well . . . well, my *God.* This only happens to *other* women. You read about it. They always live on the West Side in the nineties and no security downstairs. But not here. It can't happen to . . . not to . . . my Lord. She couldn't move her head.

All right. Hold it. Hold everything one second. Think of something fast. What? That's it: try to reason with him. You can reason; you're trained for it. It's what you do for a living. You can do that. Be rational.

Sure, swell. Except that his grip was hurting her upper teeth right through her cheeks. The pain began to fan up into the roof of her mouth from both sides.

Two thoughts at once:

One. Her nightgown was all bunched above her waist and her stomach and her, you know, everything else down there was bare. That was bad.

Two. When he started to talk, she suddenly realized that she knew who it was. My God. And that was worse.

"Everybody up," he said. "It's get-even time."

It *was* him. But he seemed to be, what? He seemed to be lisping. No, not quite; more the sibilant S, as though perhaps his mouth wasn't quite right. But it was definitely *him.* Right here beside her bed.

"Don't try to talk," he said. "Don't try to do anything. Most of all, don't plan on hitting me anymore, because you see this thing I got here? Because I'll let all the air out of you with it. You got all that?"

She blinked, but she couldn't see whatever it was, no. But it was something in his other hand—a something. And his voice wasn't right. That was more important.

What is it, my darling? What's wrong with your mouth?

"You broke . . . you almost took my head off today," he

said. "Nose is broken and I can't go anyplace to get it fixed."

Me? When? I couldn't. I would never hurt you.

"But, listen. Listen to me: I'm going to take my hand away for just a second here, and then I'm going to put this tape across your mouth. You got that? It doesn't hurt going *on*. But you make one sound and that's it."

She tried to nod. A reasoning nod. She let him put the tape on; otherwise, he would do something awful with the shiny thing in his hand. He pressed the tape back against her cheeks with his fingertips. Then he sat down beside her on the edge of the bed.

What had she done? She couldn't remember clearly. They had been sitting in her car and she had been questioning him. And she had gotten angry; that was it. And . . . oh, my God.

I didn't mean it, my dear. Not that way.

"Okay," he said. "Now. I want you to roll over on your gut. Come on. Easy, easy; you got it. Now, put your hands up under the pillow and keep them there. You move a hand, you get stuck. Okay. Are you warm enough? Come on, nod yes or no. Yes? If you're warm enough, then stop shivering."

Broken? Good Lord, was he sure his nose was broken? It could spoil the perfect symmetry of his face, the delicate balance to go with the soft eyes. If she could only see it to make sure. Perhaps touch the nose with the very tips of her fingers.

"Now, then," he said. "Here we are again, right?"

You shouldn't see me like this. It's bad. Who knows what ideas this could put into your head. The sight of a girl in her nightie, it could drive you wild with lust. Don't look at me, Press.

"And now we talk. Now we talk, like you always say. Except that this time you get to listen. You never have

123

listened to me; you just sit there with my file folder in your lap and you write things down in it about me. All those questions. But I told you: questions don't do it. They don't help."

She nodded, blinking up some tears, and she drew her fingers up into fists underneath the pillow. She could feel the fingernails biting into the butts of her hands.

His voice. If she could only touch his poor mouth, his poor swollen mouth. The swelling was what was making his voice all blurry. She would put cold compresses on his face. Maybe make him a milkshake in the blender. He could drink it through a straw or something.

"Stop shivering," he said. "Now, listen. You; everybody. All my life it's been like this. Before it was you, it was somebody else. But mostly it's always been somebody pretty much like you. Not as fat and sloppy, maybe. Sometimes some of you wear glasses, I don't know. But you're all the same person. All the same. You all start out saying, 'We're going to be pals.' It always starts out like that. I think they make you memorize that before you leave school. And then I think to myself: uh huh, we are. You bet. Pals. Listen: nobody I know has used the word 'pal' since the year of the blue snow. But, okay. Sure enough, pretty soon you all get that look in there behind your eyes and I can see it coming again: she's going to mold me into a little man again. Just like I guess it says to do in your social-worker book somewhere. Nobody tries to help me; all they want to do is bend me. But you—you are the worst one yet. You're going to write a paper on me. A *paper*, Christ, that's what I really got to have."

Lord, what if his nose wasn't fixed in time? What if it took on that terrible twisted look, a subtle shading that would cause people to turn away and miss the glory of that first look into his eyes?

"But, all right. I haven't got much time. I was thinking about this on the way over here. Thinking about what to say to you. Walk a few blocks, stop and bend over and bleed a little. It was a great trip."

Oh, Press. My baby.

"And I was trying to figure it out. But I got it—what it works out to is this: you lose. No paper this time. Mostly, no kid. Get them to run you up another kid somewhere. Do a paper on him. Because today did it. That was the end of it all."

If only she could see him. She wondered if he had bled much. On his pretty new shirt? He loved his shirts so.

"I remember that once, one time one of you told me that I was bad," he said. "Well. That's okay to say, but it's wrong. What I am now is *mean*. There's a difference. The Kid is mean. Think about it for a minute. You follow me? Nod your head. Hell, yes, you follow me. Listen: The Kid was born pissed off; pre-pissed off, even. But you, all of you, did the rest of it to me. And that's it.

"I'm gone. The Kid is gone and you lose the case. You'll never see me again; nobody ever will. Got it? And before I go, I'm going to do this."

Press! No! No!

"Lay still. You keep shaking like this and it will only hurt a lot worse."

Oh, Lord, Press!

"See, this, this is really for all of you. But you're the only one I can get my hands on—so you get it for everybody. For all the social workers. Oh, hell. Go ahead and cry. Everybody cries sometimes. Well, except The Kid. That's all over now."

She cried steadily for the next twenty minutes, wincing and trying to twist away from the pain. She swung her face from side to side against the pillow, creating a clammy half circle because her nose was running so steadily. She was afraid to sniff; it might block everything and she couldn't breathe through the tape.

He was doing it now: moving slowly. Once, when she

twisted her head around to the far left, she could just barely make out his head bent forward with concentration, the tumbled hair all dim and out of focus across his forehead.

He didn't speak again.

And then he was gone.

She listened. Be careful, now. Maybe it's all over, but maybe not.

She began to twist her body around to find a dry spot for her chafed thighs and another dry place where she could rest her face.

And then, coming on slowly like a gathering fever, the rage began to build again.

15

MARION DOLAN

"Easy now, Marion," he said. "Take it easy. I'm afraid it's going to be a few more minutes here before you can get back into your girdle."

"That hurts," she said. "Stings."

He nodded. "I wouldn't be at all surprised." He continued patting with the gauze pad, pausing to freshen it from the bottle. "But it would help if you would calm down a bit."

"Well, *damn* him," she said. She twisted her bare stomach on the examining table, making the waxy paper rustle. Then she turned her head and looked back over her shoulder at the doctor. "Calm *down*? You see what that little, you see what he *did* to me and you say calm down? And stop that, whatever that awful stuff is. I told you it stings."

"At least he didn't kill you," the doctor said.

"Kill me? That's not the point. He carved his initials into my *ass*, you old fool."

"So I see."

"Well?"

He shrugged a bit, still patting with the gauze pad. "Well, I should say that, given the rate of violent crime around here, I would venture to say that you got off luckily, my dear girl. Lucky, indeed. Have you seen this? The initials here?"

"I've got a hand mirror; I've got eyes. Of *course* I've seen them."

"Rather a neat job. Well. Medically speaking, of course."

"Stop that kind of talk. Very idea. I want them *off* of there. And right now, too. Take the skin; peel away some tissue or whatever it is you do. I don't care. Just get them off. Give me a local or something and cut them out. What's the matter with you?"

He tore the top from a fresh envelope of gauze pads and lifted them out. He spread them gently over the initials, covering the swollen, welted cuts spelling out E.P.R. against the mottled skin. A curved line had been slashed under the three initials for added emphasis; perhaps the deepest of all the cuts. He pressed at the open ridge of the cut with his fingertips, then shrugged. There was a puffy circle of pinkish area around the initials, perhaps the size of a basketball. Beyond the circle the skin looked like it had been stretched over giant mounds of farmer-style cottage cheese. He turned and picked up the tape. "I can't remove them now," he said. He pressed the strips of tape over the gauze and then flipped her nylon slip back down over the bare buttocks. "All right, Marion. You can get up and get dressed now."

"I'm not moving," she said. "I'm not *budging* from this table until you get those initials off me. Are you crazy? I can't go around, walk around like this, knowing that they're back there."

"Nobody is going to see them."

"I don't care about that. *I* know they're there. You're my doctor. I said to take them off."

He turned on the water in the sink and began washing his hands, looking across at her.

"I'm afraid I can't," he said. "Not just yet, anyway, not until this heals. But it isn't serious. Those cuts aren't really very deep; certainly not as deep as you insist they are. Let's say, ummmmm, sub-subcutaneous. Into the denser fatty region. As soon as the cuts heal—say, three weeks or so—we'll see about removing the scars, and you'll be as good as new in the buttock department. Speaking of which, by the way, it certainly wouldn't hurt for you to lose some *weight* back there, as I have told you so many times now. You really do have an overly generous backside."

"Never mind that. How do you get them off?"

"Mmmmm, probably dermabrasion. A plastic-surgery technique. Removes tattoos, birthmarks. And carved initials, I would imagine. I'll refer you to someone. That procedure will sting, too, probably."

She turned slowly, bracing with her hands, crinkling up the paper some more. She swung her legs over the side of the table, feeling for the pull-out footrest with her toes. "Ouch! Good God. I can't put my weight down on this, uhhh, on this cheek. I won't be able to sit down."

"Of course you will. Just sit carefully."

"Ohhh, that little, that little fiend, doing this to me. What did I ever do to . . . well, never mind. It was all over *nothing*. Come on, hand me the girdle there. Stockings, too. Hurry up."

"Marion, if you lost some weight, you wouldn't have to wear that awful foundation garment. Your heat rash would clear up, too."

"Oh, for*get* my weight," she said. "Just plain forget it, you hear me? You've been on me all my life about weight.

Ooohh, ouch! If you would just fix *this*, just get rid of these initials like a real doctor would, and just forget about my weight."

He nodded. "I hear you. You know, I wonder if I shouldn't give you a tetanus booster, too. No? Well. Do you want any help with that rig?"

"I can do it, I can do it."

"Mmmmm, I see. It looks terribly uncomfortable. A touch medieval; you look like you're putting on a suit of armor."

"I warned you."

"I know, I know. Oh. I guess I forgot to ask. What did he do it with?"

"Do what?"

"With what did he carve his initials into you? Is that the right way to put it?"

"Oh." She tugged at the girdle. "It was my shrimp deveiner. It's stainless steel, or whatever—a thing from Hoffritz. And it's sharp—with some sort of forked notch at the very tip of it. You know. I had cleaned some shrimp the night before. I'm going to make shrimp marinara tonight and . . . and, no. I'm *not* ever going to eat marinara again after this. Ick. Well, anyway. I had left the shrimp deveiner in the sink. And he must have picked it up when he broke in. And he took it with him when he left."

"One of your welfare cases, I take it. You knew him, of course."

She pulled the slip down and then stood up and shook her skirt into place, patting at it with both hands to stop the crackling. "Static electricity. Hmmmm? Oh, one of my welfare cases, yes. That devil. My main welfare case; I was doing my dissertation on him. That one case."

"Until he ran amuck."

"Well. He's always been slightly amuck, if that's the word. That's one of the things that's so perfect about him. Now I'll have to go back to line zero with him and start all over again. He's *frus*trating me—holding me back. And it's so important. Lord, I get my hands on that kid and I'm going, and I'm going to . . . well. Put *that* in your thesis. God, you're no help at all."

"Calm down, Marion. You're hyperventilating again; it's a long-standing problem with you."

"Well, *sure*. Sure. I take it that nobody has ever carved his initials into *your* ass, you old wreck."

"No. But if they had, I would like to think that I would take it a bit better than this."

"Well. I'm going to *get* him, understand? I'll get him, and when I do, I'm going to nail him with everything so that he can understand just who is in charge of whom. Everything: assault; battery; breaking and entering. The works. *Criminal* assault. Rape. That foul little . . ."

The doctor held up one hand. "Hold it, Marion. Hold it. You said rape?"

"Rape? Of *course*, rape, you old fool. He broke into my apartment, one. And he attacked me and beat me savagely and tied me up and cut on me and raped me. You hear all right, don't you?"

"I hear perfectly well. Thank you for asking."

"Well, rape, then. It's a very, very big offense, you know."

The doctor sighed. "Marion, Marion. It's *me*. You seem to forget that I've known you all your life. Child into adult. I've grown old and weary along the way; weary of all this, weary of difficult patients. Such as you, Marion. Now, then. You seem to have conveniently forgotten that —before I treated your newly monogrammed ass—I also examined you. Ah hah. So don't look at me in that fine state of feminine outrage. I *examined* you, remember? I can see that you do. And you most assuredly were not raped. You are still the same old Marion, as far as eye and finger can tell."

"Damn you. I said he . . ."

"No, no. I checked your innermost parts, my dear, as I always do routinely. And while your *labia minora* seem to be suffering from what one might call vibrator-fatigue, the fact remains that you are still a virgin. And decidedly unraped."

"Doesn't matter. I'll nail him for it anyway; for all of it. Get him for the works. And then we'll see."

The doctor shrugged. "All right, all right. I won't argue with you anymore. But if you decide to charge him with rape, please don't call me as a witness for the defense. Goodbye, Marion."

16

MARION DOLAN

"All fine and good," he said. "I can appreciate all the things that you propose to do with him. But first you'll have to find him."

Marion Dolan stopped in mid-sentence. She was breathing hard, aware now of the perspiration spreading in half-circles under both arms. She leaned forward and put the tips of her fingers on the desk and looked closely at the director.

"Find him?" she said.

"Exactly: find him. Now, surely you didn't expect him to stay around and wait for you? Not if what you have just told me is true. Or perhaps you expected to find him waiting in my anteroom. Or on the long bench out there in the hall. Your Boulevard of Broken Dreams. If so, you disappoint me, Miss Dolan. Which, I might add, has become something of a pattern with you." He raised his left hand and glanced at his watch, then pointed to the chair beside the desk. "Now. Sit down and let's go over this thing again."

"I *told* you. I can't sit down. I've been terribly beaten. Battered and . . . and, well, *assaulted*. And I ache all over. I have just now come from my doctor."

He continued to point at the chair. "Sit *down*, Miss Dolan. You don't appear to have been *that* badly beaten, considering the manner in which you have been prancing around this office, waving your arms and shouting. You look as . . . mmmm. You look as robust as ever to me. Sit down."

She eased into the chair slowly, supporting her weight with both arms. She settled on her right buttock, tilted toward him.

He pushed his chair away slightly. "That's better. Now, before you start your tirade again, let's . . ."

"I'm sorry, sir," she said.

"You should be. All right, then. First, there is chaos over at the Beck home. There is absolute hell to pay, as one might expect. A great deal of damage, I'm told. Plus a particularly nasty bit of business involving one of them —one of yours, no doubt—urinating on a roomful of people. Yes, that's what I said. Disgusting. Now, then. This office has got to straighten that out. But let me go on to the other points first. First: our runaway."

"He *raped* me," she said.

"Did he, indeed?"

"Yes, he did."

"You're sure."

"Of course, I'm sure."

"May I go on?"

She looked at him for a long moment, her lips pressed tightly together. Finally: "Yes, go on," she said. "I'm sorry."

"And please don't lean on my desk so intimately."

She rolled her left buttock down slowly, wincing. And gradually she straightened.

"Thank you," he said. "All right. There is the Beck

family, as I said. And, I must say, right now that item seems to be running about last on your list of troubles."

"My troubles."

"Exactly." He swiveled back to the desk and opened the file. He spread out the papers and began picking them up one at a time, looking at them. "First. First, I have here one runaway. Press Reynolds. Full name: Elvis Presley Reynolds. Age fourteen and a bit. He was so named because his mother was smitten by Elvis Presley, the . . . uhhh, the late entertainer. Not at all uncommon for people in *that* level of society to name their children after entertainers or movie stars. Now. The boy is illegitimate, of course. Came to us some eleven years ago. Via the police, as the result of a raid in the red-light district. A tenement. His mother was entertaining a client at the time."

"I know all that."

"Miss Dolan."

"I'm sorry," she said. "Go on."

"I intend to. A difficult child, Press Reynolds. Obviously carrying a great deal of undirected anger at the world for what it did to him. Becoming more and more withdrawn. We had to move him nine times; he was six times a runaway. Quite a dossier for one so young. And it's your case, Miss Dolan. Your case for the past few years. An absolutely spectacular failure on your part."

"Now, just a minute here," she said. "Listen, I . . ."

He whipped his right hand up, the index finger out. He held it almost at the tip of her nose.

"Wrong," he said. "You listen to *me*. If I have ever read of a botched rehabilitation—and heaven knows, I haven't the time to read all of these things, what with our case load—but if I have *ever* seen a classic case of mismanagement, this is it, Miss Dolan. This is it."

She shifted right, wincing with it. "He's a dirty little bastard."

135

"Aren't they all, Miss Dolan."

"Won't communicate with me. No interplay. No input."

"Indeed."

"Withdrawn. Moody. All those things you said. He has been deliberately *block*ing me. Rehabilitation? First, I'll have to get inside his head and . . ."

"Miss *Dolan*. May I go on?" He picked up another paper. "I take you now to his Stanford-Binet. One hundred and thirty-*seven*, Miss Dolan. Genius, as I'm sure I don't need to tell *you*, Miss Dolan, is one hundred and forty." He threw down the paper and picked up another sheet. "And let us consider the Wechsler, shall we? A marvelous score here. Taken before you got your meddling hands on him, I might point out. Or the test *here*, The Thematic Apper*ception*, Miss Dolan. Or the M.M.P.I., which looks frightfully above normal to me." He put the report down. "So much for whether or not somebody is *in* there."

"Well, I don't care. I've seen those reports and . . ."

"Wait. Let's get to the crux of the matter. Don't interrupt me again, Miss Dolan." He pushed the papers around and picked up a new one, the blue interoffice-memo stock. "I understand—that is, I have it right here, that you have been doing a *paper* on Elvis Presley Reynolds. Your doctoral thesis, I take it. Ah, ah, ah, don't interrupt me. There is a warning here from your section chief stating that she feels the boy was being pushed too hard because of your thesis. Constant questioning rather than a sense of concern with him. A great deal of tugging and pulling at his psyche, if you will, instead of working with his problems. Have you been doing this on our time, Miss Dolan?"

"Work with him? Who can work with him? What does the section chief know? The boy happens to be a classic case."

"Classic case of what?"

136

"He's a media child. He pulls in impulses from the world around him. He absorbs them and integrates them into his personality, don't you see it? He . . ."

"Go on. You're on dangerous ground here."

"How so?"

He shrugged. "I would think that it should be obvious to you—though I can see that it isn't—that they are *all* like that. That is, it is perfectly typical. No mother or father figure to provide guidance. Small wonder that they grow up to act entirely by instinct. Without a show of feeling. Elvis Presley Reynolds isn't special. He's typical."

"Oh, no he isn't. This kid is far and away *smarter* than all the others, and you know it. Prettier, too. He is . . . you should see him; you should look into his eyes. And . . . where was I? Oh. But he's still standing outside himself and looking back in. And if there isn't a doctorate in that, I'll . . ." She was starting to breathe heavily again.

"You'll what? I don't know what you'll do, Miss Dolan. But I can promise you one thing: you won't do it here. Not for this agency. You have done a terrible thing here."

"What?"

"You have pushed a boy too far. Leaned on him, as I think the popular phrasing has it. You are not a psychiatrist, Miss Dolan. You are a *social* worker. You are the graduate of what I would term a barely acceptable school. Mid*west*, Miss Dolan. A *land*-grant college, for heaven's sake. You are a social science and psychology major with an M.A. degree—and my records show that you had a difficult time making *that*. And now you are walking around inside the mind of one of your cases. You are dabbling in curbside psychiatry—dealt out unfeelingly from the front seat of a Pinto hatchback. My God, Miss Dolan."

She licked her lips. "All right, all right. I'll back off on him. I'll find him . . . no. We'll find him and I'll . . ."

137

He pushed the papers back into a stack, lining up the edges and patting them into place. Then he closed the folder.

"You certainly will," he said. "You'll back off, as you put it. You'll back off all the way. Let me rephrase that: You are through, Miss Dolan."

"No."

"Ahh, yes. Yes, indeed."

"But, I'll . . . wait. Maybe a leave of absence."

"Sorry. But no."

She looked into his eyes as she raised herself out of the chair, putting all her weight on the palms of her hands. She could feel the sweat running down from her collar now, forming cold between her breasts.

"So I'm through," she said. "Well, you *fag*."

"I beg your pardon?"

"Listen: you fag. Fag pansy swish. Who cares about Press Reynolds? Who gives a care about that little no-good? He was *mine* and I just about had him *down*. Who really cares about him and his damn tin psyche? Born in a whorehouse and die in a whorehouse. And you were going to let him stand in *my* way? I just about had him; he was perfect. Perfect. And then I could have had the doctorate and . . . and then maybe I could have gotten some nice college somewhere. A nice campus with trees and things. Counseling. No more snot-nosed foster kids smelling up my car. Spend a half-hour talking to one of them and get nowhere, and then I have to drive home with all my windows down. Listen: Press Reynolds is mine and you can't take him away from me."

"Please do not loom over me when you talk," he said. He brushed at the lapels of his coat with both hands. "You are covering me with spray. In fact, please leave."

"I'm going, I'm going. But don't you forget: that kid attacked me and beat me unmercifully. And he carved his . . . well. He cut me and he raped me."

"I doubt that."

"And you still say *he* needs help?"

The director nodded. "He needs help."

"Well, he's gonna get it, I promise you. He's gonna get some kind of *help*, all right. Agency or no agency. Thesis or not. I'm going to find that little bas—that little ille*giti*-mate, you hear me? I'm going to find him and then . . ."

"Then?"

"And then you'll all be sorry."

She stepped back to the desk, panting heavily. She picked up the gray folder and threw it into the air. They both watched the reports fluttering down all around them.

And then she walked to the door. Her left buttock felt like it was on fire.

TWO

17

THE KID

The hallway was too dark. First he heard the snap, and when he swung around he saw the quick chrome arc of the switchblade when it flicked open. But that was all he could see; the flash had come at about chest level. Then a hand came out of the black and pushed him back into the banister and held him there.

The figure moved in now, so close that The Kid could smell it. Sweat, mostly. A sense of lazy breath, carrying stale beer with it.

And then he saw the knife blade again. It was up close. It slid down quickly past his left eye, grazing through the eyebrow, and went out of sight. It came back up and there was a sudden, sharp stick. He went up on his toes. The tip of the blade went into his neck just underneath his left ear. Just *this* far: he could feel a sudden bubble of blood well up and start to slide down slowly toward his collar.

He stood quietly, trying to balance. The hand was still

pressed against his chest, fingers played out. The voice came from the dark just ahead, slightly to his right.

"Been lookin' all over for you," the voice said. "You a hard dude to catch up with."

The Kid nodded.

"I mean: you unnerstan' what I'm saying to you? You a slippery dude. And the Cat Man doan like that. You wasting the Cat Man's time, you dig it? Like, I'm busy, man, and I got to stop everything and, you know, places to go and things to do and like that—and I got to jive-ass all around trackin' you down. See what I mean?"

He nodded again. "Okay. You found me."

"You *know* I found you. So okay. Les' go."

"Go where?"

"Jus' go. When I say go, we go. The man wants to see you."

"What, what man?"

The breath came in closer now: "What you mean, *what* man? I mean, *the* man. The Main Man, you dig it? Like, I mean: he sees all and he knows all, you unnerstan' what I'm tellin' you? And he been seein' you from time to time. But you ain't been seein' *him*, because that's the way he do it. And right now, he doan even know yet that he wants to see you. Thing is, he wants to see *some*body, because he's lookin' for some dude to haul his ass in for beatin' up an old guy and cuttin' up the old guy's cat. Like, the man doan rightly care *who*, just so it's somebody, you dig? He gonna arrest *some*body's ass for it, 'cause he always does. And I figure it ain't gonna be me he 'rests—so it gets to be you."

"I've been seeing him, all right."

" 'Course you seen him; you supposed to *see* him, dig? But you ain't been seein' him like I mean it. He gets done wif' you and you gonna unnerstan' what I'm sayin' to you. Anyway. Anyway, lissen: like, you got any money on you?

144

I mean, as long as we're here and all. You ain't got any bills, I'm gonna cut you a whole lot worse, long as I'm cuttin.' It's like, you ain't gonna need any money anyhow, the man gets finished with your ass."

The Kid shrugged. "Back pocket."

The fingertips slid down his chest, staying in contact all the way, until they hit his belt buckle. Then the hand slid around smoothly to the small of his back. It paused there, the thumb hooked lightly in his waistband. The tip of the knife stayed in his neck.

"Wha pocket?"

"Other one."

The hand edged around further. The voice came in closer now, with the overlay of rotting teeth: "Doan move now. You jiggle, you dead. Unnerstan' what I'm sayin'?"

"Got it," The Kid said. "You're doing this all wrong, but okay. I got it. Look: I'm not moving, see?"

There was another pause, the fingers stretched out now against his back pocket. The tip of the knife slid further into his neck. He tried to stand taller.

"Do . . . uhh. Do what?"

"Doing it wrong," The Kid said. "Jesus. *Easy* with the knife, all right?"

The tip of the blade wavered. The blood seemed to be getting thicker and warmer.

"Wrong? Don't ass me aroun', man. Man, like you standin' here dead, man; you *dead*, and the Cat Man's doin' it wrong?"

"It's what I said. Maybe you don't hear too good."

"Awwwwww, man. You really askin' for it, you dig? You know that? Gah-damn, man. Sheee-it, man. You gonna talk to me or what?"

"You got it," The Kid said. "Listen, now: you just go on and hold the knife right there so it makes you feel real safe. And I'm going to talk to you. Don't run it in any

145

more; you got me bleeding pretty good already. Okay? And I'm gonna tell you what you're doing wrong."

"You dealin', man."

"Okay, look. Look: I'm not even from here, see? I mean, I'm not even from the Village here and I can tell you're all dumbed up. What the hell. Where'd you learn this horseshit number, anyhow? Jesus, this is dumb time, the way you're doing this. You're supposed to be the Cat Man, right? Big Cat Man; I've been watching you. The cape and trick hat and all. But that doesn't do it; hell, I'm surprised you're still alive. Listen: where I come from, you pull off a number like this and it's dead-time right from the start. You do it this way and you only got a few minutes to live."

"How you mean?"

"Okay. Where I come from, if we're going to get somebody in the hall, we do one thing first. God *damn*, Cat Man, you never been *up*town? I've been here in the Village, what? Three months now, and you think maybe I'm wandering around here all by my*self*? First thing we do *up*town is to make sure the guy is all *alone*. That way, nobody gets to creep up behind you and split your ass from behind—like right now."

"Wha . . ."

The hand pulled away from his waist. He could sense the shoulders twisting around in the dark.

The Kid brought his knee up fast, driving it into the space where there ought to be a crotch. The contact caught him on the top of the kneecap and jolted through his thigh. He pushed out with both hands and saw the knife blade flare away into the shadow. It fell to the floor and skidded into the wall. Then he eased away from the banister, holding his breath. He listened for the sound from the floor. When it finally came, he stepped over toward it.

"Speak up," he said.

146

The voice came up from the floor again, from just beside his right foot.

"Ooooohhhh, sheee-*it*," it said.

The Kid shifted his position a bit, fixing a bearing on the heavy breathing. Then he drew back and kicked at the voice, catching it right the first time. The kick stung his toes. He kicked some more, changing feet, shifting the pattern to make corrections for an unseen head that would be trying to flinch away. Then he stopped. He ducked down and patted around with his hands. There was hair, curly and wet. Forehead and a nose. He patted on down to the throat and put his hand around it and leaned all of his weight forward.

"There, now," The Kid said. "Do I have your attention?"

The head nodded just above the web of his hand. He eased up the pressure slightly.

"Fine," he said. "You want to hear the rest of it?"

Nod.

"Okay. Now, listen: I live around here, right? Got that part? The Kid *lives* here, and you got to learn that part by heart, because that's the way it goes down. Look: I know the man is hunting for somebody to hang some rap on. I've seen him assing around. I'm getting pretty tired of looking at that trick hair and those teeth. But we got nothing to say to each other, me and the man. Whoever he gets, it ain't going to be me. You with me so far? Nod yes or no."

The head nodded yes.

"Fine. So you got two things you can do. First thing: I'm going to be all around down here because I live here. And you can go on and do your number all you want. You know, you can dumb around in the black cape and cut up your cats and push over old folks. You can have cat heads rolling all over these hallways, all I care. That's one. Thing two is: you cross The Kid once; one time, and The Kid'll have your chili-burning ass for fair. And you can take that to the bank. You ever watch *Baretta*? So don't jive The

Kid around; I come walking by, I want to see you lookin'
the other way. You got it? You better nod."

The head nodded again, more vigorously. The Kid could
feel tears rolling down over his thumb.

"So okay. So your neck hurts and my neck hurts and
we're just about even this time out. But next time, you
lose it all, Cat Man. Next time, you get to eat one of your
dead cats, fur and toenails and all. You think about it."

He lifted his hand away from the throat and stepped
back quickly into the darkness. He waited, crouched and
shaking, holding the shrimp deveiner out front, waving it
back and forth. He waited until the outside door opened;
there was a quick shaft of light and he could see the figure
slipping out. The door hissed closed again.

The Kid stayed on his haunches. He breathed in sharply
through his mouth and got his stomach muscles set just
right so that he could stop the shivering. He shifted the
deveiner to his right hand and reached up and touched
his neck with his fingertips. It was greasy with the blood;
a pool of it was forming in the hollow of his collarbone.

He knew the way it would look from the other side,
from the viewpoint of someone watching him. Say someone holding a TV camera pointed at him. This is what the
cameraman would see: The Kid would get up and run his
hand through his hair in that special way he had of doing
it. The hair would swirl back down across The Kid's alabaster forehead. Then The Kid would shrug, putting his
fingertips to the wound and then holding them out and
looking at the blood on them. A faint look of contempt
would form on The Kid's lips. Then he would say something just right for the fade—for the part where they
would cut to commercials.

But . . . but: ohh, God. It really hurt.

He turned his back for a moment and wiped under both
eyes with the back of his left hand, getting his cheeks dry.
He breathed in deeply. Okay. Do it right. He turned back

148

to face the hallway again and he straightened his shoulders. He ran his fingers through his hair like he always did. It fell back down across his forehead. He curled his lip a bit.

"It'll probably leave a nice scar," The Kid said.

18

ICEPICK SALLY

This particular suit of long underwear was the top of the Montgomery Ward line. It was guaranteed absolutely one hundred percent cotton in the rare oatmeal color. The buttons up the front and on the drop seat in back were pure bone, not just white plastic. A little tag had fluttered from the underwear when she had first unfolded it. The tag had said that this garment was "Inspected by No. 173." And Icepick Sally had sat right down and had written a little thank-you note to No. 173 about the buttons, addressing it in care of Montgomery Ward at the Merchandise Mart in Chicago. Inspector No. 173 had never responded; well, not yet, anyway. But that didn't matter. The buttons mattered.

These drop-down seats on long underwear were the real McCoy, of course. The style was being phased out apparently, perhaps not even being made any more. The new type of long underwear featured a vertical flap in back; a

150

folded-over affair that one pulled apart like a curtain upon sitting down on a toilet. Unspeakably vulgar. No, more than that, even. It was more like the sort of thing that Norwegian farmers might wear, Norwegians being noted for their unfailing, stolid lack of good taste.

The pink fur slippers added a festive touch. They're called mules, these slippers. That's the idea, naturally: when wearing a plain costume, like long johns, you add one gay, devilish accessory like the mules. Something hinting of naughtiness.

Ginger Rogers had worn these pink fur mules. She was the only woman in the history of talking pictures who could come swinging into a room—like this, see how I do it?—who could come swinging into a room and throw herself down carelessly on the divan and kick one of the pink fur mules all the way across the room.

And her accompanying laugh would tinkle. Now that was a merry laugh, Ginger Rogers. They don't do it that way any more.

The mules had turned up very early one morning beside a garbage can on Eleventh Street. Not inside the can; just lined up perfectly beside it. Just standing there, slightly toed in. There was still dew on them and they had sparkled like zircons. Just two slippers so daintily side by side, as if Ginger Rogers had just jumped right out of them and floated up to heaven.

Icepick Sally turned slowly, looking into the full-length mirror leaned against the wall, allowing for the distortion caused by the diagonal crack through the glass. She nodded gravely back at her image: the pink fur really did set off the one hundred percent oatmeal cotton; it really did.

Then she swung around, arms out just right, and flopped down on the couch and kicked up her right leg.

The mule flew away perfectly, a high arc with the light

151

glittering off the patent-leather heel, and landed in the sink. She pushed herself up and went over and picked it out, shook it off and put it back on.

Let's see, now.

Some jewelry would be appropriate. Something nice for her boy; he really appreciated nice things. Maybe even something *bangly* to catch the candlelight over dinner.

She stepped over—these high heels are really tricky, Ginger—and looked down at the earrings and necklaces and bracelets laid out neatly on the red velvet cover on top of the dresser. There was one of each earring. People never throw away a *pair* of earrings; they lose one earring in a taxi and then they finally throw the other one away after spending two weeks trying to match it in Gimbels or Alexander's. She now owned the premier collection of single earrings, perhaps the best in Manhattan. Well. At least the Village.

Right ear. She lifted up the crystal teardrop and shook it to check the facets of light, then screwed it into place. Left ear. No question about it: she put on the little white Scotty dog. His little leash formed a chain. It had been half of a set to advertise Black and White Scotch Whisky. The little Scotty always swung around so perkily, turning to look back over her shoulder, then twirling back to look straight ahead.

Little, carefree touches like this show that you're a wonderfully aware person—but that you don't take the world too seriously.

Is that, why, my goodness, is that a little doggie earring, my dear? Yes, it is. How absolutely *cunning*.

She moved down to the left on the dresser top and lifted up the lid on the wooden cigar box. She sorted through the collection of butts with one fingertip, then picked up a half-smoked Dino. She lit it with the onyx-based Ronson desk-model lighter, puffing carefully and turning the cigar butt in her fingers to get it lit just right.

Perfectly good lighter; only a few chips knocked off the base where someone had dropped it. The sanitation men— if they had gotten there first—would have loved a lighter like this one.

She stepped back to the couch and sat down and stretched out her legs. She took a deep pull on the cigar, her cheeks concaving with the effort, and puffed some smoke rings up into the ceiling. Then she lowered her head and looked around.

This place was a *salon*, really. Well, except that nobody ever came to drink cognac and discuss poets. No, maybe it was more like a *ped a terry* in the Village, a nicely done hideaway.

It was certainly well furnished: the scraps of carpet remnants spotted here and there on the floor made for soft footing, even if a bit uneven. There was the chest of drawers that had been here when she had moved in, what? Twenty-six years ago; the chest so big in swirly oak with its feet of carved eagle's claws clutching the glass balls. She hadn't intended to have two couches in this small area, but the blue velvet camelback couch had just been sitting there on Tenth Street one morning—only broken a little bit through the middle. She had lain down on it with her arms out protectively until the sanit men had arrived. Then she had haggled and haggled with them —finally threatening to have another little stroke if they didn't let her have it. She had paid them twenty-two dollars to haul it up here. Now it was perfect. If you knew how to sit down on it.

And her treasures: the big hand-painted porcelain Cupid with the Westbury clock sunk into its stomach. It was three-and-one-half feet tall, if you counted up to the tip of his one remaining wing. Once it had been a whole floor lamp as well, the main stem rising up out of the top of its head. But that had been broken off when she had found it, and now the stem formed a sort of single little horn, like a unicorn-angel. And the clock always said nineteen minutes to three. Then there was the white birdbath that held her spider plant, a perfect, fluted Grecian column that you would never dream was made of plastic. Her Dolly Madison rocker, really a very good piece, with only one spindle missing from the backrest; why anybody would throw it out was a wonder. Her little marble statue of Diana at the hunt, always cool to the touch, even in August. So ele*gant*. And the heavy ashtray found out in front of O'Halloran's Bar. It was the White Rock club soda girl perched so daintily on her rock overlooking the pool— such lovely little bare arms and shoulders. And the precious china collection, everything from Spode to Lenox, all classified and stacked by category all around the baseboards of the room. The unclassified china and matchbooks and various newspaper clippings were stacked under the sink. She would get to them as soon as she had some time.

Her knapsack hanging on the back of the door added a nice touch of red.

She crossed her legs, waggling the pink fur mule on her toe. She held the cigar butt between thumb and first two fingers, looking up into the smoke.

The ceiling was the best part of all.

Once it had been a sport parachute, black-and-white checks like the finish-line flag they wave at Indianapolis. The idea had come to her . . . well, no. Inspiration, really, when she had had the parachute all spread open across the floor of the room from one corner to the other. She had then tacked it to the ceiling, standing on the couches and the dresser and the rocker, spotting the tacks so that the nylon billowed down between them in arches.

Well, don't laugh. No, sir. Colette had had a ceiling exactly like this. There had been a picture of it in the *Times:* Colette seated in her salon underneath her billowy ceiling like this. There was even a name for it. The style was called *Trompe Louella*.

It was like, now it was like being inside the tent of the Sheik of Araby. And the parachute shroud lines hanging down the walls made it even better, more effective and tentlike.

She hummed it, waggling her foot in time:

At *night* when you're a*sleep,* tah dah, ta *dah;* in-*to* your tent I'll *creep.*

That was one that she hadn't sung to her boy yet. She would have to remember that one. He loved it when she sang the old-timey songs to him. Sometimes she would dance along, shaking the tambourine and whapping it against her backside for emphasis. Or she would dance with the fringed shawl while singing, holding one end of it in each hand and sawing it back and forth behind her:

Lady of Spain, I ad*ore* you.

Or:

Take good care of yourself, you belong to me. Poo poo pe do.

Or "Bill Bailey," the verse and all:

Oh, late one Sunday *morn*ing, the sun was shining *fine.* An' the lady-*love* of ol' Bill Bailey was hanging clothes on the *line.* In her back *yard* and weepin' . . .

Her boy.

It was odd. It had been, ummmmm, how many weeks now? She could look it up in the marked-off days on the calendar over the hot plate.

But he was her boy.

She had stayed out after dark that day.

She hadn't planned to, but it was a long trip back from Sixth Avenue and Third Street with the knapsack so heavy. And the kids had surrounded her at Tenth. That's what had held her up so.

The sun had just about gone down behind the buildings and she had been hurrying along with her head down. And suddenly the kids were right there. No loud footsteps, just that awful cold sense of something moving fast, something rushing up from behind.

One of them had made a grab at the knapsack. But the straps had been so tight that the tug had spun her right around. Her half-glasses had flown right off her nose and one of the kids had stamped on them. It made a sound like cracking walnuts. Then she had staggered back into the wall.

She had put her hands into the pea-coat pockets. The knapsack against the wall had forced her to crouch forward. It was hard to watch all of them at once; they kept dancing in and out of her sight.

The one in the Levi's jacket with the sleeves cut off at the shoulders had stepped up the closest, holding both of his hands out front with the fingers all open.

"Where's your big-ass icepick?" he had said.

"Here. Right here," she had said. "I've got it right here in this pocket and I know how to use it. Don't come any closer."

"Ain't no icepick," one of the others had said. "What she got is a jive-ass sack full of garbage, is what she got."

"I'll stick it into your throat," she had said.

"Where the money?"

"No money," she had said. "And it's not either garbage; it's for my research." She had made grabbing motions inside the pea-coat pockets. "Icepick. I'll stick you with it. I've got both hands free, remember."

"You ain't got no purse. Got to carry your money somewheres."

"No money."

"Ol' lady, you stinkin'," one of them had said. "Icepick Sally stinks. Stink up the town. Come on."

"Don't come any closer."

"Come on: the sack. Give it on over or you a stinkin' old dead lady."

She had crouched a bit farther; now they had all been the same height.

One of them had darted around to the side where she couldn't see him, and she could feel his hands pulling at the shoulder strap. The muscles in the backs of her knees had started to tremble and she knew that she would go down.

That's when the police officer had come along.

He had stepped in among them, scattering them with his polished brown stick with the leather thong.

"Get off the old lady," he had shouted, his voice hurting her ears. "Come on. Knock it off, you little bastards. Beat it."

They had skittered away, no sound of feet, just leaving the sounds of their laughter behind them.

"You okay, Icepick?"

She had tried to straighten, holding out both arms for balance. Finally, the officer had taken her by one arm.

"Yes, okay," she had said. "Thank you."

"They hurt you any?"

"They were about to."

"Rat packs. Run wild down here. Run 'em in here, they pop up over there. Can't keep up. They *breed;* they come out full size and mean." He had helped her a few steps. "You okay now, Sally?" he had said.

"Yes, yes. Got to get home."

"Shouldn't be out after dark down here."

"I don't know that it's any more dangerous than in broad daylight."

"You can make it all right?"

"Of course," she had said. "If I sometimes seem to be a bit unsteady, it's only because I have suffered . . ."

"I know, I know," he had said. "You told me, Icepick. Now, get the hell on home." Then he had half turned, sniffing at the air. "What the hell you *got* in that knapsack, anyway?"

"It's for my collection," she had said.

And then she had made it to the front stairs, walking close to the buildings with her right hand out for support. The bricks had scraped her fingers raw. At the bottom of her own stairs outside, it had come.

The small stroke: the inside of her head had clicked on and off, just like that, and there had been a brilliant white flash behind her eyes.

She had dropped to her knees under the hammerlike punch that followed inside her head. You would think that someone could hear a blow like that.

Everything turned, what? Turned cerise, that was it, all lighted with that garish, pulsing light. Every time the light pulsed, the steps seemed to rise and fall in front of her.

She had bent forward and rested her forehead against the worn-out sandstone part of the step.

"Remember now, Lord," she had said. "Remember how I used to be good to *you* when I was a little girl."

And then she had fainted.

The hands had come later. How much later? Who could tell? The two hands had pulled her to her feet, and she felt the breath of the voice up close to her left ear. It had talked right into her ear, softly, while she had been blinking.

"Come on," it had said. "We got to get out of here."

Was it the good Lord? She had peeked downward, trying to focus.

Would the Good Lord wear green-and-white running shoes?

"Who?" she had said.

"We got to get away. You and me."

"No money."

"No, I don't want your money," the voice had said.

Maybe it was Him; He had *run* down from Heaven.

"And I've got an icepick."

"No, you haven't," the voice had said. "Come on. One more step."

One more what step? What had she been doing? What had happened here? She had been climbing her own stairs, held up by the two hands. She had turned and tried to make him out. She could barely see his face. He had had a bad nose. Terrible nose.

"Come on, now. Keep moving."

"Big dog," she had said. "I've got a big dog. Bad. A big Doberman *pincher*. He'll tear you . . ."

"No, you haven't got a dog. Are you all right?"

"Little stroke. I had a small stroke. My icepick. My dog will . . ."

"Keys," the voice had said. The hand had appeared almost at eye level. The other arm had been holding her propped up against the door frame.

And she had handed over the keys. When she did, she had glanced at them. They were all glowing cerise from the flash inside her head.

She had made it to the blue camelback sofa and had laid right down. He had picked up her feet and tucked them under her. He had covered her legs with the Spanish shawl.

And when she had awakened sometime the next afternoon, he had still been there. She had looked at him for a long, long time before he had noticed that she was awake.

And he had been here ever since.

Well, let's see, now. She would fix the turkey-neck soup for dinner. Very nourishing, with those perfect little circles of oil floating on the top. Each one of those circles would stick to your ribs.

It's all in knowing just when to get the neck bones, of course. You do it very, very early in the morning. Before the sanit men come around.

She leaned over and crushed out the cigar just under the White Rock girl's nose.

"Lovely little white arms," she said. "There was a time—you will find it hard to believe, of course—but there was a time when I had arms like that."

There was a click at the window.

She half turned on the couch, watching.

The ironwork grating swung away. A hand came into view, reaching down. Blue denim shirt-sleeve, buttoned at the cuff. The hand eased the window up.

He swung his legs inside, then ducked his head under the window and stepped into the room. He turned and swung the grating back into place.

She stood quickly, smoothing out the long underwear with the palms of both hands. Then she stepped into a model's pose, one foot forward, her arms slightly out, so that he could see how she had dressed up for him.

"Well, well," she said. "If it isn't Douglas Fairbanks, Junior."

He swung around to face her.

"Oh, *child*," she said.

His face was as serene as ever—totally without emotion. The arched eyebrows were raised slightly above the thick, heavy lashes. A perfect, *perfect* face—except for his terribly broken nose, all twisted to one side and too thick now across the bridge. But . . .

But below one ear, there was a puncture wound in his neck.

The blood was welling up slowly, forming a large bubble at the hole, then running down into his collar in a straight line. The bloodstain had spread across one side of his chest and it circled around under his arm.

He was breathing through his mouth. It was because of his nose.

"Child. Who . . . ?"

"Doesn't matter," he said. "I think it's almost through bleeding now."

"I'll fix it. I'll fix it with dry oatmeal."

"Okay. Whatever."

He walked over and sat down on the camelback couch —on the unbroken spot. He looked around the room, mouth slightly open, then looked back at her. He started at the top, looking at the Scotty dog earring swinging on its little leash, and went on down to the bottom. He nodded.

"Well?" she said.

"You're beautiful," he said.

"I know."

"I really like the slippers," he said. "Where did you get those?"

"From Ginger Rogers," she said.

19

ANGEL

"You're a nize boy," she said.

Angel nodded.

"Nize boy like you, you could be Jewish," the old lady said. "Just except for the color. So the color's a little wrong. I mean, a little lighter in the skin you need, maybe, but who's to say? It's all in the *face*, a nize boy like you. And . . ."

"Lady, I'm in a hurry," he said. He held out the flowers with his left hand. He kept his right arm and hand behind.

"But I told you it couldn't be," she said. "It's just . . . so who is going to send flowers to me? I ask you. An old lady —who even knows old ladies? Eighty-two-year-old ladies, already. It couldn't be. They just so pretty, the flowers. But . . ."

"C'mon," he said. He shook the bouquet. "Take 'em."

She reached through the door opening and put her fingertips against the wax-paper wrapping. There were brown liver spots on the back of her hand. The safety

162

chain on the door was just at her forehead level. "So I could take a little look, maybe. So nize, the flowers. There's a card, maybe."

He shifted his position when she took the bouquet, both hands behind him. The bolt cutter had bicycle grips at the ends of the long handles. He fitted his fingers into the ridges and tightened his grip.

"No card," she said.

"How about that?" he said.

"So who could . . . ?"

"Look," Angel said. "Look, lady: you gonna give me a little something, bringing them all the way up here?"

"But the flowers, they . . ."

"You jus' keep the flowers."

"A quarter," she said.

He shrugged.

"I could, I've got it, a quarter. The check came today," she said.

"I know the check came today."

"I could . . . you just wait here. Such a nize boy; such a sweet face you got. I couldn't open, I couldn't let you in, even. But just a minute. The robbing here, you wouldn't believe it. The stealing, hitting. Everybody, we're all so scared. Keep the chain on the door. But, wait. Let me get to my . . . one quarter I got."

He nodded, smiling.

And when she turned her face away from the opening, he swung the bolt cutter up and around. He took one step backward and pulled the long handles apart. He slotted the opened cutting edges over the brass safety chain, then tightened his grip on the handles and pushed them together.

The chain snapped and fell apart at the middle, each end rattling down.

He stepped in through the door and kicked it shut behind him. When she turned, her hands flying up toward her mouth, he hit her with the bolt cutter, holding it by one handle and swinging it like a bat.

She went straight down; not over backward, but straight down, her legs twisting underneath.

He stepped over closer, looking down at her. He lifted the bolt cutter with both hands, pulling the handles apart, then lowered the open blades onto her stomach.

"Surprise," he said. "Nize boy got your white ass."

He changed his grip, thumbs upward, and pressed down a bit.

"Where's it at?" he said. "The money?"

She coughed up some grayish foam. There was no pupil —only the whites of her eyes were showing.

"C'mon," he said.

She rolled her head to one side. With the next cough, some flecks of blood appeared.

He shrugged. Then he pressed down with both arms and quickly closed the bolt cutter until his thumbs met.

He lifted the cutter up and shook it. The faded cotton fabric from her apron wouldn't shake off the blades. He raised the cutter and picked them off with his fingers, looking around the room.

The purse was on top of the dresser.

He turned it upside-down and spread everything out, then picked out the money.

Eleven lousy dollars.

And before he left the room, holding the bolt cutter out in front of him, pumping his hands open and closed like a bellows, he cut things up a bit. The furniture. The walls. The chest of drawers. The old lady.

20

OFFICER KEITH LEE

The tough part was getting her by surprise. She always sensed him coming, like maybe she was wired with some early-warning system. And then, before he could get his hands on her, she would go into her poor-little-old-helpless-lady act. She even seemed to make herself shrink inside all those heavy clothes, her hands up and fingertips pressing against her throat. Looking up, like Fay Wray being approached by King Kong.

But this time he had her.

Maybe it was the street noise today. And maybe not; he had been working on making his footsteps lighter. He practiced in his apartment every night before taking his sunlamp or before putting the bleach on his hair. But walking lightly isn't the easiest thing in the world to do when you weigh two forty-one.

But now. Got you, you dirty old broad.

Keith Lee leaned in over the garbage cans and got her by the back of the neck. He pinched in with the tips of his fingers. There was a faint crackling of neck bones. He lifted up. But he kept her at a full-arm distance; already he could catch the smell of her coming back at him.

"All right," he said. "How many times I told you about this?"

She couldn't see him because she couldn't turn her head. She flapped her arms up and down, like she was trying to rise into the air and fly.

"You . . . you're *hurt*ing," she said. She coughed.

Better not pinch her old head off. That would be a little too much to explain. He eased back with his fingers a bit and then shook her back and forth.

"I told you to stay the hell away from here," he said. "How many times I told you?" He shook her again, harder. "How many times now?"

Every time she pumped her arms up and down, the smell got worse. She was pumping it up from inside the collar of the old Navy surplus pea coat. And now there was a hazy swarm of gnats around her head; he could feel them landing on the back of his hand. The gnats were swirling up from the open can.

She was trying to talk. He shook her again.

"Not . . . not bothering anybody," she said. "Please."

"Hell you're not," he said. "You're bothering *me*, for one. Scattering garbage around the sidewalk like that. I told you about that. Loitering. Trespassing on Mister O'Halloran's sidewalk here. I ought to . . . what if I accidentally mistook you for a burglar and shot you? What if I shot you in the back one time? You'd die in a garbage can."

"Don't . . . please don't shoot me," she said.

Her voice was pretty strangled; he eased up again with his fingers.

"I could do it. One shot; it could happen. You want to die in a garbage can?"

"No, sir."

"Know what they'd do? The sanit men? They'd come

166

and they'd throw you right up into the truck and then that pusher thing would push you right up inside there with the rest of the garbage and they'd haul you away to the dump. You know that?"

"Please. My neck. You're hurt . . ."

Awww, the hell with it. The damn gnats were starting to itch on the back of his hand now. He shook her again.

"Run you in," he said. "I warned you about loitering. Put you in the women's house of detention and then they send you off to the nut farm somewhere."

She was crying now. He could feel the sobs vibrate into the palm of his hand. "Please. Please, no."

"I could book you for carrying an icepick. A concealed weapon, Sally."

"No icepick. I don't have one. I just say that."

"All right, then. How am I supposed to know? Now, listen. You going to stay the hell away from here?"

She nodded up and down, coughing again.

"Promise me? One more time, Sal, and I have to shoot you. Shoot you dead. You got that?"

"Yes."

"What was that? Come on, speak it out."

She took a deeper breath and tried to say it louder. "Yes. Yes, sir."

"All right. Now, beat it."

He gave one little shove to get her going, and then shook his hand to get the gnats off.

The shove put her into a sort of lurch, bent forward and trying to keep her balance. Her knee hit one of the garbage cans and skidded it to one side. She went to the corner that way, her arms out, staggering. The faded red knapsack on her back was swinging from side to side. God knows what she had in the knapsack.

He turned and went into the bar.

"Our hero," Harry said. He was polishing a Pilsner glass, running the dish towel around the edge and then holding the glass up to the light. "I was pretty worried there for a minute, but then I figured you had the drop on her and everything would be all right."

Keith Lee scratched the back of his hand. "Your ass," he said. "You going to get me a drink or do I have to work you over, too?"

Harry put the glass down. "So what's the matter with your hand? You got the crud or something?"

"Goddam fruit flies from your lousy garbage cans out there."

"Fruit flies. It figures, this neighborhood."

"The drink, Harry, the drink."

Harry nodded. "All right, all right. Listen: you see me polishing that beer glass when you come in? You saw me, right? You want to know why I do that?" He poured from the Seagram's bottle with his right hand and added the splash of 7-Up with his left. "Seven and Seven," he said. "No ice."

"Thanks. Put it on my tab."

"Got it. Listen: you want to know why I do that?"

Keith Lee walked down to the end of the bar and looked out the window at the street. "Do what?"

"Do like I said. Polishing the beer glass like that. Why I do it is because it's expected. You ever, listen, you ever see a TV commercial involving a bar, right? So what do they always show the bartender doing? I'll tell you: he's polishing a glass. He goes like this, and then he holds it up to the light like this. Or a *movie*. You go to a movie, you got a bar in it; you got the bartender polishing the glass. So you, you're a cop. You come in here; you go into any bar, right? And the bartender is not polishing the glass and your cop's mind right away says that something's wrong—except that you can't quite figure out what it is. You got that part?"

"All right. So what are you getting at?"

Harry shrugged. "Well, I haven't doped it all out yet.

I mean, all the time, middle of the day here, with nobody in here—and I lean against the back bar here and I mostly pick my nose. Nobody has to polish the glasses any more. We got this dishwasher thing here; you put the glass over it and it goes fffrrrrzzzzz, and the glass is clean. So I'm standing here picking my nose—but let somebody come in and I automatically pick up the glass and start polishing at it."

"So?"

"So I think it's telling us something about life. You know? I haven't got that part figured out yet. You're the cop, you tell me."

Keith Lee scratched his hand again, then checked it for red spots. "What I like about this place is, we got a bartender that's a philosopher. Why don't you just make drinks like any other one?"

"Listen. I'm into thinking. I think about a lot of things. Like I just told you, about polishing the glasses. Like a lot of things about life. It stretches your head muscles; it's like taking your brain out for a walk, get it some air. Take this neighborhood. I been here, how many years now? I been here forever, is what, and I see this neighborhood turn into a goddam jungle. You got gangs; I mean kid gangs, vicious—I never see anything like it in my life. I leave here, I get right into a dial-a-cab out in front there and I go. Know what I mean? Old folks—lot of them used to come in here. All the time, I mean. They would line the bar here on afternoons. You remember those days, right? Especially on the day the pension check came in. Nice old men, nice old broads; they'd come in, dawdle over a beer forever. Tell each other stories about the old days. But now. Now they're scared to set foot outdoors. Listen, they can't even go to the *store*, get a box of Wheaties or whatever. This place is like a, they're being held prisoner by the kids around here. Got an old sergeant, lives down around the corner. World War One guy; took a shot of mustard gas in that forest, whatever the name was. He was full of good stories. Wonderful old gent. Used to come in here all the time. I could set my clock, he'd come in that door. But now . . ."

"If I got to listen to all this," Keith Lee said, "you'd better get me another drink."

"You got it. You sure you don't want no ice? Okay. But, look: yesterday. Just yesterday, some kid gets old lady Cohen. He didn't just, I don't mean he just robbed her. I mean, the kid cut the goddam chain on her door, the safety chain. A pair of bolt cutters. And then he goes and cuts her up. For what? A lousy few bucks is what. And what are you and me doing? No, I mean really. What are we doing, you and me, everybody?"

"Christ, I give up. What are we doing?"

Harry shrugged and held his hands out, the palms up.

"I'll tell you," he said. "We're standing around polishing glasses. We're polishing life's glasses and holding them up to the light, like I said. And the goddam kid gangs are murdering us. We're surrounded here."

Keith Lee went back to the window. He sipped at the drink, watching the playground. He spoke without looking back over his shoulder: "Maybe you. Not me. You see the playground? I figure he'll turn up there pretty soon. Today, maybe. Tomorrow. He won't be able to stay away from the game. I know which one I'm looking for. Way I make it, it's the one named Angel."

"Chili-burner, right? A . . . what do you call them, a Diablo?"

"They're all Diablos far as I'm concerned. But, yeah. One of them."

"So he shows up at the playground."

"So he shows up, indeed. And his next stop is going to be in the alley over there, across. And when he comes out of the alley on the way to Family Court, he's going to be walking funny."

170

"Because?"

"Because he's going to have a pair of bolt cutters all the way up his ass. Look: the juve court doesn't do anything about stopping all this. Someone has got to. Down here, it turns out to be me."

"Well, somebody, right? You know: what I said about the damn kids. If it isn't for you, it'd be worse here. You got—now, don't get me wrong, I say this—but you got a reputation as a red-ass. Know what I mean?"

"I know. Just remember that somebody's got to do it. Take that thought and stick it up your philosophy. And . . ."

They both turned when the door opened.

Harry picked up the Pilsner glass and started polishing it. He held it up to the light and squinted at it. Then he looked at the man standing just inside the door.

"Afternoon, Mister Martino," he said.

The man stood perfectly still. He looked around the bar. Then he nodded. He walked down to the end of the bar by the window and sat on the stool. He pulled the ashtray over and squared it directly in front of him with his fingertips.

Harry was there with the glass of sweet vermouth, neat.

The man nodded again. He reached into his left-side suit-coat pocket and pulled up the Rigoletto cigar. He held it daintily in the tips of his fingers and then, from his side pocket, he pulled out the silver cutter. He snipped off the end of the cigar, careful to let it fall into the clean ashtray.

Harry flicked the lighter and lit the cigar.

The man drew in deeply, turning the cigar. Then he put it on the edge of the ashtray, balancing it carefully. And finally he looked at Keith Lee.

"Officer Lee," he said.

Keith Lee nodded back. "Mister Martino."

"Won't you join me?"

171

"Thank you." Keith Lee sat down on the next stool.

The man looked up at Harry. He raised his eyebrows. Harry walked back down the bar to the center. Then he turned his back on them.

This time the man reached into the right-side suit-coat pocket. He pulled out the white, office-size envelope and put it on the bar between them.

Keith Lee picked it up and held it between his hands.

"Things are going well at the playground," the man said.

"Like I told you they would," Keith Lee said.

The man nodded at that. He raised his glass and sipped daintily at the vermouth. "Like you told me, indeed. I like things to go well at the playground, as you know."

"I know."

"It is a touchy business. Sometimes I wonder why we do it in quite this way. It isn't the largest exchange in the world; in fact, it's quite modest. The important thing is that it works. And out in the open like that. But sometimes out in the open is the best way. One sees everything; one sees nothing."

"I know."

"You have the children under control?"

Keith Lee nodded. "Control. There'll be one less of them after today. But under control."

"I understand. Just so you understand that we need them."

"I know we need them."

The man reached out and carefully turned the cigar on the ashtray so that it would burn evenly. "I realize that occasionally you have to run one of them in; I understand perfectly. But you also understand the basic need. The game provides the distraction."

"I know."

"You will find in that envelope—I suggest that you put it away now, Harry can't keep his back turned forever— you will find a little bonus in the envelope this week. It's there because this is going so well. It continues to go this well, there will be other bonuses."

Keith Lee straightened on the stool and slid the envelope under his sweater, into the waistband of his slacks. "It stays this way," he said. "Long as I'm here, it goes well."

It's all in understanding the system. Long as there's no way to beat it, you'd best understand it. He waited at the corner for the light to change, the afternoon sun warm across his shoulders.

The kids were coming faster and meaner now; they were almost in total control of the city. Brooklyn was gone, all of the Bronx. The Village would be next. The only thing was, the kid gangs didn't quite know it yet, because all they did was slash and run. They didn't communicate. Not yet. Soon as they got that part doped out—soon as they got more organization and sealed off the city into zones of killing and looting—there wouldn't be a safe grownup anywhere. But, okay. By that time, he would be out of here. He would be rich and they could have the place.

He walked across to the other side, smiling slightly, glancing into the faces passing. The faces smiled back; they always did. He could orchestrate it. If he smiled even wider and gave them more teeth, they positively beamed back at him.

All right. The juvenile court system turned the kids loose again, sometimes the same day. No problem. It only meant that you couldn't work within the system. You can't deprive a kid of his rights as a citizen. No, sir. They go around with bolt cutters now, cutting up old people.

Well, then: it's also their right as citizens to get their little heads opened up and their spleens ruptured. Sometimes, when he had to make a point to keep the area under control, a gang member would accidentally fall out a third-story window into a tenement backyard. Who the hell cared down here? Another kid belly up among the Rheingold cans and used rubbers in some yard? Show the coroner's office the kid's previous arrest report: that's one less criminal to deal with. Those dreadful bruises across the small of the victim's back? Probably hit himself on the windowsill before he accidentally fell.

And then you go around to the mother and give her the sad smile. Sorry to hear about Julio, Missus Garcia. Yes, yes, I *know* he was a good boy. Good boy, never any trouble at home; just got mixed up with bad companions. Yes, ma'am, I know.

The nice point was: the other ones knew, too. All of them, even the tiny ones, the snatchers, too small to cut and run. The moral was, you cross Officer Keith Lee and he comes to get your ass in the middle of the night.

This is called Police Science.

He turned in at the cleaner's.

Mrs. Schwartz smiled up at him, putting one hand to the middle of her breasts. She cocked her head to one side and made a small moue with her mouth. Lillian Gish used to do it that way.

"It's Officer Lee," she said.

He grinned, using all the teeth. "It's me."

"So how's my boy, my lambchick?"

He held the smile. Take it easy. You want free cleaning or not?

"What really counts," he said, "what counts with me is, how are *you*?"

She patted at her hair. "So. So, you're looking good."

"Thanks to you, I'm looking good."

"So I got your sweaters. Five this time. The bell sleeves; such nice sleeves, the sweaters."

He nodded. "I wear them only to please you. If it wasn't for you, I'd be going around here in rags. No, really, now."

174

"Fixed them like you said," she said.

"You're sure it wasn't too much trouble?"

"Trouble? I'm *here* for trouble; you should see some of my customers, the troubles I get. But, no. I did the sweaters by hand, so there shouldn't be a cleaning-fluid smell. You'll see. They still smell like you, not like the cleaning fluid. Such a *smell* you got. I do your sweaters, it makes me dizzy. I could take and bury my face in the sweaters. I could take off my clothes and roll *around* on the sweaters you got. You sure it's called . . . uhhh. What was it you said again?"

"Dunhill," he said. "I get it uptown at Dunhill in Rockefeller Center."

She shook her head. "So Dunhill I know. So I wanted to make sure. I got it; I went up there and *got* it for my Al. You think he smells like that? Lissen: he could *bathe* in it; he could take the bottle and shake it over his *head*, already. And so expensive. But he doesn't smell like you."

Keith Lee nodded. "I don't know what to tell you. I think it's the way the chemicals react on different people. You know. It works both ways: what might make Al smell nice wouldn't work on me."

"Huh. Aqua *Velva* and he should smell like you. What? Mennen *Skin* Bracer; they do it on the *television* and Al still smells like cleaning fluid. So anyway . . ."

She turned and got the sweaters, neatly folded, and put them on the counter. Five sweaters; five different colors.

Keith Lee reached into his pocket, holding the smile.

She shook her head no.

"Well, tell you what," he said. "Put these on my tab."

"Tab, schmab," she said. "So, look: I mean, you come walking past here a couple of times a day and you look in to see I'm all right—an old lady like me—and I can't do a little something for you in return? So all right, I'll put it on your tab."

175

He bent over the counter and kissed her on the cheek.

"Hoo-boy," she said. "You'll get an old lady all worked up here. Who knows what could happen?"

He turned at the door.

"Next time," he said, "I'll come right over the counter after you. Drag you in the back room and ravage you."

"So ravage," she said.

He turned toward home.

Well, there you go. He really had to agree with Missus Schwartz. He did, indeed, smell good. And he was, indeed, overpoweringly handsome. Great teeth. Killer smile. And sexy.

And not only that. He was such a hell of a nice guy.

21

THE KID

This was the kind of an air shaft it was:

Two months ago, a six-year-old girl had been stabbed and beaten and raped up on the roof, and then thrown into this air shaft. Her clothes had been thrown down after her. Little cutoff jeans, an Arbee's Roast Beef tee shirt, cotton panties, sneakers and knee-high soccer socks, white with two blue stripes around the tops. The clothing had floated down the four stories, each piece going straight through the dead air where there was no breeze and settling randomly like patches on her naked body, which had landed face up.

That was the first thing about the air shaft. But it wasn't the most important thing. The important thing was that the girl had survived. There was so much stuff at the bottom of the shaft that it had cushioned her fall: piles of wet paper sacks full of garbage, mostly. There was also a half-burned Sleep Eze mattress and one couch and two easy chairs, all with their stuffing exploded out through the knife slashes. There were a thousand beer cans, broken bottles; layers of newspapers and the burned shell of a floor-model Muntz TV set with a black hole where the picture tube used to be. There were pieces of carpeting and chunks of tar paper from the roof.

The Kid looked down into the shaft from the edge of the window. He always checked the shaft, committing everything to memory. If he ever had to jump—even in the dark—he figured that he could make it over to the mattress where the little girl had landed: just aim at the outline of blood she had left. She had apparently moved her arms after the fall. From this angle, the outline on the faded blue-and-white mattress ticking looked like a giant bird had lain on its back there, feebly moving its wings. Maybe an angel.

He had heard about the rape. Icepick Sally had told him all the details.

There is a little wooden door that opens to the street at the bottom of the shaft. It was put there for cleaning out the shaft, back in the days when anybody ever cleaned it. The police had pried open the door and had crawled in there on their bellies, pushing the garbage and junk and broken glass in front of them. They had pulled the little girl out of there and had taken her to West Side Medical, where they had kept her for two weeks.

Icepick Sally had been in the crowd of people gathered outside the little wooden door on the street side. She had seen the big blond guy, Keith Lee—the big cop in the trick clothes. Keith Lee had stopped the ambulance attendants and he had gotten right down on both knees there on the sidewalk, and he had bent way over the stretcher, face to face with the raped girl.

"Who did it?" he had asked her. Icepick Sally said that the little girl's eyes had been beaten half closed and that her mouth was all bloody and swollen. But she had taken hold of Keith Lee's sweater and had pulled him over even closer and she had said something, a name, a something, into his face. And Keith Lee had nodded at that. And then the little girl had said something else—and had actually *smiled* up at Keith Lee, a bloody caricature of a smile, grotesque to see. And she had, what was the word? She had plucked at his fancy sweater with one hand. And Keith Lee had straightened up and pulled off his pink sweater, right over his head, and had placed it on top of the little girl. It had covered her all the way down to her toes.

The rapist had been a big kid, a fifteen-year-old who lived across the street on Tenth. Officer Lee had brought in the rapist that same night before the word could get around—especially before word of the arrest could get back to the girl's family. He had hurried the boy out to a waiting patrol car.

The boy rapist had been so badly beaten that he had spent two days at the medical center before they could even book him. What had happened, Officer Keith Lee had said, was that the boy rapist had fallen all the way down the stairs trying to escape.

That was one thing. The other thing was the short, dark man who hung around the block now, always keeping an eye on the apartment building across the street. It was the raped girl's father and Icepick Sally said that he carried a sugarcane knife under his coat. She said that the moment the rapist was set free—which was never very long—that, the moment he showed up in this neighborhood, he was as good as dead. The little girl's father had quit his job so that he could stay on watch. He had told other members of the family that he planned to throw the rapist into this very same air shaft. Only in pieces. Nobody could find any fault with a plan like that.

Okay. This was how this air shaft worked:

The Kid could come in at any one of four brownstones on Eleventh Street, depending on what the security conditions were at the time—whether or not he was being followed. Two of the brownstones backed up on the shaft; he could ease up to the second floor rear, moving silently through the dark hallways. Into the janitor's closet at the end. Quickly step up onto the sink and climb out through the little swing-out window.

The hand- and toe-holds were the tricky part, especially in the rain. Because this was the back of the two buildings, the brickwork wasn't as neat as it was in front. It had probably been done by the second-string bricklayers. Norwegian louts drinking beer, Icepick Sally had said. Some of the bricks were set in crookedly enough so that you could get your fingertips on them. Some of the bricks had fallen right out into the garbage two stories down. And on his earlier trips, he had taken the back of a claw hammer and had chipped away better handholds. It was probably no worse than scaling the whatever-face-it-was of El Capitan.

Sally's window, her only window, was directly opposite. He could scale around the shaft and get to her ledge and go in. And he would be on Tenth Street, a block away from where he had entered.

Nobody ever looked out of an air-shaft window. Not even when they would yank it open to throw down another sack of garbage.

Fine: nobody knew where The Kid lived.

And that included the Cat Man and Angel and Feets and all the other members of the Diablos. And Officer Keith Lee. Well. One thing: Keith Lee could probably find out if he really *wanted* to know.

The Kid swung his feet out now and found the toehold. Then, hanging on with the fingertips of his left hand, he reached back and closed the window. He scaled quickly around the walls of the air shaft, holding the Paul Stuart sack in his teeth, and swung into Sally's window.

The smell of the place always made his eyes sting at

first. It was stale cigar smoke mostly, with an underlay of sweat and those god-awful soups she kept making on the hot plate. The soups were made out of old turkey-neck bones and some kind of bigger, thick bones that she kept scrounging out of the garbage cans. That was bad enough. What was worse was that the soups also tasted just like the lining on the inside of her knapsack and sometimes, when he sat there on the blue camelback sofa looking into a bowl of soup, little bits of lint and tobacco or cigar leaf would float to the top.

Sally would be undressed down to about three layers of clothes by that time, down to where she would be just wearing two housedresses over her long underwear. She would be pacing around the room, smoking one of the cigar butts.

"Eat, *eat*, my prince," she would say through the smoke. "This is the soup that won the West." Always something like that. Or, "You know what Ginger Rogers would say if *she* could just have a bowl of soup like that?"

He would go for the routine because it made Sally so happy: "Ginger who?"

"Rogers, *Rogers*." Sally would whip the cigar butt out of her mouth and wave it in the air. "You remember. I told you about her slippers I found. The pink fur mules with the shiny heels. Ginger Rogers, remember? I *sang* it to you the night you had the fever. The flu bug, remember? 'I won't dance, how *could* I? I won't dance, why *should* I? I won't dance, mercy bo *coo.*'" And then Sally would lean over close, her smell thick in the air between them. "Greatest dancer ever in the history of talking pictures. You couldn't be expected to remember. But me, ahhhhh. Anyway, she would say, Ginger, I mean; *she* would say: 'Miss Sally, could I just have a little more of that *won*derful soup?' See?"

He went over to the dresser and pulled out the drawer that Sally had cleaned out for him. He took the new shirt out of the sack and added it to the pile. And then he took the folded-over bills out of his right pocket. Bad day at Rockefeller Center: he had collected only thirty-four dollars on his office rounds.

He went back to the blue couch and sat down and looked around the room. In a minute he would watch some television on the little portable Sony. There would be a game show; game shows were always good to study. The head guy was always cool.

Sally would be out on her route now, collecting the Living History of Greenwich Village. She talked a lot about *that*, too, pulling things out of the knapsack and showing them to him. Pretty soon now, all the stuff that made up the Living History would crowd them right out of this room.

But, all right. Icepick Sally had been getting a little bit better ever since he had moved in. Not a lot better, but a *little*. You had to know her before you could sense any change at all:

She still smelled terrible. He couldn't get her to take a bath—even to change the long underwear. It all had something to do with Norwegians and their living habits. Saunas and all. He never could understand it. She was always muttering about Norwegians.

She still wore all those layers of clothes in the dead of summer.

She smoked cigar butts.

She never cleaned this room.

She snored and farted in her sleep.

And sometimes, worst of all, Sally would sort of blink and forget what she was talking about. Or where she was —or who he was. And when she did that, it was practically back to Square One all over again. It was one of her strokes; she really liked her little strokes.

But she was getting a little bit better.

At first, Icepick Sally had thought that he had come to kill her.

See, this thing had been easy enough to figure out. One: he had to live somewhere. He had gone down to the Village for weeks, walking around. Studying. Learning the place. And staying out of the big cop's way. But if you work it all out in your mind, check out all the options, it all comes pretty clear.

So, two: he couldn't live by himself. It had to be with somebody. A kid can't just walk up and rent a room. At first, he had just idly watched Icepick Sally; she had just kept showing up. And then, one day, he had picked up a sense of *pattern* in what she was doing. And he had started watching her more closely.

She had become perfect. Well, look: she had finally gotten her life set up so that nobody really *saw* her any more. Oh, they saw her, all right, but they just sort of looked right through her.

The old knapsack lady, that's all. She was invisible.

The kids would probably have been worse on her, but the big cop had put out the word for them to leave her alone—and that made her perfect.

Besides: she smelled bad and nobody wanted to touch her.

It had taken a couple of weeks, and finally, the night the gang of little kids had shagged her, she had collapsed on the front steps. He had helped her upstairs and had gotten her into the room. She had really been out of her tree that night.

She had slept for one whole day while he had stayed in the room, looking at all the junk and watching over her. When she had finally come around, she had started to scream a lot and to shake—even throwing up a little bit. And he had sat there on the floor in front of her, saying, "No, it's all right," over and over again.

"You've come to rob me. You've killed my *dog*," she had said.

"No, no. I need your help. And your dog's still there on the table, see? See the tape recorder there? Now, calm down."

"I've got an icepick. I'll stick it in you," she had said.

"No, no. You haven't got an icepick. But it's all *right*, believe me."

And then she had fallen silent, watching him warily. When he went to the bathroom, he left the door open so that she could see him. He moved slowly; he kept both hands in full view at all times.

Finally: "What are you here for?" she said.

"I need your *help*, I said. I told you. I'm all *alone*. I haven't got any other place to go."

"Well, you can't stay here."

"It's just a little while, is all."

"Why me?"

"Why anybody? You got to help me."

The Kid had finally gotten so tired that he had given it all up. The hell with it; sometimes you live, sometimes you die. He had fallen asleep sitting on the dumb broken-down camelback couch. All right, let her turn him in. Kill him. Something; anything.

Vaguely, he had been aware of her padding around. Once or twice she had stood close to him. And once, when he had moved his head back, there had been a sudden movement: he had slitted his eyes and he had seen her standing over him, a long bread knife held in both hands over her head. It had been poised to drive directly down into his chest.

Go ahead: he had fallen back to sleep, waiting the thrust.

The smell had finally awakened him. It was like nothing else in the world. It was Icepick Sally.

She had had her face right up next to his. She was

184

looking closely at him, examining him. She had a dead cigar butt clenched in the middle of her mouth.

"You're awake," she said. Her breath smelled like a wet rat.

He had nodded, trying to breathe shallowly. He hadn't wanted to turn his head away—not just then.

"Your eyelashes," she had said. "Your eyelashes are so long that they lie on your cheeks when you sleep. They're like velvet."

He had looked at her for a long, long time.

Finally she had nodded again.

"You're a beautiful, beautiful boy," she had said. "Your heart shows in your face. That's a bad nose; an awful nose. But still, you're lovely. I could be your mother. No, your *grand*mother. Do you know what I'm going to do? No, I can tell by the way you look at me that you don't know. Well, what I am going to do is keep you. I'll take care of you until I die. Or you die. One of us."

22

FEETS

I mean, this is what makes you crazy, man. Like, it ain't bad enough that they're old people, man. You just give old folks a little tap and they fall right *over,* man. But when they get blood on your clothes, man, come *on.*

Feets stepped back and looked down at the spray pattern of blood on his raincoat. And then he looked into the old man's face.

"You sneezin' blood on me. Look at what you just done," he said.

The old man was on his knees on the linoleum. He reached out with both hands, the fingers spread apart. There were brown spots on the backs of the hands and the cords stood out, all raised up against the bristly white hairs. But the old man didn't touch the raincoat.

"Please," he said. "Please. I'm sorry. But I . . ."

Feets kicked him in the stomach again and the old man doubled over, bringing his hands back and folding them in front. This time the blood was thicker; it flowed out evenly over his lower lip and into the white beard.

"This here is a new raincoat," Feets said. "Man, *look* at that. You know; like, you know what this here coat cost? Man, you talking about this coat, you talkin' one-*fifty*. Man, this is a *uptown* coat. Lenox *Avenue*, man. It don't jus' *clean*, you unnerstan' what I'm saying? So you gonna buy me a new one, daddy."

The old man was having great difficulty speaking now; he swung his head from side to side, trying to catch his breath.

"Please," he said again. "I told you . . . no, please don't kick me anymore. Good Lord. You came bursting in here. Look at me: I'm all alone here. And I told you about the money."

Feets shook his head no. "You lyin' to me about the money."

"I'm not. I'm *not*, and it's the truth. The money, they've got a new system. It goes right to the bank now. The Social Security check, right into the bank. No! Don't kick, *don't*, please. What I'm telling you is . . ."

"This here is *check* day, man. Don't lie to me."

"I know. I know it's check day. But, please. I don't *get* the check anymore, don't you see? Anymore. I don't. It doesn't come here as it used to. It goes directly into the bank. It's a new, it's safety for us old . . ."

Feets kicked him again.

This time it took much longer for the old man to speak. He didn't look up anymore. His head was bent forward almost to his chest and his lap was filling with the blood from his mouth. The hands were loose now, palms up.

"I . . . I'm not lying," the old man said. He coughed again. "There is no, just isn't any money here. So much robbery, old folks. We're defenseless here. Look what you've done to me. I . . ."

"Money," Feets said. "No money, old man, it gonna get worse here."

". . . all of us," the old man said. "Across the hall. Boggs, across the hall from me. Sergeant Boggs. An Army pension, and he doesn't get the checks, either. His checks go right to the bank and he doesn't have any cash in his place. He's the one who told me to . . ."

"You keep talkin' bank to me. How'm I supposed to get money from a *bank*, man?"

The old man sighed. His throat rattled. "I don't know. All I know is that I don't have any . . ."

This time Feets kicked him over on his back, sending up a little umbrella of blood.

He looked around the room and shrugged. He backed to the door, looking down at the old man. He reached behind and opened it. Then he swung his shoulder around slightly and backed into the dark hallway. He closed the door.

There was a cough just behind him. He could feel the spray from it on the back of his neck.

Feets turned, blinking to get his eyes adjusted to the dim light.

Another old man.

"Boggs," this old man said. He was even older than the other one. "Sergeant Howard J. Boggs, U.S. Infantry. Argonne Forest. Mustard gas." He coughed again.

Feets brought the knife up from his right raincoat pocket, rolling his wrist and punching the button at the same time. He heard the blade click open.

"Wait. Before you do anything with that knife," the old man said, "just look down here."

Feets looked down.

"You see it? It's a very old gun," Sergeant Boggs said. "Very, very old and very powerful. British Webley, this old piece. It's a four fifty-five, a great bear of a gun. My old souvenir; brought it back on the boat with me. And don't let the rust fool you, son. The gun still works. Yes, indeed. You *do* see the gun, don't you, laddie-buck?"

Feets blinked. "Gonna cut your old heart out," he said. "You messin' with me, old man."

Sergeant Boggs shook his head no. He was wearing his Army summer tunic. The round collar was loose around his neck. A tuft of white hair curled up over the front. "No," the sergeant said. "No hearts today. You have cut your last senior citizen. We used to handle young scum like you in the trenches. Just line them up against the dirt wall, that's all."

Feets feinted with his shoulders and started swinging his right arm up, hand bent back, the blade flickering in the overhead light.

The explosion came at the same time. It burned the bottom of Feets's elbow and it thumped like a heavy fist against his chest, right where the ribs came up together. He couldn't . . . hey, *man*. What was this? Come *on*, man: he couldn't get his shoulders away from the wall. Like, you know: like a big heavy something was just holding him there, pressing his shoulders in.

He forced himself away from the wall and turned around to see what it was that had held him there.

It was: man, the plaster was all chipped, man. Like, big, fresh *chips*. And inside each chipped-out place—just stuffed right *in* there, like somebody had done it with the tip of a pencil or something—inside each chip was a little, bitty round piece of his new raincoat, all covered with blood. Awww, *man*. He swung back to face the old man again.

The next explosion was a little bit louder and a lot hotter.

This time, Feets just slid down the wall, staying in contact with it all the way down until he got to the floor. His left leg was doubled under. And now the front of his coat—come on, man—the *front* of his coat was smoking. Just blue-gray smoke curling up from the black hole.

189

He patted at the coat carefully with both hands, his head bent forward in concentration, trying to pat out the smoke.

And the surge of blood came right up out of his mouth. He tried to close his lips tightly to hold it all in. But his lips . . . what? His lips had gone bad, shee-it, just hanging there, all open.

Then the pain came: it hit him in all the spots at once. Awwww, God. No, man, *no*.

The hurt of it all flopped him around, both of his legs kicking. He couldn't seem to stop it.

He tried not to kick Sergeant Boggs, who was squatted down now, holding the gun loosely in both of his hands, the barrel pointing down. Same blue smoke as from the raincoat. Man, what a nice *curl*. It came up just like a . . . you know, what you call them things? Just like a *question* mark hanging in the air between them.

What was that? Huh? Who that talkin'?

"Prayers. Say your prayers, laddie-buck," the old man said.

Oh. Oh, sure. Uhh, *Hail Mary, Full of Grace*. Hail . . . ohhh, God. Come on, God, that really hurt, it hurt that time. Lissen, God. Lissen to me: my feet are swelling inside my shoes, man. An' I got to play basketball this afternoon.

". . . old folks," the sergeant was saying now. "Preying on old folks. People, the people in this building live here in terror. In this entire block. We live behind locked doors. Who was it that got poor Missus Cohen with the bolt cutters? A nice, quiet woman. You couldn't meet a better woman; you should taste her homemade bread."

Wasn't me, God. It was Angel did it to her. The bolt cutters; you could go down to the playground and look. Know where I mean, God? Wait! Not more pain, no.

". . . hear me?" the old man said. "No, I don't expect you can, the way your eyes look. I don't expect you can.

190

What I was saying was: your days of kicking and robbing senior citizens are all over, son."

Feets rolled over now, trembling hard, and got to his hands and knees. He looked down at all the . . . sheee-it, what a *lot* of blood. Then he swung his head up and tried to focus. Where was . . . where are you, old man? Oh, there he was. The old man was all tinted in red. Really pretty. But, man, you know what you've just gone and *done?*

The red-tinted face came in closer.

"I can't hear you," Sergeant Boggs said. "Say it again, son. One more time."

Feets took a little bit deeper breath.

"I'm . . . I'm only thirteen years old," he said.

But the red-tinted face was gone. And now he was all alone in the hallway.

There, now. Like, man, I'll just lay me down right here a minute until I get my breath. Awwww, man, the *hurt.*

Who's there? I can't see too . . .

Oh, it's *you.*

". . . ambulance," Officer Keith Lee said. "Get you over to West Side. Fix you right up."

Way to go, man. You the Main Man, all right. Trouble is: like, the trouble is, you don't unnerstan' what that old cat just done to me. It may be almost too late.

"What's that?" Officer Lee said. "Come on, come on. Say it again."

"Tell them," Feets said. He took another breath and licked the foam off his lips. "Get to West Side, I'm gonna tell them, dig? I mean: about your deal, man. The playground. The bills you takin' for it. Unnerstan' what I'm sayin'?"

Keith Lee's voice came back very close to his ear: "What do you want to do that for?"

"I'm gonna do it for God."

"You're going to tell them everything for God?"

"Uh . . . ummmmm, yeah."

"What about *me*?"

Feets shook his head. No, not really. What he did was roll his head back and forth on the worn carpet. He tried to talk louder:

"You know. It's in case I die."

"In case you die."

"Man. Man, I'm thir*teen*."

"I know how old you are."

"You gotta take care of me."

"Be right back," Keith Lee said. "I'll take care of you, all right. See about the ambulance."

Way to go. Feets waited. He could hear the footsteps going down the stairs. And . . . what? Front door. Right, it was the front door.

And the siren. Listen to that: here come the *sireen*, man. Okay. We gonna *make* it, God.

He listened to the voices from the landing below:

Officer Lee—"Okay, okay, *hold* it. Ease up. He's already dead."

Hey, man, come on. I ain't dead.

Officer Lee—"Cigarette? No, wait. I got a lighter right here. Here. Sit down, catch your breath a minute. So, what have you clowns been up to?"

Awwww, no.

Officer Lee— "Naw. Just the usual. You know this area: you guys pull as many old folks out of here as anybody. No, what this was, this time one of the oldies shot back. That's all. At close range. What? No, no, the kid didn't say anything before he died. Hell, you ought to see the holes in him, anyway. He maybe had enough time to say 'Ouch,' know what I mean?"

Come . . . on. Come get me. It's getting darker up here.

Officer Lee— "New ambulance? What kind of mileage you get on a thing like that? You know, I got a friend has a unit something like that. It's a . . . what do you call them? It's a van. Carpet and all on the inside; a little bar and a sink. Little TV set. A little bed, even. Trouble is, he goes, oh, maybe eight, nine miles to a gallon, you know?"

Come . . .

Officer Lee— "Okay? Here, I'll give you a hand with that thing. Body's up on the second landing. Easy, now."

But Feets knew. He stopped listening to the voices and watched the hallway go completely black.

When they got up to the landing, he was really dead.

THREE

23

ICEPICK SALLY

"I was there when they drug him out," Sally said.

The Kid nodded, head down. He was sitting on the floor, dividing his money into stacks of tens and fives.

"I was there, all right. I'm most always there to watch these things," she said. "And I can always tell just about how bad it is by the way the ambulance attendants take the victim out of the building. First, they always strap them in, of course. You know, carrying the victim downstairs and all. Otherwise, the person could just slide off the stretcher. Just sort of ooze out the bottom part. But then, it's what the ambulance men do with the *sheet* that you should watch for. If they just fold the top sheet up to the shoulders and leave the victim's head and face sticking out, well, it's usually nothing to worry over and you're wasting your time watching. That's one way to tell. But then, if they pull the top sheet right up over the person's *face*, that's when it's bad. It means that chances are that the victim has already breathed his last—that God

197

has already come and taken back His gift of life. But none of that is as bad as what happened this time."

"What'd they do?"

She folded her arms and shivered. "They used the rubber *bag*. It's black rubber and it has an awful, gunmetal sheen to it. The bag folds over along the top, like this, and it has sort of a strap handle on each end. It has N.Y.P.D. stenciled on it in white. And whoever is inside that black rubber bag, well, they always make the most horrible sort of *lump* and you can't even tell which end is what. I've seen . . . I know I shouldn't tell you this, but I've seen New York policemen just *drag* one of the rubber bags downstairs. It just goes bump, bump, bump behind them; once you hear that final sound, it will stay in your mind forever. It's not at all like, mmmmmmm, what was I trying to think of? Yes: it's not at all like Christopher Robin dragging Pooh Bear down the stairs by one foot. You remember in the very beginning of . . ."

He shook his head no.

". . . you don't? The House at Pooh Corners? 'The more it snows, tiddly-*bum*?' No? I swear, you have more gaps in your childhood than anybody I know. But where was I?"

"The rubber bag," The Kid said.

"Yes. The bag. My dear, it means the very *worst*. It means blood and *pieces*. And I was there when they took him out. He was thirteen years old and they tell me, they told me that he had two small bullet holes in front—here and here—and two *enormous* holes where everything came flying out in back. He was dead, of course, when they got up to the landing."

"Name was Feets," The Kid said.

"Yes, that's what they called him, Feets. His real name was Rafael something-or-other, a Spanish-y sort of name. I knew, I had the feeling that someday I would see him in the rubber bag. He tried to grab my purse when he couldn't have been more than six years old. They start like that down here. And then he got the knife, the kind where you push a button. And he just got worse and worse and worse. You could let that serve as a lesson to you, child."

"I don't carry a knife."

"But you *do* steal."

"I *told* you about that," he said.

She shrugged. "You did, indeed. But still . . . oh. Oh, I forgot to tell you the *rest* of it."

"There's more?"

"My *dear*. No sooner had the ambulance closed its back doors and pulled away, than here came Sergeant *Boggs*. Sergeant Howard J. Boggs, walking right down those brownstone steps with Officer Keith Lee by his side. Not holding him by the arm; no, sir. No handcuffs, no *sir*. Just side by side. And Sergeant Boggs was so . . . well, so straight and *upright*, not even limping very much. He was wounded, you know. Wounded and gassed, mustard gas, in the Argonne Forest. But, no. He was so straight there, and he had his face set just right, not looking to the right or left. And he was wearing his full uniform, too. Mmmmm, the way the *belt* shined; the Sam Browne belt that comes down diagonally, across like this. And all his medals there, across his chest; you could still see the faint colors on some of the ribbons. And his overseas campaign hat, with the Infantry emblem all polished. He was, there was a time, I suppose, when his chest must have been like a *barrel*. The uniform sort of hangs now. He's shrunk as he's gotten older. But there he was: Sergeant Boggs, just looking straight ahead. And Officer Lee, that devil; Officer Lee standing there in his fuschia pants. How terrible a color for an occasion like that. And . . ."

She took several quick breaths, blinking.

"Are you all right?" The Kid said.

"Yes," she said. "Yes, but I shouldn't try to talk so fast.

It could bring on another stroke. But, still. But then Sergeant Boggs noticed me there in the crowd. Looked me right in the eyes, he did. And he, well, he clicked his heels so loudly, and he made a slight, just the tiny hint of a bow, in my direction. Really. 'Miss Sally,' he said. And I nodded and I said, 'Sergeant.' And *he* said, 'I did what had to be done up there.' And I said, 'I just know you did, Sergeant.' And then the ... along came the police car—it just double-parked right there in the street. It had a wire-mesh screen along the back of the front seat. And Officer Lee just sort of touched Sergeant Boggs lightly on the elbow; not a *grab*, just a touch. And Sergeant Boggs got kind of stiff again, the way soldiers do on parade. And he bent his head just a little tiny bit, and he said, 'Officer Lee.' And Officer Lee said, 'Sergeant.' And then Officer Lee stepped over and held open the back door of the police car, sort of standing at attention himself. And Sergeant Boggs got right in and sat down and looked straight ahead. And Officer Lee got in beside him and away they went. I cried."

"What'll they do to him?"

"Who knows? They *should* give him another medal, that's what they should do, by rights. By all that's good and holy. But I don't know. They won't ... they can't electrocute an old sergeant, can they?"

"I don't think so," The Kid said. "But I don't know. I don't think they're allowed to."

"It would be just like Officer Lee to do that."

"I know. But chances are the sergeant will be out on bail in a little while. He won't run away waiting for trial."

She looked down at him, his money stacked so neatly in front of his crossed legs, the shock of hair falling down across his forehead like a raven's wing, so shining. If there was a way, if she only could, she would jell him in transparent aspic right at this moment. Just seal him forever so that she could treasure him.

200

"How much money do you have now?" she said.

"Hundred and ten in this stack," he said. "Sixty in fives in this stack. Maybe twelve dollars more on me."

"Press?"

He swung his head up and raised his eyebrows slightly.

"Press, I ... uhhhh. You make the inside of my head light up when you look at me like that. But what I ... what was I going to say? Oh. Well, I'm getting better, too, aren't I?"

"Little bit," he said. "But ..."

"Oh, I know." She reached around in back and scratched at the spot where the long underwear was sticking. "I know what you're going to say. 'I wish you would take a bath.' Bath, bath. I told you: it robs you of your natural bodily oils that nature put there. And the oils protect you from ... listen: why do you think we have *glands*? To secrete natural oils, my dear. To protect us from chills and colds. Flu, even. Now, look: I wash. I wash what I have to wash. Not at all like those *Norwegians*. You've seen how pasty-faced they are—their saunas and all. I've heard about those saunas: they all get in there *naked* together and they whip each other with witch-hazel twigs or whatever those things are. Huh. I kept company with a Norwegian man once; it was way before your time. He smelled like a *tree*. Pink hands, pink fingernails, pasty cheeks. And he, well, I don't know this for a fact, but I understood that he took saunas all the time. And ..."

"Did you bathe then?"

"When?"

"In the old days?"

She scowled at him. "Well, of *course* I bathed. When the occasion called for it. Rest of the time I used rose water. And that's why I've lived so long."

"Okay, okay. What were you going to say?"

"About what?"

"About you are getting better."

She blinked at him, thinking. "Better, better. What?"

"Look," The Kid said. "You're the one who said, 'Press, I'm getting better,' remember?"

"Why . . . oh. *Oh.* There, you see? It's coming back to me now. What I was going to say was that, since you've come . . . well, since you've come, my life has changed so much. You make me think more, now that you're here. I used to, it used to be that . . . I don't know how to explain it to you. It used to be that my mind would sort of go *away* for days at a time, and I would forget things. The easiest things, not the big things, like the Living History. That's my life's work, the Living History. But I mean: I could go on for days not quite remembering. Little gates in my head would close, shutting off certain areas. And, of course, the series of little strokes. I've told you about the strokes?"

"You've told me about the strokes," he said.

"Well. Little strokes are very hard on a woman my age. But, since you've come to live here, I've gotten *better.* Now, when I go out on my rounds, I worry about if you'll be here when I get back. And if I'm here, I worry about what you're doing out *there.* Time was . . . well, once there was just me alone here. For so many years, Press. Here in this room, doing my work. You like this room?"

He looked around. "It's getting pretty full," he said.

"It's the History. I've got just a few more pieces to go, a few things I need. And then it will be complete. And, well. And one day, perhaps soon, there will be a knock at that door. Just a soft knock: tick, tick, like that. And I will call out, 'Who is it?' And the voice will say—that sweet, smoky voice will say, 'It's Ginger Rogers.' And I'll open the door and Ginger will be standing there in white satin. Cut low right here in front, with this ostrich boa over one shoulder, so careless. And she won't say anything; she'll just hold out one hand. And I'll *know,* see? I'll take my Doberman dog by the leash with this hand

and then I'll take Ginger's hand with my other hand. And those stairs out in the hall there—no, the ones going up, I mean—those stairs will be all chrome, sprinkled with sequins. And we'll dance up to Heaven on those stairs."

"But don't forget to put on her slippers you found."

"No. You're right. I'll have to remember that, the pink fur mules."

"They'll make you take a bath up there," The Kid said.

She pushed herself forward on the sofa and stood up. She walked over to the dresser and thumbed through the cigar butts and then picked one out. She clenched it between her teeth and whirled on him.

"They will not *either*," she said. "Very idea. In Heaven you can do what you damn well please, God damn it."

"All right, all right. But what about the History?"

"Well, that's *it*. Someone will finally come and open this door. I mean, my *temporal* body might be lying here, and all. But they'll open my door and look in here and they will be amazed. Here: all collected in a lifetime's work; here will be the Living History of Greenwich Village. All in one place, a museum. And then they'll thank me for all this work. These years of collecting."

Sally lit the cigar with the cracked onyx lighter, turning the butt carefully to get an even ash. She walked back to the couch and sat down, puffing up a mushroom of blue-gray smoke.

"You'll be wanting some dinner," she said.

He shook his head. "Oh, no you don't."

"Well. Whenever you're ready. It'll just take a minute. I've got plenty of soup stock."

"Come on."

"Well, what do you want? All we've got is a hot plate. So I have to make a hot-plate dinner. If I had a stove, I'd make you a *stove*-something."

"Couldn't we go out some time?"

"Out where? I've been out today."

"No, no. I mean out to dinner. Like people."

She clenched the cigar in the middle of her mouth and talked around it, the smoke curling up into her eyes. "Who would have me? I mean: where could I get in to eat? Name a restaurant around here, anyplace, that would let me in."

"You could clean up. I'll even buy."

"I'm just about as cleaned up as I'm going to get," she said.

"Come on."

"*No*, I said. Keep it up, just keep it up. 'Take a bath, Sally.' Or, 'Clean up.' I'm going to have another stroke, you keep after me like this."

"Okay, okay. But no soup. I'll go out in a minute and get us a something."

She slipped her fingertips inside the front placket of the long underwear and scratched at her stomach. "But, listen," she said. "You shouldn't be spending your money. I've got plenty here. You need your money for your plan."

"It's all right. I'm getting there."

"I see. How much you got there again?"

He tapped the two piles. "Hundred and seventy, all together."

"And how much do you figure you'll need?"

"Listen: the piles will have to be about *this* high before I can begin to pull it off."

She looked at The Kid through the smoke some more. He really was too lovely for words. If she had only married that Norwegian gentleman . . . what was his name again? No matter. If she had only married—no matter how disgusting the idea was then and now. But somebody; perhaps just long enough to conceive. And then, and then, Press would have come from inside her. She would have done *any*thing. She would have redecorated her womb for him. It would have had mirrored walls and Oriental rugs. And *this* would have been her own boy; her very own blood.

"I love you," she said. And when he looked up, she modified it, adjusting to the look on his face:

"I mean, I love you; you know, like a great-auntie. Don't look at me like that. It's harmless enough. You can permit that much love. Listen: I've *told* you, I have plenty of money for you. Lots." She tapped her fingertips against the money pouch sewed just inside the underwear. "And you can have as much of it as you need for your plan."

He shook his head again, the light glinting on his hair. "No. You'll need it sometime. It's okay; I'm getting there."

"But I hardly ever spend any. Here, see? Look at all this. Just look here."

"Come on. Button yourself back up. People out on the street knew you had that much money on you, they'd go ape."

"They'll never know."

"Okay. But be careful."

"I seem to have did . . . done all right, before you ever came crawling into my window."

"Well, I don't know how."

"But . . . Press."

"Hmmmmm?"

"One thing. One thing, all right? Promise me you'll tell me, you know, that you'll tell this old lady before you leave. You won't just go away one day without telling me."

He looked at her. "No, no. I'll tell you."

She closed her eyes tightly, trying to drive out the vision of this place without him. She took a deep breath.

"How much longer?"

He shrugged. "I don't know. Couple of weeks, I hope. A couple of weeks and I'm gone."

24

MARION DOLAN

There ought to be a code or something, a rule to require that all straight-back chairs in police precinct offices be bigger and stronger. Let a person of some, well, a person of some *stature* come in and sit down and the chairs always creak and make this awful snapping sound—and everybody in the whole room looks at you. They freeze for a moment, pencils poised, pieces of paper in their hands, waiting to see if the chair will shatter with a crash. It's embarrassing. Marion Dolan sat as lightly as she could, tensing her thighs. She nodded across the desk at him.

Lord, she was getting tired of all this.

"So you don't know," she said.

He was the best-looking cop so far. Well, not that looks mattered at all with any of them. But this one was a distraction, at least. He was wearing sport—no, golf clothes. The air around him smelled beautifully heavy, like new cigar and cedar. His hair was puma-colored and his tan was creamy-perfect. He had smiled at her when she had introduced herself and presented her card. Some cop, all right: it was easy to see that he used the smile as a weapon.

"No," he said. "It's like I told you, Miss Dolan. We're up to our, uhhh, to our hipbones in kids as it is. Runaways included. I wouldn't know this particular kid if you threw him in the front door."

"But surely you read our department runaway bulletins?"

He nodded at the line of clipboards hanging on the wall. "What's to check? There isn't enough time. I mean, your department, every department uptown. We've got every bulletin known to man. Runaway lists—boys, girls. Out-of-town lists. Federal lists. Rapers and what-all. Robbers, kid forgers, car thieves. Who's got time to sit around and read the clipboards every day, right?"

"I know. We're all too busy uptown, too. I just thought that maybe."

"Whenever we book a kid in here, we check his name against the bulletins. But that's about it. What we can't do is to walk all around the district and say, 'Hey, are you so-and-so?' "

She started to rub her thighs together, but the chair creaked.

"I've got a picture here if that would help," she said.

He reached across and took it.

"Just a class picture from his school; I had it blown up," she said. "Image is a little grainy, it's hard to tell exactly what he looks like. But if you squint a little you can see that he's . . . uhhhh. Well, I mean he's an extraordinary-looking boy."

"What does that mean?"

"Beautiful. No, I should say handsome. He, uhhh, he stands out. What's the word, ummm, distinctive. Don't you think?"

He shrugged. "Lady, there is no such thing as a good-looking kid."

"But this one. I don't know, he's a young Valen*tino*. See, I'm just trying to paint a sort of word-picture for you so that you . . ."

"Are you okay?"

"What?"

He was looking at her too intently now. Too closely. People shouldn't ever look at her like that.

"Shaking," he said. "You're shaking. That chair too uncomfortable?"

"No, no. I'm all right. I shake sometimes, never mind. It's hypertension. Never mind."

"Okay. But I could get you another chair, or . . ."

"Never *mind* the chair, all *right*? Just look at the *photo*graph and tell me if you've seen him."

He looked again. "What's so special about this one? You promise to take them all back uptown and I'll get you maybe a hundred boys that look just like this one."

"No! I mean, uhhh, excuse me. This one is a special case with me. With us, with *us*, I mean, at the department. It's too complicated to explain."

"I'll buy that. I've got too many complications now."

Ohhh, the hell with the chair. She started to rub her thighs together. Let the chair squeak.

"There could be some money in it," she said. "I'll pay . . . I mean, the de*part*ment will pay. We have a fund."

"A fund? For kids? You welfare people pay for runaways by the pound or something?"

"No, just this special case here. You could call me at any time. It's on my card there. Oh. About the phone number: I crossed out the department number. Call me at home, where it's written in there. I'm working out of my *home* on this one case."

The cop shrugged again. "Whatever you say. So what makes you think he's in the Village?"

"I'm not sure he's *in* the Village, exactly. But he has *been* here. I followed him down here one day. I was waiting for him ... there's a men's clothing store in midtown where he goes a lot. And I was just in the car behind him on the subway coming down here. But he moves so ... he's so sort of elusive. And when he got off I lost him."

"You lost him." He turned on the smile again, aiming it directly at her.

"Yes. I lost him," Marion Dolan said.

"I wouldn't be surprised," Keith Lee said. "All the damn racket you're making with your legs, lady."

25

THE KID

First came the smell of smoke. It worked its way into his dream and then it woke him up.

Real things do that. You can be sound asleep and hear a door slam and the same door slams in your sleep. Your mind has quickly built it right into the dream. And if it is a bad sound or smell, then your dream turns bad, just like that.

The smoke had probably set it off again: suddenly he had started dreaming about the police raid. The dream formed instantly in the same old series of flashes across his mind. He was a lot smaller. It was years ago. He was wearing a big undershirt and shorts. He was sleeping on the floor, on the plaid blanket on the floor again. That was because Mama had a man in the bed.

The plaid blanket had bedbugs in it. Ordinarily you can't see bedbugs. But every time Mama made him sleep on it, the bugs would wake up and start crawling. They would bite him all across his groin and at the backs of his

knees. Each bite left a tiny red dot that itched. But Mama
wouldn't listen. "Don't say bugs to me," she would say.
"Just lay down and shut up. Play like you're an Indian.
I'm going out for a while."

They had come in drunk, bumping into things, and
the man had almost stepped on The Kid's hand. The man
had said, "What the hell, babe, you got a *kid* on the floor
down here." And Mama had said, "Never mind. He likes
to sleep on the floor. He sleeps sound; I got to shake him
in the morning. Name's Elvis." And the man had laughed
and half sung, "Ain't nothin' but a hound dog." And then
the man had said, "Suit yourself with the kid. Let him
watch, all I care. Now, where were we?" And Mama had
said, "Right about *here*, honey-man." And the man had
said, "Wait a minute, babe. We going to do it standing
up?" And Mama had said, "We are if you don't hurry;
you're making me crazy with that thing." And the man
had said, "In just one second here, I'm going to put you
up on it and spin you all around."

And they had tossed off all their clothes. Before he
had gotten into the bed with Mama, the man had put his
cigar down on the edge of the table just above The Kid's
head. And for the next half hour, he had smelled the bitter
smoke of it while listening to the bed rattle and to the
man groan and to Mama making little meowing noises.

The cigar burned into the tabletop. It had burned out
when the police came.

They had come in with flashlights; one kick and the
door had jumped right open. The two flashlights had
swept across all the walls and then splashed on Mama and
the man. Mama and the man were cross-lighted, with their
shadows big behind them. Mama's mouth was all red-
smeary. There was even lipstick on her teeth.

The man was just fat.

One of the vice men had accidentally kicked The Kid
and then had raised his foot and said, "What the hell,

211

Bert. A little bitty kid down on the floor here." And the other vice man had said, "What is he, part of the act?"

And then the cold cigar ash had fallen on The Kid's forehead. He would never forget the smell of it.

They had taken him down and sat him down in his underwear on the long bench outside the welfare office. And . . .

Now The Kid woke up all the way.

It was real smoke, all right. He lay still for a moment, blinking, making sure that he still had all of his fingers and toes. And then he turned his head and looked over at the other couch.

Sally was asleep, curled up in her protective sleeping position in her oatmeal-colored long johns. She had her arms crossed to guard her money. She was sweating, as usual, making little gray foam at the corners of her mouth when she breathed out.

He swung his legs around and got up. He walked over to the air-shaft window and looked out. Then he looked up.

The sky was glowing pink over Eleventh Street.

He pulled on his jeans and then sat on the couch and put on the Puma running shoes.

He went out the window and scaled around the air shaft to the janitor's window at the other side. He pulled himself inside, stepped down on the janitor's sink and then paused, listening. Okay: he stepped down, went out the door and padded down the black hallway, keeping contact with the wall through his fingertips. He waited again, looking up and listening, and then headed up the stairs.

The door to the roof was unlocked.

He touched the doorknob and then stepped back quickly, hunching himself deeper into the black of the corner. He held the stainless-steel shrimp deveiner down at his side, the forked tip pointed out.

The door eased open without a sound and the back-lighting did the rest:

It was a small figure; smaller because it was in a crouch, something glinting in one hand. The glint moved in quick, defensive circles.

It was Jewel Rodriguez. Little Jewel, age eleven. Jewel who did it to cops and carried an oversize switchblade. She stopped taking the little steps and started swiveling to each side, holding the knife out a little farther.

He waited. He wished that he could breathe through his nose.

There was a long, long pause while everybody listened. Over the silence, from down on the street, there was the sound of sirens.

Finally she straightened. She brought her hands together in front and the glint disappeared, the blade of the knife folding back into the handle. She slipped it into her back pocket and turned for the roof door.

A half-step, fast, and he had her by the throat from behind. He pulled her in close and brought the deveiner around to a spot just above her belly button. It scratched a line into her stomach as it slid into position.

She stood perfectly still. She didn't shake; she just pulled in one big breath and stood there, holding it, waiting for the tip to go into her stomach. Her timing was as good as any big-size Diablo: when she determined that there wasn't going to be an immediate slice, she started breathing again.

The Kid leaned around her and kicked open the roof door with his right foot and then walked her out in front of him.

It was like an explosion: the sky was burning bright red and yellow from the flames across the street. The top two floors of the brownstones were on fire and clusters of sparks were shooting up into the night like stars rising.

He could see the silhouette a few steps away. The

213

figure was kneeling on the cindery roof surface; the derby hat was etched in outline against the fire and the cape was hanging limply from his shoulders.

The figure was holding a rifle. The barrel was resting on the ledge, aimed down toward the street.

The Kid pushed Jewel across to the kneeling figure, the sound of their footsteps lost in the whoosh from the fire. He bent her over so that they both were leaning in close.

"Hey, Cat Man," The Kid said.

The only thing that moved was the Cat Man's head. His eyes were glowing yellow-gold with the reflection.

First he looked at Jewel. Then he looked at the hand around her neck. Then he looked down a bit farther at the spot where her tee shirt was pulled up—where the shrimp deveiner was digging a hollow in her stomach. And finally, he glanced up briefly at The Kid's face. He shrugged and turned back toward the fire. He bent his head and put his left cheek against the gunstock and sighted down into the street. When he spoke, his voice came out furry:

"Sheeee-it," he said. "You some watcher. S'pose look out for me. I get through here, gonna cut your little ass."

"I *was* watching," Jewel said. Her voice vibrated against The Kid's fingers. "Watching like you said to. I didn't see him. Sumbitch was just standing behind the door there in the black all the time, wearing them go-fast shoes. Anyway, you ain't cuttin' nothing, no-body. You so dusted, man, you can't even see down there at the street. How you expect to hit anybody when, like, you can't even *see*, the way you whacked out."

The thick puffs of water from the fire hoses below hit the top floor of the brownstones across the street and the fire flinched for a second before shooting higher than ever.

The Kid pulled back harder with his right arm and brought the back of Jewel's head up to his nose. He spoke into the tight Afro curls: "Okay, here's what we're going to do. I got to talk to the Cat Man, right? So I'm going

214

to put you down, you got that part? Make one move; you go for that knife one time, and I'll gut you. I'll take this thing and carve my name all over you. You got it all? Think about it."

He gave her one second to think and then he pushed her away.

"What is that there thing?" she said. She rubbed the palm of her hand over the diagonal scratch across her stomach and then held it up to the light and looked at the faint smudge of blood on it. "It ain't no real knife. It's something else."

The Kid held the knife up in the air between them and turned it slowly.

"It's a gutter," he said. "A regular knife just cuts. But this thing reaches in *under* the cut and grabs on to things, your intestines, and drags them back outside the cut. You come all apart."

"Where'd you . . . ?"

They both jumped at the rifle shot. The smell of cordite suddenly burned into the air as an overlay to the smoke from the fire.

Jewel and The Kid stepped over and all three of them leaned forward and looked over the ledge into the street below.

"I got him," The Cat Man said. "Whoooo-eee."

The people across the street three stories below were like foreshortened marionettes, all of them moving jerkily in the firelight. The fire trucks were parked crookedly in the street and the hoses curled into the crowd like snakes.

One of the persons down there had fallen. He lay on his back, kicking with both feet. The circle of people opened and closed around him. And then one, and two— and then most all of them slowly turned to look up into the sky.

"Who you shooting at?" The Kid said.

The Cat Man swung his head around. There was a

shower of sparks from the roof across the street, and his eyes glittered green.

"That ole dude. Like, I doan know his *name*, but the old Army dude. The one who burned Feets. Unnerstan' who I'm talkin' about? Old cat; Army suit. He wasted Feets with his old Army *gun*, man." He balanced the rifle on the ledge and then held his hands about a foot apart in the air, the palms curved. "It left holes *this* big, man, where the shells come out of Feets's back. This big. Man, like I saw him down at the mortuary place; I had to carry his suit down there for his Mama. Like, that old Army dude like to blow Feets all inside-*out*, man. And Feets was my man. You dig what I'm sayin' to you?"

"I heard all about it," The Kid said. "Someone told me."

The Cat Man picked up the rifle again. He pumped out the spent cartridge. "Kill that ole dude. Ain't nobody burning no Diablo, man, I'm alive. Old Feets dead, man; he *dead*, jus' like that, and I'm the man now. I am the *cap*tain, you unnerstan' what I'm saying?"

"It's your gang now."

"You got it." The Cat Man pulled the cape around his shoulders. "My gang now. What you say."

"Well, it ain't *him*," Jewel said. She was still leaning over the ledge, looking down into the street. "It's just *some*body. You took the whole side of his head off; he ain't even kicking no more. But, shee-it. Man, you so dusted, like you can't even see straight." She leaned over a bit more and pointed. "That old Army dude is still down there; I'm lookin' at him right in the eye, man. The one you was aiming at. He's got on his jive-ass old Army shirt. But you missed him. You shot the wrong cat down there."

"I got more shells," The Cat Man said. "I'll get him next time and then I'll shoot me a *fire*man, too. Jive fireman. Where'd you put my angel dust at?"

"You don't need any more," she said. "Your eyes look like two taillights now. You look like you got a candle burnin' inside your head, man. You smoke any more, it's gonna unkink your *hair,* you dig it?"

"Who did the fire?" The Kid said.

The Cat Man shrugged. "Man, *we* did the fire. Whole Diablos, man. Burn them oldies out of there. Like, you know how much gaso*line* we put in there? Man, them oldies came spillin' on out. Half 'em, man, half 'em ain't been outside in years, man. Like, burn 'em out and take over the building. We gonna move *in* that building, you unnerstan' what I'm tellin' you? We move in and take it over, man. Old cats, them old folks afraid to move back in. They gone, and we *got* it. Where's my dust at, I said?"

Jewel pointed to her crotch.

"It's in here," she said. "Eat it."

"Cut you," The Cat Man said.

"You ain't cuttin' nobody," she said. "So whacked now you can't see to shoot. And ..."

"Knock it *off,*" The Kid said. "What about the building?"

The sparks were forming a canopy over their heads now.

"Take it over," the Cat Man said. "We take it. We move in. Like, what's a matter with you? It's what happens to a *neigh*borhood, man. To a old building. Gangs burn it out and move on in. Somebody's got to go. Somebody got to move out. It's the oldies. You think any of 'em move back in there now? Livin' scared night and day, old ears to the door, man, listenin' all the time for that splash of gasoline outside they *door.* No way. That 'partment building—and pretty soon the one next to it, man. Tear it out. The pipes; like, you sell all the plumbing, man. Good money. Just over there, the scrap man; he don't care. And stoves. Lissen, man: you want a stove? Like, twenty bills, man, you got it. 'Frigerator? All that stuff belongs to me now. Ain't no old folks movin' back into *that* building. Like, I'm gonna shoot that old dude who killed Feets. Gonna waste his old Army ass and then I'm gonna burn down this whole Village."

He kneeled down again and sighted along the barrel of the rifle. He was weaving. He pushed the derby back on his head. His forehead was shining blue-green from the fire.

He squeezed off another shot.

A window shattered in the ladder truck below.

"Look," The Kid said.

They all leaned over the ledge.

"No, no," he said. "Not the fire truck, dust-head. Look at *him*."

He was there. He was three stories down, standing in the street and looking up at the ledge. He was wearing a pink golf sweater, the one blob of color among the nightgowns and overcoats worn by the old folks. He had his head back and the spotlights from the fire trucks were making his hair pure yellow. He paused for one quick moment, his hands out. The glint of chrome in his right hand was his gun.

And then he started across the street. He sprinted up the steps.

They leaned farther forward and watched him come into their building.

"Sheee-it," the Cat Man said. "Shoot his ass, he gets up here."

"Wrong," The Kid said. "Not in the shape you're in. Come on."

"On what?"

"Look: you want to get shot? Listen: you're *about* to get shot. Remember Feets? You remember the big holes coming out of Feets's back? Well, you got holes like that coming up."

The Cat Man got up on one knee, then stood upright, weaving. He tried to pump the spent shell out of the rifle, then dropped it. His eyes were going slitted.

"Man," he said. "I'm coming down off it, man. It's like I'm moving through Jell-O. Orange Jell-O."

The Kid took two steps toward the iron door to the roof and then turned.

"Come *on*," he said. "Move it. Never mind the knife, Jewel. Shake it. Let's go."

The Cat Man shrugged, looking up at the sparks. "Man, he got us," he said.

"Not yet. I got a way out if you shake your ass."

"This time he'll kill me," Jewel said. "Throw me right off the roof, like he said."

"No, *listen*. Move it and follow me. Go where I go, you both got that? Okay?"

They started down the black staircase.

"Can you jump? Like, one story?" The Kid said.

The Cat Man was panting now, spraying the back of The Kid's neck. Jewel was coming, holding on to the cape from behind.

"Like . . . like, I was . . . I was born jumpin'," the Cat Man said. "Where I gotta jump to?"

"To a mattress. You got to hit it just exact, just right. And then there's a little door you crawl out."

"What if I miss?" Jewel said.

"Broken glass," The Kid said. He looked over his shoulder into the Cat Man's face. "Come on. I get us out and . . ."

"Wha?"

"I get us out and you owe me one."

26

ICEPICK SALLY

For the sake of the Living History of Greenwich Village, better note the exact time.

It was now 4:04 P.M.

And note the scene, so that people would understand after she was dead and gone.

It was now the day after the big fire. The sidewalks on both sides of Eleventh Street were mucky with puddled cold black water and ashes.

Poor Mister Jorgenson had been shot dead during the fire. He had fled his own building and he had been standing outside on the sidewalk. The entire left half of his head had been shot away: eye, ear, cheekbone—all of it. It had made a sound like a ball peen hammer hitting a pumpkin. Sergeant Boggs had provided that description. The sergeant was out on bail. No. No, what did they call it? He was out on his own recognizance. And Sergeant Boggs had been standing right next to poor Mister Jorgenson—just this close—and the exploding head and everything inside of it had splattered all over Sergeant Boggs.

Mister Jorgenson had flopped right over on his back there on the sidewalk, and the old folks had all bent over him. The half of his head that was left had been totally unmarked, and the one remaining eye had looked around at all of them.

"That one eye recognized me," Sergeant Boggs had said. "And it looked at me imploringly, seeking something that I could not provide. And then the one remaining eyebrow sort of knitted in what might have been a frown if there had been an opposing eyebrow to match it."

The shot had come from the roof of the building across the street. The old folks had all looked up and had seen the fuzzy silhouettes of three heads looking back down at them.

And Officer Keith Lee had looked up and had seen the outlined heads, too. He had pulled a big shiny gun from his waistband and had run into the building across the street.

Better note all of that for the History.

Sally had gotten dressed and had come downstairs and around the block, but too late for the shooting. But she had looked at and had touched the blue-gray lumps that had spattered Sergeant Boggs's shirt. The lumps were like tapioca pudding.

Too bad that her boy, that Press, had missed the fire. He had been gone, off somewhere, when she had awakened to all the noise, and he hadn't come back until this morning.

She had told Press all about it, what she knew—about the shot exploding poor Mister Jorgenson's head like that —but Press had just sat there on the broken camelback couch, not saying a word, just staring at the wall. Then he had eaten two whole Snickers bars and had gone to sleep. He was still asleep now.

At what? At 4:10 P.M.

She would dictate all of this to her dog this evening, of course. Exactly as she had said it all just now.

But first, all this work to be done. And before dark. The sidewalk in front of the burned-out brownstone was littered with fantastic treasures.

The senior citizens had gotten away with what they could, with whatever they had been able to grab and carry down the stairs when the fire broke out. Nobody had been able to go back inside for anything. No suitcases, surely. No extra clothes—it had been a nightgown-and-raincoat fire.

Funny what things people will pick up to carry out with them when their life is burning down all around them. She could picture them, frightened and crying in the smoke, spinning slowly in the center of their rooms, their arms out, looking at everything and wondering whatever to take.

Pictures: some of them had brought down photographs from the tops of dressers. Pictures of sons and daughters who had abandoned them anyway and never came to visit. All of them, the old folks, everybody had a picture of a son or daughter standing on the lawn outside an English Tudor house. The children didn't come to visit. They sent pictures.

Sally picked up a few of the photographs and looked at them. The water had puddled in the middle of most of them.

But this one was all right: nice color photograph in a sort of silvery frame. Nice house. Somebody's children. She reached to her shoulder and dropped it into the red knapsack.

And dishes. Dishes all around. This Chicago World's Fair souvenir plate. But whoever had brought it down had dropped it in the excitement and now it was . . . no, it couldn't even be fixed.

A fox collar that could snap onto a cloth coat to doll it up.

Hand-painted china figurine. It should clean up nicely. She rubbed away some of the ash with her thumb. Good china. Into the knapsack.

A lower dental plate. No, no, upper. It went in this way. Nice, broad teeth and pink gum line. Better save it; if she ever had her own teeth out, she could just hand this to the dentist. Wouldn't he be surprised—he would have been planning on some outrageous charge.

She dropped the teeth into the sack.

An ostrich boa, but it was beyond saving. The feathers would never come clean now.

Someone had brought down a tuna-and-noodle casserole. It was a good way to fix it, putting the crumbled-up potato chips on top like that. But the glass Pyrex lid had broken inward and now it was covered with specks of glass. Too dangerous to eat.

And a beaded evening purse. Black beads. Maybe she could fix the zipper.

An elastic stocking. Nice tan color, knee-high. It was for varicose veins. All right: never can tell.

And an old Norelco electric shaver, only one of the triple heads missing. Maybe Press could fix it up. Press would probably start shaving one day soon.

The things that people will carry out of a burning apartment building.

A pair of reading glasses.

Sally held them up to her eyes. She looked across the street through them and then back down into the garbage can. Too strong for distance. Fine for close work.

A Book of Mormon, the title stamped in gold leaf. Maybe the pages would dry out.

And ...

And an icepick.

She wiped the handle against her skirt. Then she held it up and looked at it.

Light-blue enameled, painted handle. Let's see:

Frank and Wanda's Bait and Tackle. Ummmm. Something. Someplace in Florida. She couldn't quite make it out.

The icepick part was all rusted. Say, mmmm, about four-and-three-quarter inches long. The tip had been broken off.

But an icepick.

She turned and looked over her shoulder. She looked both ways up and down the sidewalk.

And then she put the icepick into the right-side pocket of the pea coat. And she took a deep breath.

"Icepick Sally, indeed," she said.

27

THE KID

"All right, one more time," he said.

She scowled at him, holding the cigar in her teeth right at the middle of her mouth. The smoke curled around her head like a veil. "You don't have to get huffy about it," she said. "I just want to understand, that's all."

"All right, then," The Kid said. "What you got to understand is that I *can't* stay here. Couple more weeks of this stuff and I'll be like everybody else down here. Shooting the . . . God sake, Sally, shooting the top of somebody's damn head off. And . . ."

"Actually, it was the *side* of his head," she said. She took the cigar out of her mouth and then drew a line down the center of her forehead with her index finger. "From here on over to *here*. Took everything with it. The eyeball. One nostril and then on back to . . ."

"Sally."

". . . everything. The mortician—you should have seen it at the viewing—the mortician had poor Mister Jorgenson like *this,* see? Lying in the coffin with his head turned away to one side, turned toward the ruffled satin pillow like *this,* so that it just looked like he was taking a little nap with his head slightly turned away from you. The surviving side of his head, I think I told you, the rest of his head was just fine."

"Swell."

"What's the matter now? What'd I say this time?"

"No. Forget it."

"Come on, Press. You can tell . . . you know, you're sure acting standoffish lately. 'What'd I say,' I said?"

The Kid looked up from the stacks of money. He had them arranged in a half circle around his knees on the floor: fives, tens, twenties. He ran one hand through his hair and let it fall back.

"It isn't what you're saying," he said. "It isn't, I don't know. Listen, that's not it. It's just that all this stuff is going down around here and we're *living* with it and pretty soon we get, what? We get scar tissue on the inside of our brains, for God sake, and we just talk about it and go on living here. You know, like, 'Poor Mister Jorgenson got his head half shot away,' and then everybody gets burned out of the building over there and we just go on. And pretty soon, when something worse happens, we don't think it's so bad."

She put the cigar back into her mouth and nodded. "We get callused, you mean. Hardened, maybe. But, Press. That's life. It's the way things are. You live. You do what you can to stay alive."

"Wrong. It isn't life. It's . . . listen: you could get out of here, too. Any time. You got so much money sewed into your underwear you can barely stand up straight. You're using money for *lining,* Sally, and still you . . ."

"But I can't leave. There's my work."

"Work. Your work. Listen: your work'll get you killed, too. The goddam Diablos, the kids, all of them—they won't hold off forever. One day one of them cuts you just for no special reason. Just to hear the air come out. They've chased you already. Maybe he does it for a, for a . . . what do they call it?"

She blinked. "Initiation?"

"Right. For an initiation. 'Go cut up Icepick Sally,' they'll say one time, 'and you get to be a member.' You know what I mean. Listen, you know. You spend all your time out there half humped over, listening for the click of the blade coming out."

"True, true. But that's the way it *is*, Press. I can't change it. You can't. Are you really that afraid?"

He grinned at her. She looked at him a little closer. No, he was just baring all his teeth.

"Hell, yes, I'm afraid," he said. "But that's not it. Listen: everybody's afraid of something, but forget that part. The thing is, I've told you this before. The thing is: I've *done* all this. The whole number. All my life has been like this. Here, somewhere; I've *always* lived like this and it's crap. Listen: I've seen it all, the whole thing; all the stuff that people can do to each other. I already feel like an old . . . I feel like Sergeant *Boggs*. Now, wait a minute— just sit there and smoke the cigar and listen. Do you know —did you ever figure that there's something else out there? No, I mean really. There's another kind of life. I don't know where it is, but I know it's there. It's probably like you see on television. Look: television is crap, sure. I know life isn't all finger-snapping and, you know, Donny and Marie and the goddam balloons at the end, where they do the credits. But I mean *television*—the people in it. Listen: they get on camera and they're happy and they got places to go; you can't tell *me* they're not happy. And that makes them real and it makes me, what? I don't know. But that's what I want to be like. There's got to be . . ."

"Press, I . . ."

He held up one hand. "No. No, listen: there's got to be

another life where you meet somebody and they're not carrying a knife or maybe bolt cutters; kee-rist, *bolt* cutters. And people *talk* to each other; one guy talks, one guy *listens*—and it actually works. None of this creepy-crawly through dark hallways on the day the oldies get their pension checks. Just people talking away and looking each other right in the eye because they're both *safe*, see? If someone ever came up to me and said, 'Hey, if it ain't good old Press. How are you doing, good old Press?' I'd probably flash on him. But around here? Are you kidding me?"

The cigar had gone out. That was because she was crying and not puffing.

"All your life?" she said. "All your *life*?"

"Forget it."

"But you're still a little . . . what of your mother?"

"Your nose is all runny."

"Never *mind* my nose," she said. "If I wipe it on my sleeve, it makes you mad." She sniffed in hard, making a bubbly rattle. "What about your mother?"

The Kid shrugged. "She does it to men for money. No. No, she does it to men for drinks. For pats on the head, whatever. When I was a baby, she used to do it to guys with me lying right there on the other side of the bed. Once I jiggled right off. Then, later, she made me sleep on the floor. There was a lamp on the nightstand. I could lie on my back on the floor and look up and see their shadows moving on the ceiling. It was my way of going to the movies: watching great big shadows doing it to each other."

"Press."

"And once there was a guy who used to hit her a lot; he was the one who took the money. Then he'd hit me. I'd curl up into a ball. He'd keep hitting. He had a high voice for a man. 'Cry, you little bastard,' he'd say. 'Don't pull that stuff on me. You better cry or I'll kill you.'"

228

"And you cried?"

"Finally I had to."

"Press, I . . ."

The Kid smiled the nonsmile again. "Another guy was going to commit suicide. Took our big bread knife. But he couldn't do it, he chickened out. So he got me by the hair instead and he held the knife at my neck for a long time, crying and talking crazy."

"*Press.* Stop it."

"And then, one night, the vice guys came. And it was all over. But, see, it was too late."

She sniffed in again. "Too late?"

"Sure. I was already an old man by then. I felt like I must be a midget, going around, looking up at all the big people. They put me in a lot of foster homes. The Germans treat you like a, what do you call them? A slave. The Catholics believe in beating a kid into Heaven. Another German family once. They called me a Jew because I was so cunning, they said. Jew-baby."

"Are you Jewish?"

"How the hell would I know?"

"And then?"

"And then social workers. They don't see you as a people; they see you as a *case.* The last one, the last one wanted to know about playing with myself. Her mouth was all slobbery and wet when she asked me about it. I wouldn't tell her and she broke my nose like this."

"Good Lord," Sally said. She stood up and brushed the flats of her hands over her skirt. "I've got to have another cigar. In fact, I'd better have a drop of brandy, too. You want a drop of brandy, darling?"

"No, thanks."

She looked over her shoulder from the chest of drawers. "But you're safe here with me now. Sally will look after you. Anybody so much as looks cross-eyed at you and I'll icepick them."

"Swell. Except that you haven't got an icepick."

"That's all you know."

"Anyway," he said.

"Anyway. Put it all behind you. Come on, now. Change the look on your face. I still don't understand where you're so set on going. All this stuff you're collecting and all."

The Kid nodded. "All right. One more time. All together, now: I'm going out *there*. Away from here. All of this. Listen: you said all this stuff. Okay. I've broken *through* at Paul Stuart. It's important; it's like graduating. I walk in there now, straight up, and I've got them worked out. The steady stare. A lot of it is in how you walk and look and maybe hold your mouth. It cost me a lot of dough; it took a lot of trips in there—but now, I walk in and if one of them looks at me like I was just some kid or something, I cold-stare him until he coughs a little bit and looks the other way. And nobody lays anything dumb on me; the guy makes a move for a dumb shirt and I can stop him with an eyebrow. And the Italian guy, the one with the curly mustache. 'Ahh, it's Master Reynolds,' he says to me now. 'What may I get for you?' He doesn't know who I am, see, but I've got him figuring that I'm somebody and he'd better not screw it up or maybe I tell my old man. You see?"

"It's that important to you?"

The Kid nodded. "It's only everything. It's got to be that way for the plan. I *told* you, Sally. The luggage there. It's got to be Mark Cross. No other luggage does it. Not Gucci, which is for dagos in from Bayside. You do the Gucci, you're out of the contest, see? No, Mark Cross. And the E. P. R. stamped in gold stuff on the strap. Not big letters; just so you can barely notice them with the corner of your eye. Big letters are bad; I don't know why, I just know. Okay. I got the ace suitcase. The shirts. Ties. And pants and shoes, right?"

She pointed with her cigar stub. "And such a fuss over the coat."

"Blazer," he said. "*Blazer*. I told you: it's got to be Brooks. I know that you told me Max Linowitz. Sure, cheaper at Max Linowitz. But I told you: it's got to be Brooks Brothers because, I don't know, their blazer has got a look to it—it's the way it hangs—and people can make it all the way across a room. They see it, they know it. And it says something to them. You sew that thing on the pocket yet?"

"I'll do it tonight," she said. "It's called an escutcheon. Es-*cut*-cheon. Burke Academy, indeed."

"Who cares? It's important. People don't *read* it; they just see it and they nod to themselves, inside."

"You've thought of everything."

"I hope so. All right. And then it's the Plaza."

"It must be the Plaza? Not the St. Regis? Or the . . ."

"Come on," he said.

"All right. The Plaza."

He nodded. "And you call and make the reservation for me. My mother calling. And I go to the Plaza and I get out of the cab there, across from Central Park, and I catch the dooman's eye and . . . uhhh. Listen: did I tell you what they do at the check-in desk there?"

"No."

"I've been there and studied it." The Kid straightened his legs and stood up. "You're at the check-in desk, see? Like this. And the guy who signs you in, whatever they're called, the guy snaps a quick look over your shoulder at your suitcase. Where it's sitting there, where the doorman put it down. And just while he's snapping that quick look, you turn—a little move like this, like you've been doing it all your life—and you slip the doorman a bill. You turn back slowly—and the check-in guy has got the luggage *made*. I mean made: the Mark Cross pure leather;

231

God, he can smell it. And the guy raises his eyebrows a bit; not much, but he's now got the luggage made and the blazer and the whole number. And if he was to lean over the edge of the desk and look down, he would see that the loafers are just right, too. Black loafers, you've blown it. But brown, see, and scuffed, not shiny. Rich kids always wear kiss-my-ass shoes like that."

She nodded. "And what do you do then?"

He smiled and shook his head so that the hair swooped down like a wing.

"And then I go into the Palm Court. This is the important number. I go into the Palm Court and I get seated. And the waiter, I tell the waiter, like this: 'Some coffee, if you please, and I'd like to see the pastry cart.' Not just 'Coffee and a piece of cake.' You say, 'I'd like to see the pastry cart.' It *has* to be done that way. And then. And then I'm going to spend a long, long time just drinking that coffee and eating whatever the hell it is, I don't know. And looking around. And nobody there will know what's happening. It won't be anything they can see or hear. But The Kid will be changing. And when I've paid the check, I will get up and slowly walk out. But, get this: it won't be The Kid walking out of the Palm Court. The *Kid* walked in and sat down. It will be E. P. Reynolds walking out and nobody will ever see The Kid again."

Sally sat down on the camelback couch, legs apart, her elbows resting on her knees. She was holding the brandy glass between her hands.

"I swear, it's just so beautiful," she said. "I mean: I don't even know if it will work. But, Lord, the way you *tell* it. The pastry cart and all. I can just close my eyes and see you doing it: 'I believe I'll have one of *those*. No, on second thought, what are these little things? This rather baroque looking little thing? I think I'll have one of those.' It will be just right. The arched eyebrows the way you do it. The icy control you have: looking at people the way you do. Well. The people there in the Palm Court could only think it was a Rockefeller heir in there eating cake. Maybe a young Kennedy. Though they're just too scruffy, the young Kennedys. But a *some*body. So tell me: the one who comes walking out of the Palm Court. The boy who goes in, I know him. But the one who walks out?"

"It won't be me. It'll be *him*."

She sighed. "It's wonderful. You make me feel like, mmmm, like Lennie."

"Who's Lennie?"

"He was a man. Just a man; little crazy, maybe, like me. He was in John Steinbeck's *Of Mice and Men*. And once he sat on the riverbank and . . . well. I've got it all twisted around, but Lennie liked rabbits, see? Because they were so soft and furry or whatever. And he would tell the *other* guy, Lennie would say, 'Tell me about the rabbits, George.' And then they would . . . Why are you looking at me like that?"

"You've lost me," The Kid said. "You having another little stroke or something?"

"No, dummy. What I meant was: I feel like Lennie when you tell me about your plan. I just love hearing it. I want to sit here and say to you, 'Tell me about the Plaza, George.'"

He scowled. "I still don't . . ."

"You had to be there," she said.

28

ICEPICK SALLY

That would be one dead cat. Run, poor cat.

And it was a Siamese, too. It appeared to be a seal point, and they're by far the prettiest. It was wearing a collar with shiny things studded on it, light blue jewels to match its eyes. The cat was standing on its back legs, stretched up toward the top of the garbage can outside O'Halloran's.

But as good as dead.

That was because the umber-colored boy in the black cape and derby hat was standing just between them—just between her and the cat. The boy had his back to her. He was watching the cat; he had his hands in his back pockets, his elbows pointing out.

"Don't," Sally said. "Don't you do it."

No. No, that was not quite right. What she had done was to move her mouth saying it—move her mouth and shake her head back and forth—but no sound was coming out. The inside of her head was roaring with the effort of trying to say it out loud in time. The roof of her mouth had suddenly gone dry.

Now the boy bent over and reached into the top of his knee-high boot.

Sally could see the glint of the knife coming up out of the boot. It was a thin and polished blade—long, oh, Lord, was it long!

The boy straightened and flipped the knife in a half circle in the air and caught it by the blade. He held it with the tips of his fingers, waggling the handle back and forth just alongside his right ear.

"Oh, God, *don't!*" she said. And this time, the voice just came right out of there. Out loud.

The Cat Man turned and looked at her. The cape swung around with him and then settled in folds against his hips and the backs of his legs.

There was something . . . what? There was something wrong with his eyes. They looked like they were being lit from the inside. Like someone had sprayed fluorescent glycerine on them from behind. He took forever to blink— one long blink with both eyes closed in the middle of it like he was napping—and then he opened them again. And he smiled at her.

"Hey. Old jive-ass Icepick," he said.

She reached out with her right hand and steadied herself against the corner of the building.

"You leave that poor cat alone," she said.

He slow-blinked again. "Ol' Icepick. You lookin' good, Mama. I thought I smell someone creepin' up behind me. Lookin' real good. An' I hate to have to cut you, you dig?"

"Show some mercy," she said.

The Cat Man nodded.

"Hey," he said. "You got it. You *got* it. What I'm gonna do is, what the Cat Man goin' to do is to get you this jive cat for your dinner. I gonna put him in your *back*-sack for you, dig? An' you get to *eat* this ol' cat."

"Please. Don't."

But he swung away now, bringing his arm up into throwing position.

There is a sense that warns cats. Some kind of danger-crackle in the air that only cats can feel. The Siamese suddenly swirled away from the garbage can. It was a pirouette, really, with both front paws still up.

The knife made a shining turn in the air when it left the boy's hand. The blade went into the cat's chest directly between the front paws. The force of it raised the cat higher on its hind legs. There was no sound; the cat stayed balanced, opening and closing its mouth and blinking the blue eyes.

Watching, Sally opened and closed her mouth in unison.

The cat looked down at the handle of the knife. It brought its paws together slowly to touch it. The soft touch; it kept its claws sheathed. And then, slowly, it sank back to the sidewalk. It rolled over on its left side with all four paws facing them, making fluid swimming motions in the air.

The Cat Man stepped over and squatted down. He reached in between the cat's front paws and pulled out the knife. Then he picked up the cat's tail and doubled it over in the palm of his hand. He drew the knife blade through it. He held the knife up and looked at both sides of the blade, then did it again. He put the knife back into his right boot and stood. When he looked at her, his eyes were more glittery than before.

She took a half step toward him now, her hands out.

"You beast," she said. Then she stopped.

He . . . what? He didn't see her, that was what. The wet eyes were focused on some middle distance between them and he was half smiling.

"Beast, beast."

And he didn't hear her, either. He stood and adjusted his cape. Then he turned and walked away. He stopped at the curb, looked both ways for traffic, and walked over toward the playground.

Awwww, dear Lord. Come *on*, Lord. Don't you ever look in on Greenwich Village? She braced her right hand against the side of the garbage can and slowly lowered herself down to one knee beside the cat. She reached out and patted it. The eyes were the last to die; one minute they were burning blue and then, slowly, they turned the color of milk.

"There," she said. "There, there, kitty-cat."

She nudged the cat's head backward and unbuckled the jeweled collar. She held it in both hands for a minute, turning it back and forth, watching the light shine on the blue stones.

"I'll wear it for you," she said. "My wrist, I guess. One of us will carry on. Just don't you worry."

She put the collar into the knapsack and then got up slowly, steadying herself on the can. She rubbed under both eyes with the sleeve of the pea coat.

She walked two stores down past O'Halloran's Bar and then stopped. She half swung around and looked over at the playground. The Cat Man was over there now.

"Animal-beast," she said.

She put both hands in the pea-coat pockets.

Ahh, the smooth enameled square handle. The icepick, that's what it was. Her icepick, dear Lord. She squinted at the boys playing basketball. She could make out the red satin lining on the swirling cape.

I wonder, Lord—I wonder if you would be kind enough to help me across the street and then guide my hand in a stroke of vengeance. One of us has got to be strong enough to do this, God. Or are you still out of town?

Then came the footsteps. Out of all the people on the sidewalk here, out of all the traffic, she would always know that step. She waited, listening, until the steps came right up to her left side. Then: "Hello, Press," she said.

"What are you doing?" he said. "It's too hot out here."

She was afraid to turn and look at him. It had been this way for the last week or so. She was afraid that when she turned her head to look at him, that he would be wearing the going-away clothes. Carrying the Mark Cross suitcase. Wearing the blazer with the escutcheon on the pocket.

So she looked down and sideways at his shoes first. The wrong shoes. All right.

"I said, 'What are you doing?' " he said.

She sniffed in deeply and then drew her coat sleeve across underneath her nose.

"I'm standing here," she said. "I'm just standing here contemplating doing something that you wouldn't believe. You would not think that it was in me to think what I am thinking about doing right this very minute."

He glanced across the street. "The playground? You thinking of going over and getting in the game?"

She rubbed her thumb along the smooth handle of the icepick inside her pocket. "In a manner of speaking, yes."

"What's the matter?"

"Matter with who?"

"Are you crying or something? Come on, look at me."

"I don't want to look at you," she said. "And, yes, I'm crying. It's allowed. I'm *old*."

He stepped around in front and looked into her face. "Listen, Sally . . ."

"Will you leave me *alone*? Go away. Go on, just get. Go to your damn dumb Plaza. I'll pastry-cart you one right alongside the head."

"Somebody did something to you," he said. "Who?"

She wiped her nose on the sleeve again. "Never mind."

"Look, Sally: I told you it would be like this. It doesn't get any better. It gets worse all along. And now you're standing here crying in the middle of Sixth Avenue. What the hell, Sally."

"Poor little cat," she said. "Poor kitty-cat. It just took hold of the knife handle with its poor little furry hands. I wonder if cats can cry?"

"What?"

"Oh, never mind. It's over now."

He walked a few steps away and then turned back to her. Then he walked back up and leaned his face in close.

"I told you," he said. "You got to get out of here. Now, listen to me one time: you're getting crazier by the minute. And you're going to get hurt. Killed, maybe. Standing here and crying. Something happened; somebody has hurt you. And you won't let me help. Who knows what's going on here?"

"Oh, don't worry. God knows."

"Sally, will you just knock it off? Look: let's go. Come on with me. Let's just get the hell out of here before something bad happens."

She took a deep breath. Here came that awful roaring inside her head again. That was the way the poor cat had felt when the pointed knife went in. Couldn't catch its breath. She couldn't catch her breath.

"You said we haven't got enough money," she said.

He shrugged at her. "It's all *right*. We'll work it out. Just come with me, okay?"

"Some people have all the money," she said.

He looked at her and then turned his head to see where she was looking. "Who has? The Diablos? Hell, they haven't got any more . . ."

She shook her head. "No. Not the boys on the basketball court. No, there. See?"

It was the two men making the exchange again. They were already seated side by side on the bench; she hadn't noticed them come into the park. They had their shopping bags lined up side by side between them. The younger man was reaching into one of the sacks for the cans of beer.

He frowned. "I don't see . . ."

"Exactly. That's exactly it," she said. "You don't see; nobody sees. It's the way they want it. Now look again at the two men sitting on the bench and watching the game. Well, they came into the playground from different directions—one from over there. The other one from over *there*. We weren't looking at the time. Now, then. They come in with their shopping bags and they meet and they put the bags down and they sit down and have a little bite of something together."

Press glanced back at her. "So big deal."

"So you bet big deal. You know what's in those two shopping bags?"

"Beer. Looks like couple of heroes in the other one. Who knows?"

Sally nodded up and down. "I know, is who knows. One of the bags is full of *money*, my dear."

She could have sworn that he jumped a little bit inside his clothes. "Money?"

"Of *course*. And the other bag is full of goods."

"What goods?"

"Whatever it is that the money is paying for. Dope, of course. Cocaine, perhaps. Or heroin. In fact, heroin, I'm pretty sure."

"But I still don't . . ."

"Darling," she said. "Dear boy. The two men approach. They meet. You've got that part? Well, it takes close observation; I'm usually back there in front of O'Halloran's at the garbage cans. But all right. They meet. They put their shopping bags down on the bench, just so. And then they shake hands. They sit down. But what they have done while shaking hands is a small turnaround. Almost like a little waltz step. The young man peeks into his bag and lifts out the two cans of beer. The older man peeks into *his* bag and lifts out the sandwiches. But what are they really doing? What they are really doing is double-

240

checking what it is that lies *under* the beer and the sand-wiches. The beer and sandwiches are just what is sitting on *top*. See, Press?"

She could see that he saw. In fact, his face had fallen into that look again. His face had turned perfectly serene, as if the Mormon Tabernacle Choir was singing inside his head. But all he did was nod slightly.

"Got it," he said.

"Well, all right then. One bag contains the goods and one bag contains the money to pay for the goods."

"How much money do you think it is?"

"I have no idea, my dear. But I suspect that it's quite a bit."

"A sackful?"

"The sackful, yes."

Press nodded, still not looking at her. She looked over at his profile. If it wasn't for his terribly smashed nose, it would be absolutely *Grecian*. Hawklike. The Look of Eagles. Now he swung around to face her.

"And when they leave," he said, "when they leave, the one guy takes the other guy's bag and the other guy takes the *other* guy's bag. Because they've switched."

She nodded. "Sometimes they change positions while they're shaking hands. Sometimes it's all in the way they set the bags down on the bench. Either way, they get up and go, and each man is carrying a different bag from the one he brought in."

"How often do they do this?"

"Once a week. Every Wednesday about sundown."

"He didn't even eat all the *sand*wich," Press said, watching them leave.

"Would you?"

"Sure. Why not?"

She took him by the arm and tugged gently. "Come on. We'd better be on the way. Don't pay any attention to them. They're criminals. Dope. The worst kind of scum.

The Village is full of dope. The mob, I suspect. You know, Mafia, I think. In fact, I'm pretty sure."

Her head hurt so. She couldn't get the cat out of her mind.

The image of the cat with the knife in its breast kept intermingling in her mind with the image of herself: she was on her knees in front of O'Halloran's Bar. The boy in the cape—the tan-colored boy with the terrible, glittery eyes—was standing just in front of her. He was striking a pose, with his arm out toward her.

No. Not a pose. He had just thrown his knife.

And she could see, she could imagine herself looking down at the handle of the knife jutting out just *here,* at her chest. She would slowly bring her paws together to touch the handle and . . .

"Press," she said.

They turned the corner on Tenth Street.

"Mmmmm?"

"Press, I wonder if . . . oh, I don't know. But, you know, I wonder if I could really . . . well. If I could really go with you when you go."

"You're coming," he said. "I can't leave you here by yourself. Hate to tell you this part, but you'll have to take a bath."

"Oh, come on. It isn't as if I've never had a bath."

"Not since I've known you."

She held on a little harder to his arm. "Walk slower. Tell me about the Plaza again. We could change the wording. The waiter comes up. And you say, 'We'd like to see the pastry cart.' "

"Fine."

"Tell it to me."

"Not again. I'm thinking."

There was the sound again now. It was so strange: she could hear it over the traffic, just like she could pick out and identify Press's footsteps. Keen old ears.

Strange sound. There it went again. Raspy. It was going shhhhhhhpppppp, shhhhhhhpppp, shhhhhpppp.

Something rubbing together.

She glanced over at Press to see if he had heard it. But he was obviously far away in thought, looking down, his eyebrows drawn together.

Sally glanced back over her left shoulder.

Nothing.

Well, nothing special that she could see.

Just a great big fat lady walking along quite a way behind them.

But it wasn't anybody she knew.

29

THE KID

The Cat Man had all of the good moves—plus a couple of extra touches that were right out of Earl Monroe. Another life, another city somewhere, maybe, and the scouting guys would already be coming around to watch him play. They would be shaking his hand a lot and saying not to worry about the high school transcripts; they'd fix up the transcripts—and, listen: does your old man need a job? The Cat Man would be thinking about Indiana, thinking about Rutgers. Well, stuff it, hoop fans. To get to Rutgers, you got to show them a little more than your stutter-step. It would have to be another life, all right. Because in this one, the Cat Man couldn't even read.

He always wore the black derby and his silk cape while playing, and now, bringing the ball up to midcourt, he dribbled between his legs from right to left and then fired a behind-the-back pass from left to right. With the cape swirling around him, there was a quick flash in there when nobody knew where the ball was. Angel picked it off and went in for an easy lay-up. The Cat Man glanced over at the bench.

The Kid nodded. "I saw it, I saw it," he said.

He was sitting easily, legs crossed, his arms stretched out along the back of the bench. He watched the game without changing his expression, breathing through his mouth the way he always did when he was thinking. He was letting the afternoon sun shine on his broken nose.

The Cat Man always showed up at the playground early with his own string of kids. One kid to carry the new Converse sneaks. One kid to carefully hold the Cat Man's satin shirt while he played—and one to guard the pointy-toed, high-heeled boots. Another kid to hold the fresh towel so that the Cat Man could dry off his torso and under his arms after every game; the Cat Man was fastidious about that. The little kids stole a fresh towel for him for every game.

The Cat Man's boots were always lined up precisely beside their young guard. Several times during the game, the kid would pick up the boots and polish them with a handkerchief.

There was a built-in holster inside the right boot for the throwing knife. The Cat Man was fastidious about *that*. After each game, when he gave each one of his kids a dollar bill, no matter how much they begged and danced around him, he would never let any of them touch the throwing knife.

"Too sharp, man," the Cat Man would say, shaking his head. "Just the right swing, man—you got to roll your hand like this here—just the right swing, babe, takes a cat in half, just like that. Nothin' to it, you dig?"

And all the little kids would leave the playground practicing the big swing, rolling their wrists so that the pretend knife would turn once in the air. There were very few stray cats left in this section of the Village.

But okay. Time to shake it one more time. The Kid

recrossed his legs and started counting to himself. He bent his head forward and looked at the game: thousand two, one thousand three, one thousand four, moving his lips slightly. And then he nodded when the Cat Man glanced over at the bench.

Twelve . . . no, fourteen. One thousand fifteen; come on, *move* it, and, uhhh, what? Say one thousand twenty, and . . .

To his right, the Cat Man came down with the rebound, his legs spread wide, the cape billowing up in back. He head-faked toward the fence and then spun quickly and started pounding up-court to his left. At center court, Angel set the pick and the Cat Man spun around him. But the picked-off kid switched and came around on the same side. They crashed.

The Cat Man palmed the ball, his knuckles arched over it, holding it lazily in front of his stomach.

" 'ference," he said. "I'm gonna take me two. Both, I get three."

The picked-off defender, whose name was Juan, shook his head no.

"Nothin'," he said. "S'matter with you, man? Ain't no 'ference; you plain-ass *chargin'*, man. No shots, man. We takin' it in right here, man." He spit on the asphalt between them.

The Cat Man shrugged. "Chargin'? Ain't no jive-ass chargin', man. What it was: you standin' flat in my *way*. Like, I'm movin',' you dig? And you *blockin'*, unnerstan' what I'm sayin'? Move your ass, baby, I'm takin' me two free."

The other players closed in now, looking interested. And from the far side, coming off the wire screen, the little kids began to circle. The one guarding the boots bent quickly and picked up the right boot and held it out in front of his chest like an altar boy carrying the eucharist. He walked directly toward the Cat Man.

Juan, maybe six three and lean at thirteen years old, swung his right hand up and held it in the air between them. Then he slowly drew all the fingers down into a fist. He used the fist to make a living—hitting old people in hallways. Each one of the knuckles was clearly defined, covered with whitish scar tissue. This time when he spoke, he enunciated each word perfectly.

"Your Mama," he said, "takes it in the ear, man."

And with a quick flash of his left hand, he knocked the ball away.

It bounced toward The Kid's outstretched legs.

The fight started in the center, with both Juan and the Cat Man moving fluidly at the same time, and it exploded outward to each side. There was a flash of the red satin lining inside the cape; the Cat Man ducking smoothly from the waist with his left hand up to protect his face, his right hand reaching out for the offered boot. Then he spun back into a crouch, the sunlight catching the side of the blade on the throwing knife.

They spilled over toward the bench, some of them falling, others rising high and coming down crookedly. Inside the circle of dust and fists, the knife flickered on and off like a spotlight.

The bench disappeared inside the fight.

The Kid folded his arms in front and pulled in his legs.

"Shoes," he said. "Watch the shoes, *puñeta.*"

The knife blade glinted just beside his right eye.

One thousand fifty-one, one thousand fifty-two. Or whatever the hell it was. "Okay, okay," he said. "Hold it." He ducked his head slightly and picked off an incoming punch with his left hand. "*Hold* it, all right?" He pushed himself upright and looked around. Below his waist, the little kids were still fighting, rolling around and under the bench.

"Time," he said. "*Time.* Knock it off."

The Cat Man's face loomed up close from the right.

247

"How 'bout it, man?" he said.

The Kid shook his head. "Sloppy. Listen: we got to, you know, this wasn't near fast enough. We're supposed to be done and all the way across the street by this time."

"Awww, man. Your ass, man."

"No, listen: what do you think this is? What do you call it? A goddam ballet? You guys are staggering through this thing and I'm sitting here yawning. I don't know. And anyway—besides, I think we got to have a few more. Three, at least. Maybe five. I think maybe you can watch this and maybe still see through to right inside here."

The Cat Man nodded. "Five? You got five."

"I mean five that we know."

"Ain't no jive *strangers* in this park, man. I mean: like, I got 'em, you know 'em, you dig it?"

The Kid kicked out with his left leg, shaking one of the little ones off his ankle. "The shoes, watch the *shoes*," he said. He looked up. "Somebody here, all right, somebody get these little bastards to knock it off. We're up to our ass in little fights here."

Angel whistled once sharply. "*Mira, maricón, aguanta*," he said. "Damn *coño. Puñeta*. I'll bust some *cojones* here."

"Okay," The Kid said. "Who got the other knife?"

Angel nodded and patted his back pocket.

"I didn't see it."

"Ain't s'pose to. Doan worry, I could have had it in your nose three, four times; you wouldn't have seen it."

The Cat Man snapped his fingers. "Towel me," he said.

The towel boy stepped up and handed over the towel. He was holding it out so that the blood from his nose wouldn't drip onto the white terrycloth.

"Where's my main bootman?" the Cat Man said.

The boy got to his feet slowly, hugging the boots. He turned his head carefully to one side and spit up some pink foam.

"Awww, man," the Cat Man said. "I *tole* you. I'm talkin' and you ain't hearin' again. Man, I tole you, you ain't supposed to be doin' no fightin'. We *got* folks to fight, man. You take care of the *boots;* you jus' stay out of the way and handle the boots, man. Look at that. Now, go wan. Get your black ass over there and clean 'em *off,* you unnerstan' what I'm sayin' to you? I'm s'pose to wear boots lookin' like that?"

He turned back to The Kid. He shook out the towel and checked it carefully, turning it both ways. Then he began to dab carefully under his arms with it, blotting delicately at the crinkly hair.

"Okay," he said. "Okay, so we pick it up some. Man, like you cuttin' it pretty close if we s'pose go any faster."

The Kid shook his head. "No, you're still a little bit off. But, all right. It's coming. What I think we'll do, after today, what I think we'll do is to run a *play* through here. Right on through. It'll go faster that way all by itself, you got it? Same thing, see, except we run the play through here like this—and then we keep it moving right on over there. And across the street and out. You follow?"

They both turned and looked at MacDougal.

"I can dig it," the Cat Man said.

"All right,, day after tomorrow," The Kid said. "I mean, tomorrow you watch the bench here. You know, make sure you see how they do it with the shopping bags and all. Don't let them see you watching; just watch. Like I told you. Day after that, we work out again."

The Cat Man swung the towel out and a little hand was there to take it. He snapped his fingers and the satin shirt appeared in another hand. He shouldered into it and began on the buttons.

"This doan go like you say," he said, "an' somebody gonna get burned. Those big cats, you know, like they gonna haul off and *waste* a few folks around here."

"Not if they can't find 'em, they're not."

"You sure it's like you said?"

The Kid nodded. "It's like I said."

"I mean, you know: one whole sack. Like, full."

"Look: you saw the guy carry it in last week; he was all leaned over to one side from the weight of it, wasn't he?"

"Maybe he jus' built crooked."

"Your ass."

"Sheeee-it." The Cat Man adjusted the cape around his shoulders, looking down to make sure the gold clasp was squared just at the center of his shirt collar. "If it's like you say, man, I'm gonna be the king dude of this place, you dig? The king Diablo, man. Here's the way they gonna say it: they gonna say, 'Here come the Cat MAN.' Like that."

"I thought you already were," The Kid said.

"You got it." The Cat Man snapped his fingers again, and then looked at his fingernails. "Boots," he said.

The bootboy stepped up, holding them out. They glittered in the light.

The Cat Man turned and sat on the bench, swinging the cape out of the way. He bent over and began untying the Converse sneaks.

And when he spoke, it was without looking up. "What you do," he said, "when this is all over, I mean—like, what you do is, you take you a pile of them bills, see? You jus' take you a mess of them and you cut on out somewheres and get you a new *nose*. They got cats who do that; you find you one of them dudes and, like, you tell him, 'Lissen, my main man, you jus' make me a fine nose, hear? An' when you get it put on, you can jus' throw out this ol' smashed one.' You dig?" Now the Cat Man raised his head and looked. "Because one thing about you. I mean, you smart, all right. Like, you thinkin' and you talkin' and sayin' it *right*. You smart. But, man, I mean you sure some ugly."

250

The Kid looked at him for a long moment. And then he nodded.

"See you around," he said.

Icepick Sally had mentioned it, too. There are people, specialists, who rebuild noses.

He walked along slowly, glancing across the sidewalk at his reflection in the windows.

"The doctor has a lovely polished mahogany box," Sally had said. "Not a very deep box; just about this thick. It's hinged on one side. And the doctor swings it open and there are all these noses—all of them just sitting side by side inside there. All displayed on crushed mauve velvet, I think it is. One side of the box is a mirror. And you just reach in there and try on noses until you find the one that suits you best."

"How do you know all that?" he had asked.

"Sally knows everything," she had said.

And the image had stuck. Sally's stories did that to him. Sometimes at night he dreamed about reaching into the display box and trying on new noses, turning his head each way while he looked in the mirror.

He raised his head now and glanced into the faces of the people passing. Those few who glanced back didn't seem particularly shocked. Well, nobody jumped. Nobody turned away and puked. Maybe it wasn't . . .

But, see, that wasn't the point.

The *point* was, the whole goddam idea was, whether or not people in real life, real people, would go around looking like this. The people at the Plaza: hell, all their teeth were straight, too, and when they walked away, the air smelled like them where they had been standing. And they walked evenly, toes all lined up. They came out of the Palm Court and their lives were folded over neatly and sealed. It showed in their faces. Nothing bad happened to them. Otherwise it would show, somehow: a twitch, maybe. A downcurve at the mouth, maybe. A something.

And don't let them lay that bullshit on you about television. Who said, Miss Dolan, somebody—somebody said that you can't believe what you see on television. Easy to say; people were always going around saying it—but it was wrong. It doesn't take a lot of heavy figuring. Look: real life is crap, got that part? Okay. Television is not. What it is, it's the way things are supposed to be. Jesus, nobody seems to really understand that part. You don't look at the screen, you look *into* it, and you can see in there what life is supposed to be like. And that's it: if you can't believe in television, there's nothing to believe in.

He squared his back a bit more, as if maybe the camera truck was rolling alongside, the camera crew taping him in action. He could imagine just about how he would look from up on the truck:

The kid there, that one. Walking in the crowd. That's him. You got him; now zoom in a touch, give me a bigger image. Right, you got it. Clean faded jeans, the running shoes. Can you get me a closer shot of the shoes, Harry? Fine. They're Puma Tigers, see? Nice touch. Very Americana, Harry. Nice-looking shirt the kid is wearing. Maybe J. Press, would you say? Umm, Chipps, maybe. No, got to be Paul Stuart.

The Kid slowed down his pace now, turning his face slightly toward the street. That would be a better camera angle for someone in a camera truck.

If Dan Rather were to jump off the truck now. You know, come off the truck carrying the microphone with the long cord trailing behind, The Kid would be able to handle it. The Kid was getting better and better at handling stuff.

Dan Rather would probably fall in step alongside; it

would be that kind of an interview—with both of them walking casually side by side, street sounds in the background. And Dan Rather would do the intro:

"Since last we talked to The Kid," he would say, "the scene has changed. We are now in Greenwich Village. Art colony, literary hideaway, gay community, true—but more recently the turf of vicious kid gangs. When last we talked to The Kid, he was at Rockefeller Center, some twenty-five or thirty blocks away in terms of distance, but a world away in lifestyle. What are you up to now, Kid?"

And The Kid would raise his eyebrows, not smiling.

"I'm coaching a basketball team," he would say.

Awww, balls. Put Dan Rather back on the damn truck.

Some basketball team. He could take the Diablos right now and play, who? And play North Carolina State. Scrub them up a touch, you know. Get them to stand still for the national anthem. And then send them in. Never mind plays. *Plays*, for God's sake? You've already got the fast break and you've got a center who wears a cape and who can go up for a rebound and come down with a knife out.

Or a guard. You've got a guard who does a little Calvin Murphy spin on you at the top of the key—and you look down and there's a red line right across the middle of your stomach. And coming right along behind the red line, everything suddenly falls right out onto the floor. Everybody looks shocked. The college guys lose, North Carolina State. That's what kind of team he had.

He had had them at it for two weeks now, ever since that day Icepick Sally had showed him the exchange at the playground.

He had gone straight over that evening. Over to the new Diablo clubhouse in the burned-out building on Eleventh. The gang was still in the process of stripping it, selling the pipes and tearing out the plumbing. They had already sold all the stuff that had been left behind by the old folks.

The Cat Man had been full of PCP again.

He called it Angel Dust. Sometimes he called it Busy Bee. It was also called Elephant, but the Cat Man couldn't say Elephant.

What it was, it was, what do you call it? It was phencyclidine. Faster than T's and V's, Tuinals and Valiums. And no waiting: just sprinkle it on and suck it up with the smoke, man.

The Cat Man said it made the inside of his head sing.

It had taken a long time to get through. The Cat Man had been sitting huddled inside his cape in a bare apartment. He had been sitting on a mattress on the bare floor, the derby down to the bridge of his nose. He had been admiring his long, graceful hands. The introduction had gone about the same as always:

"Cut your white ass," the Cat Man had said. "You didn't carry 'at thing. What you call 'at thing?"

"It's a gutter," The Kid had said.

"Like, it pulls out . . ."

"One snick," The Kid had said, "and I can string your stomach from here over there to the door. Got it?"

And then they had talked business.

The Cat Man blinked his way through it: "What you tellin' me, what you sayin' is, you can fix it so's I can get my hands on that bagful of stuff."

"Right, right. Now, listen," The Kid had said. "The way I make it is this: it's got to be pure. Got to be. Because they wouldn't go to all that trouble with making the switch if it was already cut—if it was already street stuff. They could just drive up in a car and throw it out the window."

"Pure. If it's pure, you know what you talkin' about?" the Cat Man had said. "You standin' there talkin' about a shopping bag full. A load that size, man, a load like that.

254

You cut it—you jus' cut it *normal*, man—and you know how much stuff you end up with to sell?"

"A lot."

"Lot. Sheeee-*it*, man. Lot? You talkin' about a *room*ful of stuff. You talkin' big money, man."

"Do you know how to cut it?" The Kid had said.

And the Cat Man had shrugged grandly under the cape, his fingers all spread out. "Like, do I know how to cut it? Like, do Pinocchio have a wooden ass? What you askin' the Cat Man, you askin' do I know? '*Course* I know."

"All right, then. You got it all."

"You in?"

"No, I'm out," The Kid had said. "You get to keep all the stuff—the whole bag. I get the other bag. Now, your stuff is un*cut*—are you following me here? Uncut. So you cut it and you end up with ten—maybe twelve times more money than is in the bag. Got it? But okay. I can't wait and you can. So you get to take the stuff. I take the other bag and I'm gone."

The Cat Man had shaken his head no.

"But, man, they got, they got somebody watchin', man. You know, you talking about 'at stuff, you talking about the big men, man. They ain't gonna . . ."

"What's to watch? You ever see anybody watching? That's the idea behind them doing it that way—right out there in the open. There's nothing to watch for if there's nothing to *see*."

"Jive-ass cop," the Cat Man had said.

"What cop?"

"Man, what cop? Keith *Lee* cop, is what cop. Man, like he's their Main Man. *He's* watchin'. He *paid* to watch."

The Kid hadn't known about that. So he had put it this way: "I *know* that," he had said.

"So?"

"So I got a plan. Look: I'll take care of the cop."

"You gonna . . ."

"Listen," The Kid had said. "You come down off the dust; you just burn down off it and then come and see me."

Well, all right. He did have a plan.

Officer Keith Lee could watch what he liked to watch best.

The Kid would watch the basketball game.

Very nice. That way, everybody watches, everybody wins.

30

JEWEL RODRIGUEZ

She could hear him breathing. It was just the same as it always was when she did this: he was breathing through his mouth and it sounded wet.

She pulled the tee shirt up over her head and held it there for a moment, letting the bracelets slide down her arms toward her elbows. Then she dropped the shirt and shook her hair loose.

She was now naked in the dusty yellow light.

His feet twitched, suddenly going sort of toes-out. The only thing she could see was his feet in the tasseled golf shoes. The darkness cut off the rest of him. He was sitting on the floor with his back against the wall, just where the shaft from the skylight cut off into total shadow.

She held both arms out and turned slowly. She looked down at her stomach. The glass up there in that old skylight above was all dirty, man, and it had gone all yellowish over the years. And where the beams of light slanted down onto the grayed carpet, the air was full of lazy specks of dust.

But she was pure gold now. And she was shining gold all under her arms where she was sweating.

You dig that gold color, don't you, pig? You jus' want to rub your head against all that mellow yellow, right, big pig?

And she could smell him, too. Man, that heavy leaf tobacco and cedar smell drifting out, just sort of oozing out of the dark where he sat. Sometimes it took a couple of days to get the smell off of herself after she did one of these. Man, she would lay in bed at night and still smell him. The fingermarks he left on her arms smelled like him.

She turned again, snapping her fingers and swinging her hips. Now the backs of her knees were slick with sweat. In this light, they would look like gold lightly coated with olive oil.

Mama had taught her to dance like this. Mama used to do this uptown at the *Met*rople, man, and Mama said that the men used to half climb up on top of the bar, spilling their bottles of beer, just to stuff bills down into her G-string. Mama would dance until two o'clock and turn tricks until five and then come home. Mama would be asleep when Jewel got up, the G-string all rinsed out and hanging on the bathroom doorknob.

Shake it for him. Show it to him.

He was breathing wetter now. Heavier. Fine. You jus' keep sittin' in the dark and blinkin' and breathin', man.

She wondered if he would see the scratch across her stomach from The Kid's whatever that thing was—the thing he carried that cut you and pulled your guts out. The gutter. Officer Keith Lee didn't like for her to have any marks on her body anywhere. He had warned her.

Well. Except for his big old fingermarks.

Man, like The Kid was bad news; you could feel it about him. He didn't laugh, he didn't cry. He didn't shoot up and he didn't even smoke Elephant. Didn't sell T's and V's to get money, man. You couldn't tell what was going on behind his face. Didn't live anyplace. Man, you'd jus' sort of look around one time and there The Kid would be, his eyelids half down, jus' lookin' at you. An' you talk to him and you could tell that The Kid had all his feelers out, man, even if he jus' seemed to be, like, talkin'. The Kid liked to know where everybody was all the time. Every time she asked The Kid for money, he would just give it to her; no jive-ass about it—just hand over a couple of bills, never changing that god-awful face of his. Man, that flat ol' smashed face that looked like someone had hit him straight on with the back of a coal shovel.

Keep dancing: she was sweating all over now. She bent her knees slightly, legs far apart, swung her pelvis forward and rubbed the palms of her hands down the tops of her thighs, the way Mama had showed her.

You dig that, Officer Lee? You see the owl, baby?

She had been surprised that The Kid had known about her doing this under the skylight.

"How'd The Kid know?" the Cat Man had said. "Like, man, everybody in the worl' *knows*. I mean, like you doan have to show them the bite marks on your tiny ass for them to know. Like, you could sell *tickets*, you dig it? Ain't no secret, you and the man up there on that top landing. But that ain't the point. What the point is, you jus' do what The Kid says you s'pose to do. No jive-ass now: Kid says you go up there an' dance, you go dance."

So she had gone and gotten Officer Keith Lee.

And now she glanced over at his feet in the golf shoes. They were pulling back slightly. That meant that he would be leaning forward from the wall now.

Sure enough: his two hands slowly came out of the dark. Two disembodied hands coming out into the shaft of light. You couldn't see the arms, just those two big hands.

The backs of the hands were covered thick with red-

259

dish-tan hair. The hair was standing out now, all curly and bristly. And his voice came out of the black. "Come here," it said.

She swallowed hard twice. She stepped forward into the two hands.

"I don't care if he makes you want to puke," The Kid had said. "You just do what, whatever it is he wants. Don't tell me about it. Just do it like I told you."

The palms of the big hands were hot and wet around her hips. The thumbs pointed inward, pressing down into the matching hollows of her groin.

"Now, then," he said. "Now, then. You goddam little criminal. We're going to . . ."

Then the left thumb swung inward, sliding along her wet skin. And there was a pause.

She waited, swallowing some more. What the hell was he going to . . . ?

He was looking at his watch. That's what he was doing. With his hands in the light and his face back in the dark, he was reading his wristwatch. No. Not now.

"God *damn*," he said.

She staggered back when he pushed her away. She could sense an uncoiling in the dark and the tobacco-and-cedar smell rose with him as he stood up.

His voice came from way above the top of her head. "Got to go," he said. "Damn. I forgot about today. The hell's the matter with me?"

Okay, Jewel-babe. Like Mama always said. Time to do your move. Lay it on him.

She left the pillar of gold light and stepped into the dark with him. She put both arms around his thighs and put her cheek against his stomach.

"Not yet," she said. "Don't go now, man. We gonna have the fun part now. Like, now the show starts. It's show time."

"Come on. Move it." One of the hands came around fast and caught her on the neck.

She fell away, hitting the wall with her head, and slid down to the floor. She doubled over, curling up into a ball to protect her stomach in case he kicked.

But his footsteps were clattering back down the stairs.

"Damn," he said at the first landing. Then, on the next landing down: "Damn," he said.

She rose to her knees, rubbing at her neck. Then she stood and looked around. She stepped over to the pile of clothes and kicked them apart with one toe. She bent quickly and grabbed the cotton underpants and stepped into them and pulled them up. Then the cutoffs. Where the hell was the tee shirt? There wasn't much time.

Time to go, man. Got to *go*. Miss the show.

She wheeled and started up the stairs that led to the roof.

She had done just a little bit better than The Kid had told her to do.

"I want you to keep dancing," The Kid had said. "And then, whatever else it is. But make it last a long time."

Dig it. She had danced. But never mind the other part.

Man, that was because, when she had come away from him in the dark, she had come away with his gun. Right out of his waistband.

Look at that muffkin' gun. Shiny, goddam *heavy* goddam gun, man. Lord, look at it shine so.

But there wasn't much time.

It was 6:30 P.M.

31

THE CAT MAN

6:30 P.M.

The knife turned once in the air. Blade down—and then blade up and around. It drove through the sandwich in the man's hand. Through the salami, the baked pimento, the provolone and on into the man's chest, carrying the rounded half of the hard roll with it and pinning it there like a medal.

The man looked down at the knife handle in surprise. He still had his empty hand in the air, the fingers apart in exactly the space where the sandwich had been.

Perfect. Like, only *perfecto*, man. The Cat Man had thrown the knife on the run, a full-arm, bad-ass, all-power swing, the kind of swing with that knife that could pin an alley cat to a steel beam, man.

The knife had flashed just alongside Angel's neck on its way to the target. Which was also *perfecto*, since Angel had been setting a sort of pick on the man sitting on the bench so that he wouldn't see the Cat Man coming.

And now Angel was bringing his own left hand up on the other man, the man holding the beer. Angel was all crouched and swinging up fast from his knees. His switchblade was already open.

The blade went full length into the man's stomach, just between his hands. The man was holding a can of beer in each hand.

The Cat Man half turned in the air, his cape swinging open, and tossed his right boot to the bootboy. "Take on off," he said. "Scat."

The players had already encircled the bench when the Cat Man had thrown, and now they closed in more tightly, creating a thick jungle of waving arms and bobbing heads. From outside the moving jungle, from the bar across the street or from up close, it was impossible to see through to the bench.

The basketball rolled off alone to the right.

"Get 'em up on they feet," the Cat Man said. "Gimme them shoppin' bags. Come on, shake it."

The two men came off the bench fast, lifted by hands in front and hands in back. The circle of players closed in around them.

"Okay, les' haul it," the Cat Man said.

The sandwich man was already dead. His head was down as if he was still looking at the half sandwich pinned to his shirt. But the head rolled back and forth loosely, negatively, like he couldn't believe what he was seeing.

A single track of blood started down from underneath the bread, moving slowly, carrying a piece of lettuce with it.

The players dragged him along on the tips of his toes.

The beer man was shuffling, toed in, forced along by the hands holding him. He was swinging his head from side to side, licking at his lips and saying, "Oh, God, oh, God."

The Cat Man held both shopping bags in his left hand and swung the cape around them.

"Get the ball, the ball," he said.

And the tight knot of players moved off toward Mac-Dougal. Two players danced out in front of the pack, dribbling the basketball and passing it quickly back and forth between them.

"Oh, *God*," the beer man said. "Lissen: put me down just a second. I got to breathe."

"Keep him up," the Cat Man said. "Up, *up*. Man, like somebody get this dude by the ass, somethin'. Lift. Come on."

"Lissen," the beer man said.

"Ain't no way," the Cat Man said. "Jus' keep dancin', pop."

"Best not to kill them," The Kid had said. "You don't have to waste anybody, all you got to do is get the shopping bags. Look: you burn one of those guys and there's going to be big trouble around here after I'm gone. Not me, it's you they're going to be tracking down. Just the bags."

But hump the humpin' Kid. What did The Kid know, man?

The circle of players reached the street and started across. To the left, a taxicab slid to a stop, the horn howling.

"Lissen to me," the beer man said. "This is . . . oh, God. This is bad trouble you got. You know who it is you're messing with? Who you're . . . oh, Jesus, my gut. Who you're dealing with here? This shipment, oh, oh, those guys won't let you get, oh, get away with, oh, oh. Oh, *God*."

"Man, like somebody shut him to hell up," the Cat Man said.

Angel drove the switchblade into the beer man from behind, right up under the left shoulder blade. The breath came out of the beer man in a sudden whoosh. He stopped talking. He began to huff reddish-yellow foam out of his mouth.

"Lift," the Cat Man said.

The circle of players went up and over the curb, undulating like a humpbacked animal. They moved into the alley.

The Kid stepped out from where he had been leaning against the building.

The circle of players came to a stop.

The Kid looked inside the circle at the two men. He looked at them for a long moment. Then he looked at the Cat Man. With both looks, his expression stayed the same.

"You doan like it?" the Cat Man said.

The Kid shrugged. "It's your game. I don't play basketball."

"Here's your bag," the Cat Man said.

"Okay."

"You losin'," the Cat Man said. "You unnerstan' what I'm sayin' to you? Like, I mean this *here* bag is heavy, man. I cut this stuff, I got like, you know, I got big money. You got a few bills in there is all, man. Doan look like much. You run through that, you got nothin' left to *sell*, you dig? 'Less you wanna stay and cut, man."

"Can't."

"You stupit, man."

"Maybe so."

"Stupit." The Cat Man reached over and picked up the beer man's limp left arm. He looked at the watch on the wrist and then let the arm fall away. It hit against the man's side and bounced once. Now he looked back at The Kid.

"Better shake your honky ass," he said.

"How come?"

" 'Cause in 'bout five minutes, I burn this place down," the Cat Man said.

"Down where?"

The Cat Man looked back over his shoulder. "Like the whole block where you live at. You unnerstan' what I'm sayin' to you? Look: I *know* where you live, stupit. I known for a while. I see you comin' and I see you goin'. So I'm tellin' you now: your whole muffkin' block coming down s'evenin'. And, like, these here two cats here gonna be found like burned ashes in the roons. You dig it, what I'm sayin'? Like, say they couldn't get out of the *build*-ing, man. Ain't no Mafia gonna chase nobody, his man jus' goes up in smoke, dig it? And anyway . . ."

"Anyway?"

"And anyway, man, you know I dig fires, man."

The Kid nodded. "I know."

The Cat Man nodded back at him, grinning. "So if you stayin' wif' me, stay. But if you runnin', like, you better run now."

The Kid looked back down the block, back at the distance he had to run.

It was 6:35 P.M.

32

OFFICER KEITH LEE

Damn bench was empty. Look at it: nobody there.

It was 6:35 P.M.

It figured. It had to figure. He had known that the bench would be empty all the time he had been running down the block. In fact, about the minute he had gotten to the bottom of the stairs back there and had discovered that his gun was gone, he had known that the bench would be empty. And that was item number one.

Item number two was that there wasn't any basketball game going on. Empty playground. Empty bench. It frigging *fig*ured.

Not now. Not today. Cóme on, Lord. If there's a God that looks after cops—you know, even horny cops, all cops —then be there just this one time.

You know: maybe it's nothing. Maybe those two guys just made the switch a little earlier today. You know: maybe nobody just happened to be playing basketball today. One time, okay, Lord? You got it?

No way.

He pushed open the door and stepped into O'Halloran's.

"Never mind shining the glasses," Keith Lee said. "Put the glass down. Listen: where's Mister Martino?"

Harry blinked at him. "Ain't come in today. He don't always come in. You know. He leaves it to you."

"Where're the two guys?"

"Mmmmm?"

"God damn it. The guys. Come on. Two guys across the street over there. Playground. The two guys on the *bench*, right?"

"They were there."

"But not now."

Harry looked out the window. "No. Not now."

"They were there early?"

"Mmmmmm, no. Same time."

"And the game?"

"What game?"

"Come on, come on. Come *on*. Basketball game, damn it."

"What's a matter with you, Lee?"

Keith Lee put the flats of both hands on the bar and leaned over it. "The bas–ket–ball game, Harry. In a minute, I take this whole bar and, this whole bar, and it goes right up your ass."

Harry wrinkled his forehead. "All right, all right. So calm down, already. Lissen: you got veins standing out on your neck like *snakes*, Lee. Sure. They played basketball. Like always. Big deal. They just left, just now. All in a bunch. Headed over to MacDougal."

"In a *what*?"

"Bunch."

"What does that mean?"

"Bunch," Harry said. "A circle of kids. You know, all at once. They . . ."

"And the guys. The two guys on the bench?"

Harry thought about it for a moment. He absently reached for a glass and the dishcloth. "I din't see them after that, the two guys."

Keith Lee turned and walked to the window.

He sighted through the O in O'Halloran's painted on the window, looking at the empty bench across the street. He moved his head slightly and looked out through the uprights on the letter H, like football goalposts.

What it was, it was trouble time if he didn't do something here.

Okay: think. *Think*, for chrissakes. Come on. Think of something.

Okay: he could go home and get the other gun. His regulation service piece. And take out Mister Martino. Make it look like, you know, like somebody else . . .

. . . and then, mmmmm. Okay: Martino goes. And then, uhhh, then . . . oh, *Christ*. There was Jewel. Okay: Jewel, too. She would be sure to show up somewhere with the Magnum. Sure as hell, and then everybody would know that it was his gun. Damn kid. Not worth it, tiny buns and all. So, okay. First Jewel and then Martino. She'd go tonight. Off the goddam roof.

He spoke without turning around: "What'd you say?"

"I said sirens on Tenth Street," Harry said. "You hear all the sirens?"

"Screw the sirens," Keith Lee said. "Screw you, too."

Come on: think of something.

He moved his head slightly again and looked out through the little o in the O'Halloran's sign.

And he stiffened.

The kid was coming across the park at a full run. And he was carrying one of the shopping bags.

Well, thank you, Lord. By God, you've *done* it.

He wheeled around on Harry. "Gimmie your gun."

Harry's eyebrows went up.

"Gun?" he said. "I ain't got . . ."

"The gun, the *gun*," Keith Lee said. "Don't give me any of that you-ain't got. Just gimme the *gun*, man."

Harry reached under the bar and lifted up the sawed-off. "I know it's illegal and all," he said. "But, you know. It's just in case we . . ."

Keith Lee grabbed it and ran for the door. He paused for one step and broke open the shotgun and glanced down at the round butt ends of the two shells. Then he snapped it closed and kicked open the door and stepped out onto the sidewalk.

"Freeze," he said.

The kid skidded to a stop.

"Hold it right there," Keith Lee said. He swung the shotgun up to hip level, holding it slightly away from his side.

You don't really have to aim a sawed-off. Any place will do: a sawed-off shotgun is a hamburger-maker.

The kid stood there. His chest went up and down regularly with his breathing. His hair was swirled down across his forehead. His face was exactly the way his face always was.

Keith Lee nodded at him. "Just drop the bag," he said.

Thank you, Lord. Boy, Lord, I'll tell you. One minute you've got a guy down and in trouble and the next minute everything is okay. And now it would be okay. Part of the secret of being a good cop is being lucky. Right, Lord?

The kid turned his head slowly and looked to the side.

Keith Lee turned his head slowly and checked where the kid was looking.

Jewel Rodriguez was at the corner.

She was on her bare knees on the sidewalk, her legs braced apart. She was holding the chrome-plated Magnum in both hands. She was holding it at arm's length and aiming it.

Keith Lee saw the flash. He didn't hear the sound.

Then he could feel the stuffing coming out of his back.

And then he heard the sound: it was O'Halloran's window shattering behind him.

Okay, okay. Just a second here and we're gonna have *two* dead kids.

He looked down at his golf sweater.

There was a small hole there now. It was precisely—by God, look at *that*. It was exactly where the little alligator symbol would go if this was a Lacoste golf sweater instead of a Sears Men's Store Johnny Miller sweater. The little alligator would go right where the hole was now. In fact, if there *had* been a little alligator on the . . .

What the hell?

He couldn't seem to get his shoulders out of O'Halloran's window.

And the back of his sweater. He had forgotten. When the Magnum had flashed like that, the whole damn *back* had come out of his sweater.

Old Missus Schwartz at the cleaners would have a fit when she saw that.

He sank to his knees. He looked at the kid.

The kid was sliding into soft focus. Back to you in a minute, kid. Don't go away.

He swung his head around and looked at Jewel.

Golden girl. All shimmery and pure gold. You should have, you should have *seen* her up there, all naked under that skylight, Lord. I mean: all sort of salty and slippery with sweat and all shiny and . . .

He smiled at her. Give her the big smile. It did it to them every time. Women of all ages the world over. Everybody in the Village. All he had to do was smile and they all loved him. Johnny Miller should only have a smile like this one.

And Jewel smiled back at him, sighting down the pistol. It flashed again, brightly.

The shell took out his two front teeth going in, and all of the back of his neck coming out.

Keith Lee went over backward, until he hit the wall just underneath O'Halloran's window. Then he sat with his legs twisted under him.

What was that? Come again. I can't hear you over those damn sirens. Somebody yelling at somebody.

Oh, oh. That was it: someone was saying: *Run*, kid.

It was the last thing he heard.

33

THE KID

Things to think about while running:

Thing number one: it was 6:45 P.M. Moving time.

And two: the first bursts of fire were already starting to show, glowing pink in all the top windows. Jesus, the whole block was going to burn. There were fire trucks down at the far end. Guys in those black raincoats with the white lettering stenciled on the back. And people—the old folks—were starting to look out their windows.

Come on, let's go.

Three: Jewel had kept on shooting that gun. After she had yelled for him to run, she had swung around and leveled it on the big cop again. God, the look on Officer Lee's face: he had bared all his teeth like a trapped animal—maybe he thought that he was smiling or something —and Jewel had shot his face in half. The Kid had looked back over his shoulder once at the corner. Jewel was still firing, hitting the cop with every shot. She was turning him into pudding.

Where'd she get a gun like that, you suppose? All she had been supposed to do was dance. And maybe whatever else. Hell, she could have gotten away with it. They all could have pulled it off, even the Diablos. But this whole place was crazy now.

Step it up.

Four: The Cat Man and the players would be circling around here somewhere now. Stash those two dead guys in one of these buildings and let them burn. That probably wouldn't work, either. Cat Man's problem. Cat Man had the stuff, and The Kid had the cash.

Five: it hadn't looked like very much money in the shopping bag. And he hadn't figured on the denominations. How do you go and cash brand-new-looking hundreds without, you know, without somebody saying something? But okay, no time to worry about that now. If there was any place in town you could do it, you could do it at the Plaza. You could do anything at the Plaza.

He swung in at the hollowed sandstone steps and started up. Hell with Eleventh Street and going around the air shaft. This was going to have to be a front-door day.

He started up the inside stairs.

Even more things to think about:

Icepick Sally was going to look just goddam great coming along in her pea coat and long underwear. What the hell was he going to do about that? Well, thing is, she'd *have* to come with him now, want to or not. Only way to get her out of this place was to burn it down around her head.

All right, something. She was coming and that was it. Stop off somewhere on the way uptown and run her through a car wash or something.

You know: first get her all clean. Then get her hair fixed; whatever it is they do. Get her some clothes somewhere. Some really nice-looking old-lady clothes.

Tell her to remember not to smile and show those teeth.

He put the shopping bag down outside the door and got out the keys.

It still said:

YOU

AIN'T

GOT

NO

DOG

scratched on the door. The super had said, he had told Sally, that he would paint it out maybe if he ever got hold of some paint, but with the rents they were getting here, you couldn't expect a body to just go around painting things any time somebody wanted something painted.

He unlocked both locks and pushed the door open. He picked up the shopping bag and walked in.

"Sally," he said. He was breathing hard through his mouth.

She was already talking. She was standing at the hot plate with the enameled teakettle in one hand and one of the good Lenox china cups in the other. She poured boiling water into the cup.

". . . history of Greenwich Village," she was saying, "and it's all right here in this room." She stopped and squinted at him. "And, uhhh. Press? Mmmm, it *is*. Press, it's you. How very nice."

"Sally," he said. "Now, listen. Just listen. We got to go and we haven't got much time. Just put the teapot down— don't drop anything—just put it down and I'll tell you what we have to do."

She blinked at him. "Go? Where?"

"The Plaza. It's time now."

"But, my dear," she said. "I told you that I . . ."

"The *build*ing's on fire," he said. "Diablos are burning the building down. They've got the whole block on fire."

Sally turned and put the kettle back on the hot plate. She shook her head. "But . . . but, they can't do that. Why, that's *terrible*. Not when we've got *company*."

"Comp—" He turned and looked where Sally was nodding.

And there she was:

Marion Dolan was standing in the shadowy part of the room next to the chest of drawers. She was holding one of the teacups in her hands. Her head and shoulders were in the darkness; the front part of her stomach pushed out into the light. She made a slight forward nod with her head.

"You've got company," she said. "It's good to see you again, dear."

He took some shallow breaths, using the time to get his face into exactly the right look. "How did . . . ?"

"How did I find you? It wasn't easy. And no thanks to the police. They're terrible in this district. Or did you want to know how I got in here?" She stepped forward into the light. "Press, dear, you look so wonderful. Every time I see you, I just . . . ummmm, well. Never mind. How did I get in here? Well, I simply introduced myself to Miss Sally here and she was kind enough to invite me in."

"Isn't she marvelous?" Sally said. "Miss Dolan is here to help you; she told me that. It's just like a *fairy* tale, really. You need help and suddenly she . . ."

"Tell me," Marion Dolan said, "is the building really on fire? Or is that another one of your little fancies?"

He shook his head. "It's on fire."

"And where is the fire now?"

"Top floor."

She came another step into the center of the room. "Then we've got some time?"

"Not much."

"Well, I'll just put on some more water and make us some more tea," Sally said. "Here, Miss Dolan, I'll take the cup."

Marion Dolan handed it over without taking her eyes from The Kid's face. She came in another step.

She had grown a lot bigger since the last time he had seen her. Her hands and arms were puffed, like they were filled up tightly with water under pressure.

"You'll never know how terrible it's been," she said.

He backed up one step. "Miss Dolan. The goddam *building* is on fire."

She reached out with one hand and it filled the air between them.

"You did a terrible thing to me," she said.

The hand stayed there, but she spread out all the fingers. Each one was thick. She was now looking at him through the spaces between her fingers.

"Terrible," she said.

"Will everybody want cream and sugar?" Sally said. "Well, milk, I mean. I haven't got any real cream."

"But that's not why I'm here," Marion Dolan said, not moving. "Not at all, my dear boy. I forgave you *that*. I do not forget, but I forgive." She began to reach forward slowly with the big hand. "I am here for another reason. I have, I have thought only about you since . . . do you know what that means? Can you comprehend the way you dominate my thoughts? No, of course you can't. Through the night, every hour of the day. My child—and my failure. My pèrfect child. I haven't been able to think of anything, anyone else."

"Water'll be hot in just another minute," Sally said.

And finally the hand arrived: the fat fingers got him by the shirt collar and the hand began to pull him toward her.

"My perfect boy," Marion Dolan said. "You didn't know it, but you were. You were perfect. Not another child like you. Perhaps the advance model of the child we'll be breeding in generations to come. You are created entirely by what you see and what you take in. Unable to react to anything. Unable to react to love, because you didn't have it when you needed it. They wouldn't believe me about you. And then you took me down with you when you left. Down into your other-world."

She pulled him all the way in. She was breathing through her mouth and her breath smelled black.

"Unstable," she said. "They called me unstable, did you know that? Of course you didn't. My psychiatrist, he . . . the talk about paranoia. I could have been *famous*. But not now; now I'm ruined. Well. Nobody ruins Marion Dolan."

He thought about Mama. Why do you suppose Mama, at a time like this? It just jumped into his mind: Mama's big shadow on the ceiling, straddled over a fat man, riding him like a horse. Mama, who wouldn't come and get him when they took him away and sat him down on that long bench. She never came, ever, Mama. And he thought about the street: looking into all the faces and nobody ever looking back. And television. Dan Rather had never seen his Mama's shadow on the ceiling.

"So tell me, perfect child," she said. "What do you feel now? At last, now? What are you thinking about behind your serene little mask? An honest emotion. Not a *reaction*, Elvis Presley Reynolds, my love. An emotion. Tell me."

He took in as much breath as he could get in.

"You'll never know," he said. "You'll die not knowing."

She hit him with her other hand. The class ring on her little finger punched a hole into his cheek.

"What in the *world*?" Sally said from across the room.

Now, quickly, the big round face in front of his was going all blotchy. It was exploding into patches of milky white under the rouge. A long vein rose up across the center of her forehead like a piece of pinkish string pasted there.

Off to one side, he could hear the teakettle whistle. It was whistling on the same level as the sirens outside.

Marion Dolan hit him again while he twisted, trying to break her grip. He saw her hand draw back: more blood was collecting all around the outside edge of the college graduation ring on the little finger.

"What are you . . . ?" Sally said. "Miss *Dolan!* Stop!"

They fell. The broken section of the blue camelback couch was cutting him across the shoulders. His legs were straight out in front. And then Marion Dolan was on her knees, hitting him.

"Kill you," she said. There was gray spit swinging at both corners of her mouth. "You're mine. Always have been mine; I invented you." She struck again. "I'll throw, I'll drape your body over the director's desk. I'll throw you down there dead and we'll *see* who wins. I *loved* you."

She hit him again, putting more weight into it.

She rose up on her knees. She lifted the front of her skirt with both hands. He could see the thick white ribbing on the corset running down her legs. She swung one leg over him and lowered the knee on the other side of his waist, pinning him between her thighs. She began squeezing inward. And then she began pumping her hips back and forth. She was trembling—big shivers that were shaking her clothes while she hit at him.

"Loved you," she said. "Loved you, my tiny love. My baby. Ohhhhh, God, my baby. Love-boy. Love, love, love . . ."

She was squeezing his life out. His vision was getting shadowy. He tried to blink it away.

Who, who was that?

It was Sally. She was just squatting there, looking on. Sally, for Christ's sake, Sally . . .

No. No, Sally wasn't just looking. She was lifting her right hand out of the pea-coat pocket.

Marion Dolan's fist blocked out his view. And then her hand drew back again and he could see.

It was an icepick. A rusty, broken-tipped icepick.

Sally gripped it like a dagger. She swung it high over her head, rising up on her knees with the motion. And then she drove it down fast, straight into one of the giant thighs. She bent and pulled at it with both hands, twisting, straining to get it back out. She raised it and drove it in again.

"...love-baby." Marion Dolan stopped hitting, her hand drawn back alongside her ear. She blinked several times. She looked down at her leg.

She swung her arm and swept Sally aside. There was a swirl of cotton skirts and legs in long underwear.

Marion Dolan was panting hard. Her chin was shining with spit.

They both looked at the blue enameled handle of the icepick planted in her thigh. They both reached for it.

Marion Dolan got it, closing her hand around it and pulling it out with a twisting wrench.

She bent forward again, until all he could see was her wide shoulders turned inward toward him.

And she drove the icepick into his stomach. She leaned her weight forward on the handle, rotating it in a small circle. Then she leaned back and pulled it out. She held it up and looked at the rusty shaft, as if she was seeing it for the first time. She looked back down at him. She squeezed in again with the thighs.

"I loved you," she said.

She half rose again on her knees and hunched over him. She held the icepick between the palms of her hands and she came forward slowly, until the broken point rested just at his abdomen. She hunched her shoulders forward. Closer, until one breast was draped on each side of his face.

"Did you ever love me?" she said. Her spit was dripping down into his face.

Okay, where was everybody? The pain kept coming in

280

hard, stinging waves. The inside of his mouth had gone all dry.

But, all right, then. One time. One final time for all the guys on the camera truck. And one time for Dan Rather. See The Kid take a shaky breath. See The Kid blink hard and try to get things in focus. This one is for you, Dan Rather, and for the guys working on the camera. The ender, while the second hand sweeps around. The program has gone bad, but what the hell, as we say in television. Never show them how you really feel. Show them some class. He twisted his head back and looked up until he could see into her eyes.

"We're a little late, folks," he said. "So goodnight."

And she came forward slowly, shoving the icepick in all the way, leaning against it.

He could feel all of his breath go out.

He rolled his head to one side.

He could see Sally now. Fuzzy, but there she was. And all in slow motion.

Sally was standing up. She was standing just at Marion Dolan's shoulder. All in slow motion, Sally was reaching out with one hand. Slowly, she was sinking all her fingers into the back of Marion Dolan's hair. And slowly, she was bending the head back.

And back and back.

And with her other hand, Icepick Sally was slowly tilting the teakettle, which was still whistling with the boiling water.

And slowly—really so slow and pretty—Sally was pouring the water down onto Marion Dolan's face.

34

THE KID

The Kid does tricks. See The Kid lean against the banister so casually. See The Kid raise his eyebrows so easily and nod his head slightly forward at the approach of the fireman in the black rubber raincoat.

The trick is that The Kid can't really stand up. That's why he is leaning against the banister. Otherwise The Kid would fall down the stairs to the bottom.

"You okay?" the fireman said. "You hear me all right? I was asking you if there was anybody else up here."

The Kid shook his head no. "No," he said. "I'm the last one."

"Well, then move it," the fireman said. "Come on. I come running up here, you're standing here like you're taking in the sights or something. Damn building, whole building's gonna come down on your head here in a minute. Let's go."

The Kid nodded. He bent and picked up the Mark Cross bag, the genuine leather, golden tan, with the initials E. P. R. stamped in gold on the strap. He started down the stairs behind the fireman. He held tightly to the railing and he blinked to keep the fireman in focus. The white-stenciled letters kept wavering in and out, getting all soft.

The fireman turned his head again.

"You're sure nobody else?"

"Nobody else," The Kid said.

The roar of sound came behind them. A puff of hot wind came down the stairwell.

"Well, doesn't matter now," the fireman said. "There goes that ceiling anyways. Come on. Listen: am I gonna have to carry you out of here?"

"I can make it," The Kid said.

Come on, then: one foot down, then the other foot. The backs of his legs were shaking. His stomach was starting to swell out. The pain was swinging away and then in again hard, so hard that it hurt all the way down the fronts of his legs.

He looked down to see if any blood was showing through the front of his pants yet.

No, not yet.

He went out through the broken glass doors and down the hollowed sandstone steps.

How beautiful: the whole sky was yellow and red, all of it filtered through smoke. All the way across. The fire went all up and down the block. The fire was coughing, making a giant breathing sound.

Who was that talking? There was the voice again:

"Listen," the fireman said. "You gonna get your little ass out of here? You want to lean against things, get the hell off this block and lean against anything you want, all right? Now, move it."

The Kid moved it, walking down the sidewalk, wearing the new blazer and carrying the Mark Cross bag. One of the other tricks The Kid does: walking like he knows where he's going.

There was Sergeant Boggs. Sergeant Boggs was dragging an Army duffel bag on the sidewalk behind him.

The Kid nodded. "Evening, Sergeant, sir."

The old man nodded back. "Young man."

The Kid walked on.

Sally would have liked that. A very civil touch, she would have said, approvingly. Too many kids aren't at all courteous to the old folks these days.

Sally was very dead now, and he wondered what it was that he should feel. The things that Miss Dolan had been talking about. He was very sorry that Icepick Sally was dead—but he wondered if there was something more that he should feel that maybe he didn't know about.

And Marion Dolan was even deader.

He didn't feel anything about that.

First Sally had burned Marion Dolan to death with the boiling water. And Sally had kept on pulling hard, until Marion Dolan had gone over backwards.

And then Sally had helped him up, not knowing about his icepick holes. She had kept telling him to stand up straight, stop hunching over like that; only Norwegians had such bad posture. But that was because she had been so distracted and excited.

The excitement had killed her.

The Kid had finally gotten his face sponged off and had gotten the blood to stop coming out of the hole in his cheek. He had fainted twice over the sink, hitting his head on the faucet. And then he had pushed himself upright and had gotten turned around, holding the index fingers of both hands tight against the two icepick holes.

And Sally had been just sitting there. Looking right ahead, her face perfectly composed. No. No, more than that: a sort of, you know, a sort of very pleasant look. The Big Stroke had finally come and got her. No wonder.

It had taken so long to get into his Plaza Hotel clothes. Sometimes the pain in his stomach would hit like a hot,

284

firing jab, and he would have to pull one leg up. When he had tried to stand up, he could feel the blood leaking down on the inside of his stomach.

His hips. No, his what? The, you know, the pelvic structure: it sits there like a sort of big bowl.

Right now the bowl was filling up with blood. Two little spigots of it were splashing inward and filling up the bowl.

He had talked to Sally while packing the Mark Cross bag. It doesn't matter; you can talk to dead people. First, the money, all the hundreds from the shopping bag. Then his own money. All the money from the offices in Rockefeller Center. Sally's money, all the bills inside her long underwear, she would take into Heaven with her.

"Don't you worry," he had said to Sally. "Listen: just sit tight. Ginger Rogers will get here before the building comes down. Just listen for that knock on the door."

He had put on the blue oxford-cloth button-down shirt. And the tie, the red stripe tie.

And then he had stopped, panting like a dog, his tongue out slightly, waiting for another wave of pain to roar through.

And then the school blazer.

"Ginger Rogers is, too, coming," he had told Sally. He had gone back over and leaned down in front of her, looking into her eyes that weren't looking back. "Just like you said. And when you open that door, you know, it'll be like you said. With the . . . ohhhhhhh, *God*. Excuse me. With the diamond stairs and all."

And then he had dragged the suitcase to the door. But he had stopped one more time to look back at her.

He had doubled over to make the walking a little bit easier and he had gone back and gotten the pink fur slippers with the patent-leather heels. And he had shuffled over to Sally. Her feet were hard to move. But he had pulled off both of her outdoor shoes and he had put on the pink fur mules. That way, she would be ready to dance away when Ginger Rogers came.

Whoever Ginger Rogers was.

And then he had turned at the door. Just at the time the ceiling had caved in on the floor above them. There had been a rolling crash on the ceiling. A lot of the plaster had broken loose up above the parachute draping.

And when he had taken one last look before closing the door, it was falling down just like sequins in the light. The sequins had been drifting down gently, covering Sally's head and shoulders.

Now he was at the corner. At the fire line. There was a crowd of people behind the police barricades on the other side of the street, all fuzzy faces looking in at the block-long fire.

He blinked into a hand-held spotlight.

It was, what? It was a television crew. They were filming the fire.

The pain pulled him down for a minute. He forced himself back up straight.

Man, they sure were well dressed. Probably had just come from a television party when someone had called them and told them that Greenwich Village was burning down. Television people have parties and laugh a lot.

Maybe it would be Dan Rather. The Kid couldn't see the network symbols on the sides of the cameras yet.

It *would* be Dan Rather, with his split-tail coat and nice tie and the microphone with the black sponge-rubber ball on the end of it. And Dan Rather would wave The Kid over.

"The world, the world that is Greenwich Village, is burning down," Dan Rather would say. "And here, coming out of the fire into our spotlights, walking toward us now, here comes The Kid. He is, in effect, walking away from a burning past, a troubled past, into the future. The metaphor, the symbolism, is apt here: here is The

286

Kid, burning his metaphorical bridges behind him and stepping into a new . . ."

It was hard to see who it was, with all this smoke so thick in the air. But it might, you know, it might be Dan Rather.

The Kid pulled himself a little bit straighter after glancing down at the front of his pants. No blood was showing yet.

The Kid walked directly toward the hand-held spot-lights. The Kid allowed a slight smile to play at his mouth; the shock of hair was hanging down across his forehead.

He was almost into the lights, smiling, when he heard the voice:

"Hey, Max, somebody," it said. "Will you get that god-dam kid out of there. What the hell is this? Somebody. Hey, *kid*. Will you for chrissakes get the hell out of the way? We're trying to cover a fire here, we got you walk-ing right into the camera like a goddam King Kong or somebody. Move it."

The Kid stopped.

He could feel the bowl filling up with blood. The pain was starting to pull him back down into a crouch. It was bringing tears to his eyes.

It isn't you, Dan Rather?

No. It isn't you. It never is, really. Not really.

"Hey, goddam kid. Will you . . . ?"

The Kid nodded at the lights. "I'm going," he said. "All right, I'm going."

Ohhhhhh, *God*.

He turned now and squinted into the dark. The build-ings were swaying, sliding in and out of focus. Looking out through his eyes, everything looked black and wet.

But, okay. Okay, let's go. Come . . . on.

The next thrust of pain came in harder. He could al-most hear it.

He straightened just a bit. He pressed the palm of his left hand against his stomach and then doubled all the way over to hold it in place.

The walk was a shuffle, pushing one foot at a time, the Mark Cross suitcase dragging.

Keep moving. What would the guys on the camera truck say?

No, no. Not those guys back there at the fire line. You know: the other camera truck, the one that was always with him.

Ohhhh, God. He stopped and coughed.

Here's what they would be saying right now:

"Beautiful kid there, Sam. Get me a tighter shot of him. That's it. I mean, this here is Americana, Sam. Know what I mean? Class kid, right? You can spot the breeding. Good schools, fine, rich family and all. You can actually spot them, these kids; I mean, they stand out, it's something in their bearing. You ever see anything classier? Look at him run."